GHOST WARRIOR

Jimmy Morrill

Laurence Joseph Murphy

ISBN 978-0-9923046-2-1

Ghost Warrior, - Jimmy Morrill
is also available as an Ebook.

Published by
THUNDERBOLT PUBLISHING

Acknowledgement of Country

The author acknowledges the Aboriginal peoples of this nation as the first inhabitants and traditional owners of the land and wishes to pay all due respects to ancestors and elders, past and present.

Grammatical Format.

Where it is obvious that English is being spoken in this narrative the speech is shown thus;-

"I am speaking in English." (Normal text and double quotation marks.)

Where any Aboriginal language is being spoken, or the text is meant to imply that it is a translation into English of any language group, the speech is shown thus;-

'*I am speaking in the Bindal language*' (Italicised text and single quotation marks.)

Apology

Like the translation into English of many ancient languages only an approximation of sentence construction can be made here due to complex differences in syntax that are beyond the scope and intent of this book. It is also not the purpose of this book to initiate debate on the variations in dialect of the many tribes that inhabit or inhabited North Queensland, as proposed by different researchers of the subject over many years. Basic differences in syntax are best explained by several examples;-

'*Balbamu   birban-du ya-na*'
'*Wallaby   fast   go*'
("The wallaby is running away quickly.")

'*Abu-nggu   bala   gugay-a*'
'*Father   walk   camp*'
("My father is going to his camp.")

These examples are quoted to hopefully avoid any contention that I have disrespected the intelligence of the speakers by inferring that they possess a stilted or restricted conversational capacity. I can assure the reader that this is not the case and that I have only attempted to make the translation into English as realistic as possible to maintain the authenticity of the narrative.

Laurence Joseph Murphy (Author)

Dedication

This book is dedicated to the memory of my brother

James (Jimmy) Murphy
1947 – 2011
May your spirit forever wander free amongst the spinifex in the
wilderness that you loved, released as you are from the burden of life's
toils,

Contents

Introduction

This is a work of fiction that is based on the true story of the 1846 wreck of the barque, *Peruvian* and its aftermath. The story is centred on the subsequent experiences of a survivor, James Murrells, (also known as Jimmy Morrill) and many of the events described actually took place. Some fictional characters have been introduced, however, in order to provide substance to the narrative as it may have unfolded, but several of these characters have also been created by the author from fragments of information about real life individuals who are thought to have played a role and who, subsequently had a major effect on Jimmy's life.

The Aboriginal persons named herein, apart from the well-known Bennelong, are fictitious and do not relate in any way to any Aboriginal persons either living or dead.

The non-fictional characters whose names are mentioned throughout the narrative have been personified, as far as possible, as history has recorded them and their exploits are factual and chronologically correct.

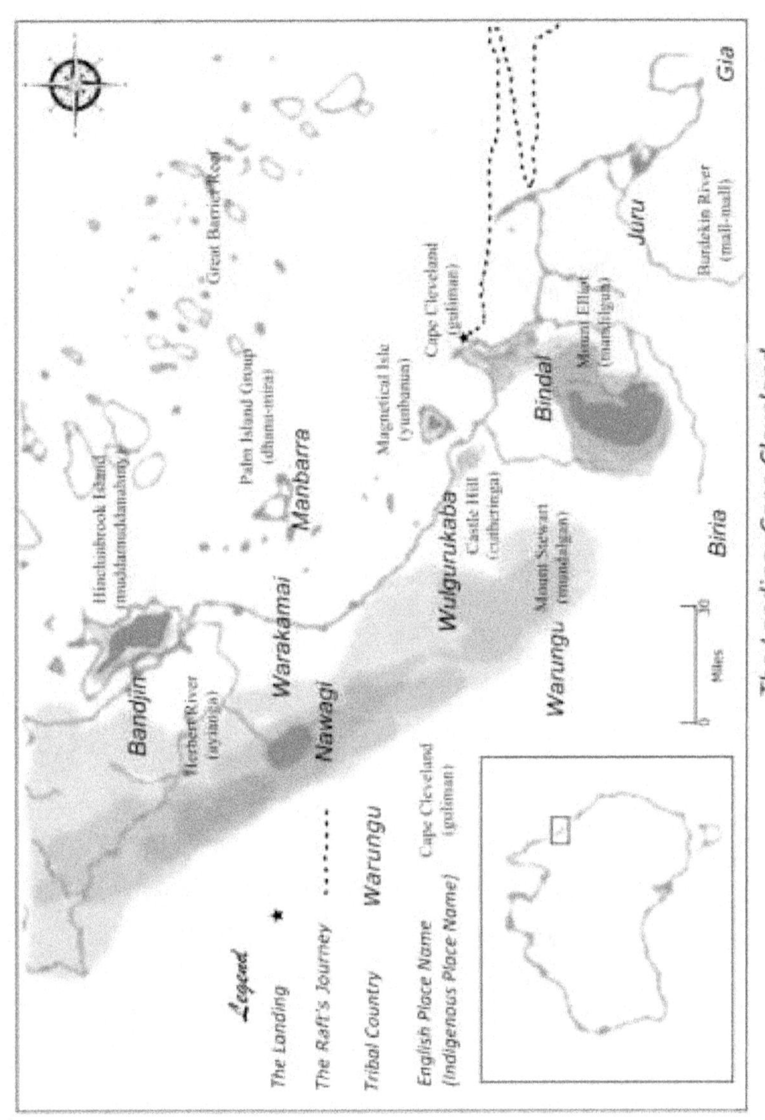

The Landing: Cape Cleveland

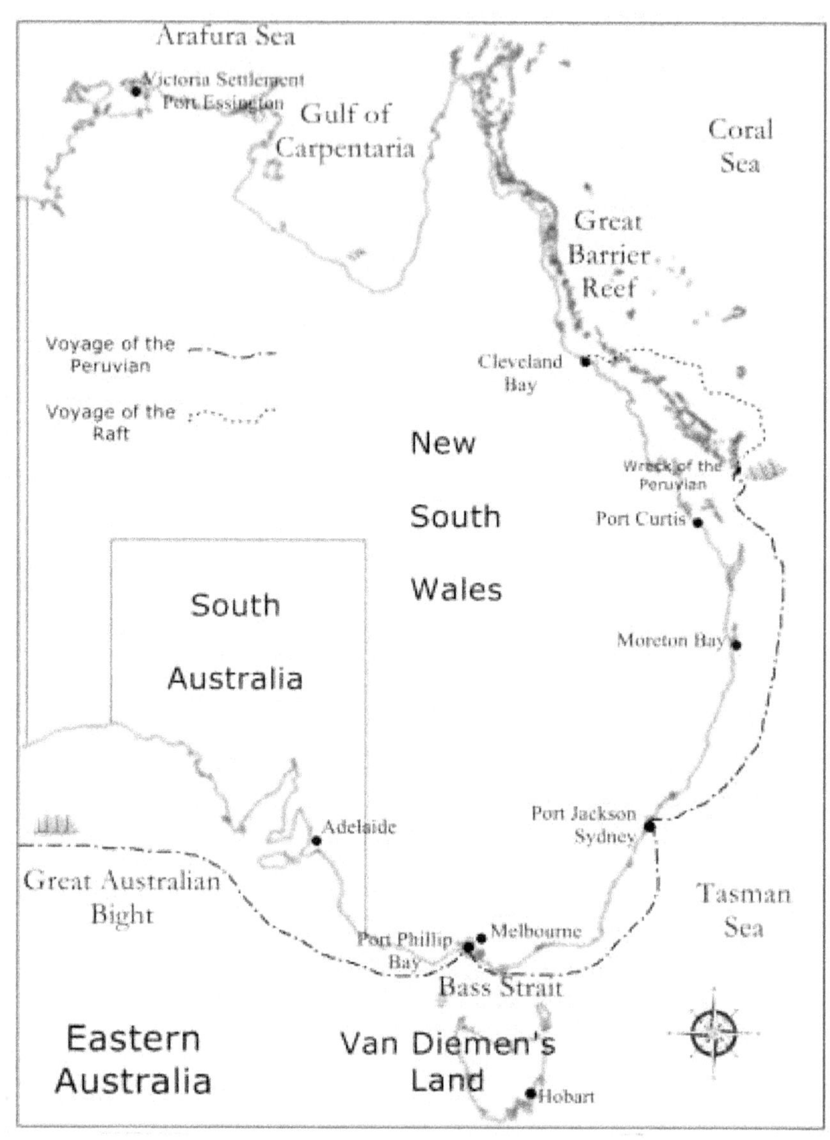

Eastern Coast of Australia 1846

Foreword

CLEMENT ROSS
1798 – 1880

The flowers on my father's grave had not long withered when my thoughts returned once more to the chronicle that had consumed the latter part of his life and that he wished me to make public after his death.

Let me make it quite clear from the outset that this story is *not* primarily about my father, Clement Ross. I must, however, set up my introduction to Jimmy Morrill, the main subject of the account, by telling you a little about the man whose obsession with the disappearance of the barque *Peruvian* and the fate of its passengers and crew led me to become personally involved in the accomplishment of his project.

The man known to his friends and adversaries alike as 'Rossie' was born in the year 1798 in old Sydney Town in the Australian Colony of New South Wales. Sydney then was very much different to the great maritime city that it is today more than eighty years later, for it was no more than a small port clinging to the low rise above the beautiful and natural Darling Harbour, and it had been hewn out of the surrounding scrub only ten years before Clem's 'inauspicious' (as he called it) entry into this world.

My father's final days were free from stress and his death a painless release from the minor tribulations imposed by nature on his timeworn body. And deservedly so, for Clem was one of those unacknowledged men and women who held noble thoughts for all mankind and who tried, without any public honour for his efforts, to be a champion of the underdog.

My father always acknowledged that he was fortunate in having the opportunity of a good education, certainly better than most of his peers. It was because of that privileged training, coupled with an active mind and a good memory that he was assured of a straightforward path to a commission in the Marine Corps following in his own father's footsteps. He shunned the prospect of such a dull career, however, for although it was a well-paid profession and assured him of a comfortable life he knew he was likely to be desk-bound, and Clem wasn't a sedentary sort of youth. Instead, he embarked on an adventure that took him to many great ports of the world as a merchant seaman, and his only real regret from that exciting period of his life was that if it hadn't been for an unfortunate incident that cut short his seafaring adventures he may yet have had an opportunity to captain a vessel in his own right.

As much as Clem always loved his home town, he spent the latter part of his life in the small town of Gladstone, which was established in 1863 and is located three hundred and forty miles to the north of Brisbane as the crow flies. Long before that, however, it had its beginnings as Port Curtis, the first port to be established north of Moreton Bay when that port was still in the Colony of New South Wales.

Despite the ravages of time on his old, infirm body, my father's mind was still active up to the close of his life, and his memory impeccable, - or so *he* believed it to be. If, however, what I am about to relate to you about the fascinating story of Jimmy Morrill finds fault with the research of some historical sleuth at any point in the future, I beg of that determined agent to remember that my father was an elderly man whose only objective was to set the record straight at long last and to recount Jimmy's story forthrightly as he remembered it.

Why, you might ask, would Clem have left it so close to the end of his life to request me to assemble the notes that he had compiled many years before, and release them to the world as a journal? Well then, the answer to that question would be that the death from cancer last year of his long-time friend, the Honourable Sir Maurice O'Connell, presented such an opportunity.

You see, Maurie (for that was what Sir Maurice preferred Clem to call him) held the position of President of the Queensland Legislative Council, and Clem knew how vital it was to protect his friend's reputation from any hint of irregularity that might proceed from publication of his name in his reminiscences.

The notion of ascribing a fictitious name to conceal Sir Maurice's identity had certainly crossed his mind, but he finally rejected that strategy as an unacceptable risk. After much soul-searching and many attempts to re-enact the circumstances of the tragedy without revealing Sir Maurice's involvement, he took the safest option at the time, which was to remain silent.

Clem also made it clear that Sir Maurice never deemed himself an outstanding individual in the many submissions to the British Government on the vexing problem of the protection of the indigenous people of the Colony of Queensland, and in the colonies in general. Any credit for the success of that noble cause, Sir Maurice always insisted, must go to the combined efforts of the members of the prestigious *Clapham Sect,* and not to any single individual. In fact, his good friend Mr William Henry Walsh, Member of the Queensland

Legislative Council, continues his strongly worded opposition to the inexcusable presence of the blight on humanity that is the Queensland Native Police Force. This is despite conflict over the issue with Queensland's first Governor Sir George Ferguson Bowen and many other prominent graziers who continue to justify the ownership of *their* land, based on the concept of *Terra Nullius,* or *'Nobody's Land',* to its most extreme and barbarous conclusion.

You will probably already know that the illustrious Mr Edmund Gregory, Esquire, an Assistant Manager of the *'Courier'* who also fulfilled the role of Government Printer, published an account entitled *'Sketch of the residence of James Morrill among the Aboriginals of North Queensland for seventeen years',* a rather long-winded title to a document which briefly attempts to cover the entire saga of Jimmy Morrill's experience in something less than thirty pages of foolscap. This is not to say that I am unimpressed with Mr Gregory's work. I *have* read it thoroughly and I agree with much of what has been written. His account covers such issues as the nature and useful properties of the botanical specimens that Jimmy was able to identify, for example, - but Mr Gregory didn't know Jimmy as my father knew him and probably coaxed the story from him piece by piece by asking many pointed questions that were within the sphere of his own personal and perceived public interest.

The first issue of that pamphlet was published in 1863, shortly after Jimmy's extraordinary return to society, and it was republished in 1866 with minor alterations. According to Clem, however, Jimmy was not a talkative man even before the *Peruvian* saga began and, for reasons which will become clear later in the narrative, he was even less loquacious when it was over. It remains to be imagined if it ever *was* over for him, but you can judge that for yourself. It would indeed have been painstaking work to extract any information from him that he felt was not in his, or his *friends'* best interests, and what he deemed to be not necessary to share with the public at large at that time in his personal struggles on their behalf.

Clem, on the other hand, was a friend with whom he could converse freely and with the unspoken pledge of confidentiality. He was sure Jimmy Morrill felt, as he did, that they were kindred spirits even after such a long absence from each other's company, and that almost *familial* relationship that they had established briefly long ago in Sydney was rekindled without any apparent effort from either of them.

I have also been in the privileged position of acquainting myself with several of Jimmy's family and friends in Maldon, and indeed with those who remain of the Pitkethly's in Dundee, to whom my father had once had the onerous task of informing, through the agonisingly slow medium of international mail delivery, of the disappearance in 1846 of their kin, together with the other passengers and crew of the *Peruvian*. Many of the latter, I might add, had very little or no information on record by which their family could be identified.

Now, of course, with the installation of the wonderful new international electric telegraph line, which has been in operation for only the past seven years and connects the colonies of Australia with the rest of the world, I have been able to send swift messages to those same family members in England, Scotland and across Australia, and receive a reply within days or even hours. I have utilised that service sparingly, ever mindful of the need for thoughtfulness regarding the feelings of those whose lives I have intruded upon and for whom I have possibly dredged up reminiscences that had been long ago consigned to the realm of fond memories.

Those that I *have* managed to contact, however, have responded good-naturedly and with graciousness to my requests for assistance in connecting those small details that have enabled me to shed light on the everyday lives enjoyed by their long-lost loved ones before the calamity of the loss of the *Peruvian* erupted in their midst.

I have acquired some confidence from their prompt responses and eager questions, that the sad events of that fateful time are forever embedded in their recollections as much as they are now in mine.

The remainder of the material contained in these pages and not told to Clem directly by Jimmy has also been gleaned from a source that Mr Gregory certainly would not have had access to at the time that he wrote his pamphlet; a source that is so scarce now that even though its stories have been accurately conveyed in dance over thousands of years it is now in danger of dying out altogether. I speak of the few who remain of the people who became Jimmy's self-proclaimed *other* family for seventeen years of his life, the Bindal of Mount Elliot.

Eliza Ann S---H. (nee Ross.)
Gladstone,
Colony of Queensland
July, 1880

THE INCREDIBLE JOURNEY OF
JAMES MORRILL

AS DOCUMENTED FOR POSTERITY
BY
ELIZA ANN S---H. (NEE ROSS)
JULY 1880

1

"Ah Juanita, there you are, love. Where's young Jimmy this morning? I want him to run an errand for me." The man stood in the open doorway wiping his hands on an oily rag. His voice was gruff, but not unkind.

Juanita Murrells looked up from her sewing. "He's down by the Heybridge Basin again, Davey. Can I run your errand instead?" She laid the quilt she was mending on the table beside her armchair.

Davey Murrells looked into the tired, dark eyes of his wife of almost twenty years and frowned. "No, no, don't get up. I know you've always been happy to run the errands in the past, Juanita," he said. "I was hoping that young Jimmy might start to show a bit of interest in the engineering business now that he's finished his education. Edward has taken to it very well, and we're so busy I can't spare him to make the trip into Maldon."

"Oh, we mustn't rush Jimmy into making a decision on his future just yet Davey. He's only fourteen after all's said and done. Edward is seventeen and a much more settled type of lad altogether." She pushed a strand of greying hair that had fallen over her forehead back behind her ear.

"I thought we agreed that it was not a decision *he* had to make, Juanita," Davey said quietly. It was a conversation they'd had once before and he didn't want to upset her again, - not in the weakened state that her body was in at the moment. "I'll be needing another assistant soon and he and Edward will be taking over the workshop one day."

"Jimmy's a sensitive lad, Davey, and he's still getting over the tough time he's had at Heybridge National School." Juanita shook her head and her face took on a touch of melancholy. "Children can be so cruel to those who are even *slightly* different," she said.

"Jimmy's not *that* much different to any of them. Maybe a shade darker, that's all. They're a pasty looking bunch anyway," Davey said emphatically. "I'd rather see the boy with a bit of his mother's colouring than looking like a ghost who's escaped from the Maldon cemetery."

Juanita brightened up. "You're right Davey, and I know I shouldn't get upset with children playing their silly games. When Jimmy grows up and mixes with other people of the world he won't look out of place." She thought about her own experiences in Heybridge village when Davey first brought his *'coloured'* wife home. She'd come to the cold and damp metropolis of London to find work as a housekeeper, but her first job turned out to be with a repugnant and lecherous old tyrant who had hired her for purposes other than housekeeping. Thankfully she'd escaped his clutches and it was soon after that bad experience that she'd met Davey Murrells.

He was a good, hard-working and reliable husband, but he was blissfully unaware of the innuendo and whispering that had gone on behind his back and she'd had to bear the impact of it mostly alone. There were no other *'Caribs'* in Heybridge or across the river in Maldon either that she could share her feelings with, for the thirty miles between London and the village on the River Blackwater may as well have been as wide as the Atlantic itself. The lack of suitable work in the country areas was enough to dissuade others of her kind from leaving the relative security of servitude in the dreary kitchens of upper-class Londoners to venture into the unknown of the English countryside.

The underhanded smirks and sly jeers that she'd experienced back then from the middle-class ladies, however, had only served to make her stronger and in fact she'd quickly established a small but close circle of friends amongst the fishermen and their wives, some of whom, although born and bred on the Blackwater, were as swarthy looking as she was. She had no doubt that young Jimmy would rise above any adversity he encountered in his life just as she had.

"He doesn't *have* to mix with other people of the world, Juanita. There's plenty of work for him here in Heybridge and it's a steady, comfortable living he'll have in the workshop." Davey had moved to his wife's side and made to place his hand on her shoulder, but drew it back quickly when she recoiled away from his touch.

"Don't you dare touch me with those oily hands, Davey Murrells," she scolded him. "I suppose it's a bucket of grease you want picked up in Maldon?"

Davey looked down at his hands and then back at his wife. "How'd you guess?" he said with a knowing wink.

"It wasn't difficult, since you seem to have most of the last tin all over your arms and on that filthy rag you carry about with you." She laughed. It was a loud hearty sound that came from deep in her ample midriff and was characteristic of the race of people she had left behind in Jamaica. "You could almost be mistaken for a *mulatto* yourself, you know."

Davey laughed too, but then was suddenly serious. "Send young Jimmy down to the workshop when he gets back, will you?"

Juanita nodded, hoping that Davey would leave quickly as she could feel a fit of coughing coming on.

He walked to the door. "I really want to have a talk to the boy soon. We're not getting any younger either and I know your chest infection is still causing you a lot of pain too."

"I know, Davey." Juanita managed to wheeze. "I'll be fine in a few weeks, truly I will." She tried to sound positive, but she knew as well as Davey that the English climate had never been good for her health although she loved the lifestyle that it afforded.

She and Davey had lived with their two sons and ten year old twin daughters Mary and Gracie in this big old comfortable house one street back from the Heybridge wharf for the last fifteen years. Davey's workshop was on the wharf too at Swan Yard, just around the corner, so he was always close at hand if she felt really bad, something that seemed to be happening more regularly lately. After Davey had gone she sighed deeply, pulled a shawl over her legs and tried to concentrate once more on her sewing.

2

Jimmy Murrells knew that it was past nine o'clock, for he'd clearly heard the sombre peals of the clock tower bell calling the faithful to prayer in Maldon across the River Blackwater. He could usually see the church, standing on its own little hill with its steeple towering above the town.

'Ma' said the churches were always built on the highest point of land above the town so the parishioners would think they were that much closer to God than the heathens down in the valley.'

He grinned. His ma' was always relating little philosophies like that and he never knew whether she was serious or not until he heard that well-known laugh.

Today, a warm Sunday morning in July, a grey fog hung low over the river, shrouding the steeple and even obscuring his view of the ships he knew were tied up at the wharves, and the small pleasure boats that were anchored in the shallows off the main channel.

He walked along the well-trodden track between waist high river rushes. It was a path that he'd taken more often of late since his liberation from the physical exertions of the schoolmaster, Mr Bridge, a former soldier whose enthusiastic pursuit of exercise was evidence of his belief in the old adage that *a healthy body is essential for a healthy mind*. The discipline hadn't done him any harm though, he realised, for he'd grown into a stronger than average fourteen year old with a good reading ability and maturity beyond his years.

After the final peal of the church bell had reverberated across the three hundred yard wide channel from Maldon, an eerie silence descended on the river. The nineteen year old Queen Victoria, just over a year into her reign, had already stamped her tiny foot and demanded that her subjects follow her example and purge themselves of the excesses of her uncle's Georgian reign. It was not surprising then that Sundays were now commonly reserved for quiet prayer and contemplation by the majority of the population who seemed captivated by every moral value expressed by their young monarch.

Jimmy looked further along the path that followed the north bank of the Blackwater downstream towards Heybridge Basin. There was nobody in that direction, he concluded. He turned around and scanned the track back towards the village, and when he was sure that no one else had decided to take a morning stroll instead of attending church he stepped carefully off among the reeds, treading lightly to minimise any flattening that would alert a later passer-by to the presence of a deviation from the main track. A few yards further on he sat down on a grassy knoll on the riverbank, his back against an ancient Yew that obscured any view of his position except from out on the river itself. He realised that his effort at concealment was a little extreme, but he'd come to think of this as his own special place, somewhere he could come to think and indulge in his dreams for the future.

A ghostly shape slowly emerged from the fog and slipped silently along the centre of the channel, and suddenly a single blast from a foghorn echoed across the water. He stood up and waved to the dim outline of a man who appeared on the deck of the vessel, not knowing if he could be seen, but it didn't matter. There were still some jobs that had to be done on a Sunday and the man was Mr Firman, captain of the Pilot Boat, heading down the dredged channel towards the estuary of the Blackwater to guide the first of the North Sea freighters to its moorings at the Maldon wharves.

Mr Firman would know he was there on the bank and always sounded the horn as a kind of greeting, for he was one of only two other people who knew of this special place. The second was the one individual he loved more than any other person in the world, his ma'. She'd accompanied him here on a couple of occasions when she wasn't too sick to undertake the mile long walk and it was here underneath the spreading branches of the ancient Yew that he had gained his first insight into her tough upbringing. He'd been unburdening his own troubles on to her about what he felt was his unfair treatment at the hands of some of his former school friends when she cradled him in her arms and told him the harrowing story in a soft and composed tone that rendered his own worries insignificant.

"My father," she'd said, "was a rather handsome Afro-American slave who worked on a sugar plantation in Jamaica. Like the majority of slaves, he worked long hours for a master who was brutal and regarded cruelty towards all the slaves, men, women and children, as his divine right. My father had thought many times of escaping, but he knew that the ruthless ex-soldier who owned him had many friends and would hunt him down and kill him as a warning to others who might try to do the same."

Jimmy had seen his mother's eyes mist over as she recalled the events that led to her receiving the right to call herself a *free person of colour*.

"One day an adjoining plantation owner came to visit and brought with him his teenage daughter. How the daughter came to meet the slave and contrive to keep meeting him in secret is still a mystery to this day," she'd said, "but love and willpower prevailed and in the end the young couple absconded and were secretly married in Kingston."

Jimmy had giggled at that. "Love and willpower," he'd repeated, his young mind trying to comprehend some hidden meaning to the innocuous phrase. "How could their love and willpower alone be enough to escape from the plantation owner, Ma?"

Juanita had remained patient. "Of course they needed some luck too," she'd said. "It was a perception amongst many slaves at the time that they must simply accept any situation that they were thrust into in life, no matter what it was, and that their new-found Christian God would eventually deliver them into some imagined salvation. My father didn't agree. God was too slow in answering *his* prayers. Sure enough, he said, if you can't change something, accept it for what it is and make the best of it, but if you *can* make a change that you are certain will grant you true love and happiness you must have the willpower to follow it through."

His mother had hugged him then. "I love you, Jimmy and you're father does too, and we know that you love us; that's the simple truth," she'd said. "But you're too young to appreciate the effect that love can have on a person's happiness. Later in your life you'll know what I mean. *In the end, love, whether it's love of another human being, or simply love of life, will be what defines your future happiness for the rest of it.*"

Jimmy had been intrigued. "And did the big bad plantation owner try to catch them and bring them back?" he'd asked breathlessly. His jaw had dropped at his mother's reply.

"Indeed," she'd said, "and he *did* catch up with them too." But then she'd laughed that hearty laugh that he'd always loved. "Oh, it was all highly unusual, but not entirely unknown. They'd gone to the local authorities for protection from the gang that had come after them. The authorities didn't know what to do, but the young white woman, my mother, told them about the new Slave Laws. She'd probably heard her father discussing them with other land owners, and there was provision in the laws for that very situation. You see, by marrying a free white woman my father became automatically free too, and any children of that marriage were free as well. I don't think my father's former owner or my maternal grandfather ever spoke to each other again."

"So you became a free person of colour," Jimmy had said. "Didn't that make your life a whole lot better?"

"Not really." His mother had shaken her head and her sad look returned. "The Slave Laws were in place and their intention was clear, but after my father became a free man none of the land owners would give him any work. My mother had to support us by working as a servant to one of the families that she'd previously been the equal of in rank. They were very good to her, but her own family would have nothing to do with her. When I came along I was called a *mulatto* and that only gave me limited rights as I grew up."

"*Mulatto*, that's a strange word, Ma," he'd said.

She nodded. "I'm not sure of the origin, Jimmy, *but a mule is a cross between a donkey and a horse.*"

Jimmy had looked at her with a wry smile, waiting for her characteristic laugh, but it hadn't come. His smile had faded then and was replaced with a stunned frown. "They were comparing you with an *animal?*"

"Probably," she said," but that was the least of our worries. The plantation owners were beginning to get frightened, because the Empire's dependence on slave labour and the plantation economy had resulted in the slaves outnumbering the plantation white people by about twenty to one and the anti-slavery movement was in full swing. The British Government had already passed laws to improve conditions for the slaves. They'd banned the use of whips in the field and the flogging of women, but the House of Assembly in Jamaica resisted the new laws and we, - the free persons of colour, - were persecuted almost as much as the slaves."

Jimmy had hugged his mother then. "You're safe *now* Ma," he'd told her. "Dad and Edward and I won't let anything happen to you now."

The Pilot Boat passed out of sight and he looked down once more into the grey water, imagining that he too was the captain of a ship sailing to far off places that he'd never heard of. It was a dream that he'd had often in this special place, but he knew in his heart that that's all it was, a dream, for in reality he was destined to spend his life working in his father's workshop.

It wasn't a pleasant outlook and he cringed when he thought of the look on Edward's face each morning as he readied himself for the long day ahead with the whirring machinery as his only companion, but he remembered his mother's words and the words of his grandfather.

If you can't change something, accept it for what it is and make the best of it, but if you can make a change that you are certain will grant you true love and happiness you must have the willpower to follow it through.

3

George Pitkethly, or *Geordie* as he preferred to be called, had come from a long line of seafarers and had been destined to become a sailor from the moment he was born. That event had occurred in a thatched roof cottage in the small, picturesque fishing village of Newburgh, in Fife on the east coast of Scotland in 1816.

The call of the sea had revisited Geordie's father, Alexander, when Geordie was ten years old. He'd signed on as a crew member on the survey barque, *Beagle*, out of Plymouth, bound for Patagonia and Tierra del Fuego on a voyage of Hydrographical Survey under the command of the Australian, Captain Phillip Parker King. It was a journey that took him away from Scotland for four years. On his return in 1830 he'd been devastated to find that his eldest son, Thomas, also a sailor, had been drowned at Yarmouth several months before and it was then that Alexander had decided to give up the rigours of seafaring and look for a less dangerous enterprise on dry land.

He prudently bought into the Dundee Shipyard of McKenzie Brothers and eventually became sole owner, but the family continued to live in the same cottage in Newburgh, just five miles from Dundee, for despite his acquired wealth, Geordies father was still first of all a simple sailor and the village life of Newburgh suited him.

Geordie's grandfather had served as an articled seaman aboard the *Endeavour* under the command of Lieutenant James Cook on his first voyage of discovery, first to Tahiti to observe the transit of Venus so that measurements of the Sun's distance from Earth could be calculated, and then, on the top secret orders of the Admiralty, to find and take possession of the great South Land in the name of King George of Britain, that is - if the elusive Great South Land existed at all.

With his father away at sea for long periods and his grandfather retired and living in a room attached to the cottage, the old man, quite naturally, had become Geordie's teacher and mentor. He'd learned to read navigational charts and maps almost before he could walk and consequently, as he grew into adulthood he'd maintained such a great respect for accurate and meticulous chart reading that his grandfather had prophesised, *'It will be the saving o' yer skin one day'*.

Geordie, at twenty-one years old, was a strong young man of average height and placid disposition when he met Elizabeth Ruxton, two years his junior, in Liverpool, England. Elizabeth, known to her family and friends as *Betsy*, was petite, fair-skinned and had blue eyes and long black hair, which she usually wore tied up with colourful ribbons.

Her father, Robert Ruxton, had been a wine importer from Dundee, and coincidentally, had known Geordie's father through their related business interests, but he had departed this life not long before the couple met, as had Geordie's mother whose name was also Elizabeth. It was a stressful time for Betsy, for her two brothers had also perished at a young age and her mother, Jean, alone in Dundee, was ailing.

Geordie had already secured a berth before he'd met Betsy, which he knew was a once in a lifetime opportunity. It was to be a voyage to explore the parts of the coastline of Australia that Matthew Flinders, in his 1802 voyage, had left uncharted and it was to be embarked on board none other than the *Beagle*, the barque that his father had shipped on in *his* final berth as a sailor.

Geordie and Betsy were very much in love, but they both accepted their responsibilities without question. They knew that the time was coming when they would be required to spend time apart. In an act of enduring devotion, however, they affirmed their love and absolute commitment to each other and were duly married in Liverpool in April 1837. Geordie left on his voyage of exploration on the ninth of June and the newly married Mrs Betsy Pitkethly returned to Dundee to care for her ailing mother.

It was six long years before Geordie Pitkethly returned to his home in Newburgh. He had matured into a heavily bearded, black haired and weather-beaten sailor, and his softly spoken Scottish accent, had been modified over the years as a concession to the problems of communicating with associates of various nationalities.

His dignified bearing and the astuteness that emanated from his deep blue eyes had commanded respect from the sailors who had served alongside him and his acumen had not escaped the notice of his superiors either, for he had gained the position of Master's-Mate on the *Beagle*. That rank required him to assist the Master in the navigation of the ship by plotting the Captain's requested course from daily solar observations. He also kept the official log of weather conditions, wind speed and direction, and ship's position. It was a responsibility that he took great satisfaction in and he knew his grandfather would have been proud of his achievement.

Betsy had waited patiently for the first four years, which had been the planned duration of the voyage, gratefully receiving the infrequent letters hurriedly scribbled and dispatched by Geordie from faraway seaports on British ships returning to their home anchorages. It was little enough comfort though, and as the extra months dragged by her stoicism faded. To make matters worse her mother, Jean, had passed away several years before so she was forced to endure the heartache of the prolonged delay on her own. She vowed then that she would never allow herself to be separated from Geordie ever again.

Geordie's homecoming was a grand event in the ordinary lives of the villagers of Newburgh, where the fishing boats set off each day before dawn to cast their nets in the River Tay estuary, and he was treated with the pomp and ceremony that was deemed fitting for a representative of such a prestigious and successful exploratory voyage. Eventually, however, the speeches and tributes became little more than the occasional slap on the back and coarse greeting from some old Jack-tar on the wharf and he and Betsy were able to settle into the simple, but gratifying daily existence of a *newly* married couple that had eluded them for so long.

Both Geordie and Betsy had come from devout Presbyterian families and Geordie was invited to take on the role of a deacon assisting the local pastor of the Scottish Presbyterian Church. His father, Alexander too, as expected, insisted that he take over as captain of one of his ships plying the coastal trade in the North Sea.

Geordie accepted both assignments gladly, as it meant he was never away from home for more than an overnight voyage. It was a time of bliss for Betsy and the only cloud on the horizon was that they seemed unable to produce the child that she and Geordie had hoped for.

Of the ships owned by Alexander Pitkethly, the *Peruvian*, a four masted vessel of 304 tons was the largest in the fleet. It was 100 feet from bowsprit to stern, had a beam of almost 30 feet and had been slipped only four years earlier in 1841 in Dundee, its home port. Geordie had been dismayed, however, to learn that it lay moored idle at the dockyard much of the time with smaller coastal vessels sailing up and down the Tay fully loaded with cargo for the North Sea ports.

It came as no great surprise when, midway through 1845, Geordie's father admitted that the construction and fitout of the *Peruvian* had been too much of an ambitious venture from the beginning, and that his small shipyard was losing money and may have to close. It was the idle *Peruvian*, of course, that was the main cause of Alexander's financial woes. There was, however, a small chance that he could still trade himself out of debt, for he'd struck a lucrative deal with the British Government to supply various goods and equipment to the government store at Sydney in the colony of New South Wales, Australia. It was the only prospect that would stave off bankruptcy, and

Geordie, having already spent considerable time in the Antipodes, was the most experienced sailor in the shipyard.

Geordie sat in the small front parlour of the cottage with his elbows on his knees, his face a mask of dejection. "I don't have any choice, my love," he explained to Betsy. "I *must* take on just this one voyage tae save my faither's business. My wee brother Alex is going as well an' I need tae make sure he gets back without any harm coming tae him. It would break my faither's heart tae lose another son tae drowning after Thomas, an' then losing my mother after that."

"Alex is twenty-five, Geordie. He's only four years younger than you an' he's quite a big lad. Thomas was just nineteen." Betsy reminded him.

"Aye, I know, but Alex is a wee bit hot-headed, as ye' very well know, an' he's apt tae jump in tae things an' get himself in bother."

Betsy had never revealed to Geordie her long held desire to journey with him to the interesting places that his voyages had taken him. She'd listened with wonder and perhaps a bit of envy as he revisited them with her in his entertaining tales by the warmth of the blazing fire in the hearth at their cottage, for she fully expected that she would never get the opportunity to fulfil her wish. Now, with the pain of her mother's passing well behind her and the prospect of Geordie being away for almost a full year, she realised that the time had come to make a stand. She couldn't bear to be left alone again. Her smile was sympathetic, but her tone was defiant. "I can understand that ye' must go, Geordie, for yer faither's sake an' tae make sure Alex comes tae nae harm, but I can tell ye' something right now laddie, - yer no' going anywhere without Betsy Pitkethly alongside ye' tae see that *you* come tae nae harm either."

4

Betsy Pitkethly walked along the wharf and up the gangway of the *Peruvian* with mixed feelings. She was excited at the prospect of the voyage ahead, of course, but also a little anxious that the preparations for departure might not all be going to Geordie's plan, for there seemed to be confusion and mayhem all around her and it was not in her nature to easily become accustomed to such chaos in her usually neat and well-ordered existence.

Men and boys in diverse workmen's outfits, from young pimple-faced deckhands and swarthy wharf labourers in black oilskins, to bearded seafarer's in blue working uniforms, shouted directives or bellowed advice in gruff, impatient voices around her. They were almost drowned out by the din coming from the hen-coops and pig-pens, and the cranes that hissed and belched steam as bags, chests and trunks were hoisted aboard. She carefully avoided the coils of rope, sailmakers canvas and various other tackles and riggings that lay about the deck in untidy disarray and made her way along the railing towards the back of the ship. *'It's not the back; it's the aft end,'* she reminded herself with a smile, *'just like fore is the front, starboard is the right hand side and port is left. Learn the words or you'll sound like a goose instead of a captain's wife. Aye, aye sir.'*

She glanced up at the rope net that held the pallet of baggage as the crane lowered it on to the deck, hoping to recognise some of her own hampers of clothes and cosmetics. Her greatest fear was that she would be the sole unfortunate victim of a misplacement of luggage and be forced to spend the next four months in an oversized sailor-man's uniform with rolled up sleeves and baggy leggings. She'd conveyed her concern to Geordie, but he'd just laughed at her and promised that he'd make sure that nothing of hers would be left behind. She was relieved just the same, when Geordie met her on the stairs to the raised aft deck, opened the door to their cabin and she found her hampers neatly stacked inside. He laughed again as she heaved an audible sigh of relief.

"I hope yer no' going tae worry for the whole voyage about wee things like that, my love," he said.

"Aye, Geordie, I know yer right an' I shouldn'ae worry, but it *is* my first time after all. I'll soon settle down, Captain, *sir*." She saluted him, then laughed and glanced about the cabin. "Oh look, we've got two windows and a nice skylight up there."

"I told them we'd have the stern cabin, Betsy. There's more air an' light in here, - unless we're forced tae put the shutters up in a storm, an' ye' won't be annoyed wi' all the cooking odours from the galley. I had the *bulls-eye* caulked too." He saw her puzzled look and pointed to the skylight above her head. "They usually leak, an' ye' cann'ae imagine what it's like tae have a cauld seawater bath when yer trying tae get tae sleep in yer bunk."

"No, I cann'ae imagine that, Geordie, an' the single bunks wi' the high side-boards look a bit snug fitting. I don't think we'll be getting up tae much mischief in these wee beds." She giggled.

Geordie grinned. "Ye'll find out soon enough that the side-boards *are* a necessity, Betsy, as well as the rail in front o' the book shelf, an' the swing tray above the table. They're all there fer a purpose, ye' know." A worried look creased his brow. "I hope ye' don't come tae regret yer decision tae embark on this trip wi' me, my love? Ye' still have until the morrow tae change yer mind ye' know."

Betsy clasped her arms around his waist and buried her head in his chest. "I'm no' letting ye' out of my sight ever again, Geordie, I told ye' that an' I mean it. I cann'ae say truthfully that I'm no' frightened at what might lie ahead o' us, but I'd be more fearful o' staying here praying every night by myself an' no' knowing what's happening tae ye' or when yer coming back tae me safe an' sound." She sighed deeply and hugged him more tightly as if to make the point quite clear. "Whatever the future holds fer us from now on, it will happen tae us together, an' if through some dire circumstance that we cann'ae comprehend at this moment we don't survive this voyage we'll go tae our graves together. May the Lord protect us from harm."

One of Geordies strong arms encircled her shoulders and he upturned her small face with his free hand so that he could look into her eyes. "That's a very sobering thought, Betsy," he said, in a subdued voice that carried a hollow quality. "I know yer a bit scared, lass, but ye'll soon get used tae it all, an' I swear to ye' on ma holy bible that this'll be the last time I'll ever put ye' in any danger. When we get back home again after this I'm going tae become a Minister o' the cloth full time. May the Lord protect us."

Betsy smiled. "My very own Minister, indeed; I'm a lucky wee woman."

The Peruvian beat down the North Sea in favourable winds, but a contrary and variable breeze in the English Channel rendered its progress very sluggish for the following three days. In the heavy swell the *Peruvian* swayed and rolled and Betsy soon found out the reason for the single bunks with the high side-boards, for she quickly surrendered to the miserable curse of sea-sickness and, were it not for Geordie tucking her in with pillows wedged on either side, she would have rolled weakly and helplessly from side to side with the movement of the ship.

Weary, but sleepless and with a queasy stomach, she lay on her back dizzily watching the swing tray doing its eccentric waltz above the table in uncanny timing with the cloaks hanging on their hooks on the back of the cabin door, and listening to the alarming creaking noises that seemed to come from every nook and cranny. The yelling of the crew as they repeatedly trimmed sail and tacked in a zig-zag pattern towards, and then away from the French coastline, did nothing to alleviate her discomfort either, and Geordie's obligatory absence on duty left her to contemplate her misery alone.

His words echoed in her mind. *'I hope ye' don't come tae regret yer decision tae embark on this trip wi' me, ma love?'* He'd been so concerned for her welfare and she'd been adamant that she could cope with anything that nature and the elements threw at her, but here she was, lying prostrate in her cot, feeling sorry for herself, and it was barely five days into a voyage that could take them a full year to complete.

The weather improved after the Peruvian left the channel and in the Bay of Biscay it became so favourable that Betsy was able to spend a good part of each day reading her favourite poetry on a deckchair on the aft deck outside her cabin, but the contentment she felt then when she looked out on the white crested waves with the occasional seabird gliding overhead was not destined to last.

After rounding the cape, her world again became a nightmare of cold stormy weather that banished her to her cabin, where with shutters securing the stern-windows and bullseye closed tight she slept away as much of the day as she was able to, and sat shivering, wrapped in cloaks and furs the remainder. There was not a stove in the cabin to keep warm by and, she thought gloomily, if there *had* been one, its glowing embers would have been distributed to all corners of the room with disastrous results.

The cabin was pitch black, for the lamp that she'd had lighted for her and placed on the swing-tray had long since crashed to the floor amidst the debris of cups and saucers, and cloaks and oilskins from their hooks on the cabin door. Every plank in the vessel complained in its own particular tone of creaking, cracking or groaning and with the wind howling and screaming in her ears it made such a frightful racket that she cowered in a corner of her bunk with her knees pulled up under her chin.

She was alone in the cabin again, for Geordie was up on deck struggling to maintain control of the ship with the rest of his crew, and oddly, it was there in the cold blackness as she prayed for *his* safety and that of the whole ship's complement that she suddenly felt the nausea evaporate and a warm wave of peace and calm flow through her body.

Without consciously realising it she released her vicelike grip on the edge of the bed rail and lay back, stretching her legs and letting her arms relax by her sides. The peculiar sensation that she had lifted off the bunk and was floating weightlessly in a radiant emptiness that was pleasurable against her skin overwhelmed her and, in that sublime state of calm serenity she accepted *absolutely* her fate, because no matter what the final consequence of this terrible storm might be, she realised once and for all that she never wanted to be anywhere other than by Geordie's side.

5

It was a warm summer day in Sydney, a continuation of the fine weather that they'd encountered all the way up the eastern coast of Australia since passing through Bass's Straits, and a far cry from the foul weather that had plagued the voyage since rounding the cape.

Geordie Pitkethly stood, arms folded, looking over the deck rail of the *Peruvian* down to the uniquely and aptly named Circular Quay, where cedar logs were being loaded by the dockside labourers under the supervision of his brother, Alex. The cedar logs were destined for Hong Kong, a well-regarded and profitable back-load for ships that had brought goods to the colony and were travelling back to Britain via Hong Kong and Batavia. The raw logs would be sawn and kiln dried and would eventually find their way back to the colonies as finely crafted furniture.

Darling Harbour, in which the *Peruvian* gently swayed at anchor amongst a flotilla of other craft, was considered to be the western boundary of the main city area, which was positioned on the southern shore of Port Jackson about seven miles from the Pacific Ocean and at the head of Sydney Cove. With at least three miles of deep water frontage, where ships of the heaviest cargo could safely approach the wharves, Sydney had become known as an unrivalled maritime centre.

The main streets, of which George Street was the principal, ran north and south parallel with the harbour. They were intersected at right angles by shorter streets in a neat rectangular pattern that perhaps could have been regarded as too formal by a man more used to the narrow winding lanes of a Scottish village, but Pitkethly quite liked its tidy uniformity and he'd noticed how much the city had grown since his previous visit aboard the *Beagle* five years ago.

The extent of progress in the suburbs had been evident from the moment the *Peruvian* entered the harbour, when he'd observed many fine villas and cottages that had been recently built on the north shore of Port Jackson, the verdant greenery of their well-tended gardens making a pleasant contrast with the brown scrub that surrounded them. It had come as no surprise to Geordie that the houses, shops and businesses in the main city now stretched in an unbroken line to the south for more than two miles.

Pitkethly had taken the opportunity to pay a duty call to the Post Office in order to forward his sail plan to the principals of the shipping company in London. It had quite bewildered him on his first visit that a voyage from Sydney to London could take a ship four to five months, depending on the inclemency of the weather, and yet the mail would unfailingly take only eight weeks to reach the same destination. It was, he'd been cheerfully informed, due to the fact that the voyage undertaken by the mail ship took it to the port of Suez on the northern shore of the Red Sea. The mail was then transferred to a camel train and transported across the sandy plains to Port Said on the Mediterranean. From there it was transferred to another ship and finally to London via the Strait of Gibraltar. *'How difficult would it be to cut a channel through the desert to join the Red Sea with the Mediterranean?'*

The Post Office itself, perhaps the most important building in the colony to many, particularly those in the remotest extremities of the land, was a plain enough stone building, but its exterior had been enhanced by the addition of a handsome portico, its pediment supported by six Doric columns and emblazoned with the Royal Arms in the centre of the tympanum.

The postmaster, a man of a pleasant and agreeable demeanour, had been more than enthusiastic in his analysis of the future prospects of the city. His vision of impending great achievements was perhaps boosted by that part of the city that he proudly admitted he worked and lived in, for that part of George Street facing the eastern wall of the Barrack Square between Hunter Street and the Post Office, embraced some of the finest houses yet built in Sydney. He was, moreover, equipped with a sound knowledge of the figures that confirmed his belief in its continuing growth, a fact that Geordie conjectured was a necessary part of his profession. A census had been recently completed, he'd said, and the number of houses in the city was now 7100, but in recent years the suburbs had also grown considerably in size in every direction and accounted for a further 1715 households, the total population being in excess of thirty-eight thousand people.

Geordie's gaze swung towards the imposing façade of the new Government House, an elegant stone edifice built in the Tudor Gothic Revival style with white, marble, castellated turrets and tall chimneys of elaborately carved stone. It had been under construction at the time of his previous visit, when the old Government House, built in 1789 using English bricks and native stone, was still in use, but since last year had been the official residence of Governor Gipps.

He knew that the interior was just as imposing as the exterior, for in 1840 he'd been fortunate in being invited to a ball in the unfinished building to commemorate the marriage of the young Queen Victoria to her beloved Prince Albert, and he remembered his initial surprise at the spacious and lofty halls and state rooms, the great ballroom with its large orchestral stage and the grand staircase of highly fashioned Australian cedar.

A pair of sentinels stood in the shade on either side of its colossal entrance doors, their red military jackets and black bearskins looking absurdly out of place in the balminess of the day. A well-maintained lawn surrounded it and on this expansive green sward tall, sombre Norfolk Pines grew alongside noble English Oak trees whose verdant yellow-green leaves were in stark contrast to the decaying brown autumn carpet that lay beneath the bare branches and naked trunks that he'd left behind in Dundee in October of last year.

Geordie, having satisfied himself that the loading was going smoothly under Alex's direction, left his vantage point at the deck rail with the intention of fulfilling a pre-arranged meeting with his wife. Betsy had already gone ashore to wander among the fashionable emporiums of George Street and he advised the watch that that's where he could be found in any emergent situation.

Sydney had fascinated Betsy from her very first day in the city. The long thoroughfares packed with first-rate shops offered every variety of merchandise to the ladies who arrived and left in carriages of every description, from genuine London built coaches brilliant in paint and varnish, to the showy barouche and the more humble four-wheel chaise or two-wheel gig.

"It seems tae me that the ladies here are no' keen tae walk all that far, Geordie." Betsy, a strict disciplinarian for maintaining a healthy regime, had said of her initial impression. "An' all those carriages coming an' going wi' their horses kicking up the dust in yer face is a right nuisance, but I have tae agree wi' ye' that there's some lovely buildings here an' I cann'ae believe it's such a young town – less than sixty years, ye' say?"

Geordie had been quite worried at the commencement of the voyage that Betsy's Scottish accent might cause her problems in communicating with the inhabitants of the various countries at which the *Peruvian* was due to dock, as he himself had experienced in *his* early travels. He was amused and relieved at Betsy's ability to divest herself of the least intelligible part of her Scottish brogue and assume a reasonable Queens English accent at will, although she would revert immediately to her native pronunciation when they were alone together. They'd met in Liverpool, so she'd had some experience in conversing with people outside Scotland, but the English spoken by the residents of that city was scarcely ideal as a model for representing the English language as a whole.

However exuberant she may have been at the opportunity to travel with him, and despite her steadfast denial of any excessive level of stress during the voyage, the journey *had* taken its toll on her, Geordie felt sure.

Her innocently declared delight at just being able to walk steadily without the floor seeming to heave about and hurl her over, and even the simple enjoyment she expressed at being able to use two hands to brush her hair instead of having to keep one free to hold on to the dressing table amused both of them. It also made him embarrassingly aware though, that those little inconveniences on board a pitching and rolling ship that *he* took for granted, she had probably found frustrating and perhaps even distressing.

He managed a sly smile though, as he remembered how proud she had always been of her table manners and how horrified she'd been when her wine-glass toppled over on to her plate at the dinner table somewhere in the English Channel in a heavy swell. After that humiliation she had fastidiously used the swing tray above the table to avoid any repeat mischance and even when they dined at one of Sydney's most highly regarded public houses, he'd noticed that she unwittingly propped her wine-glass against the salad bowl for support.

It was also Betsy's idea to spend their first night in Sydney ashore in that same respectable establishment, something that would never have occurred to him, for their cabin on the Peruvian was sufficient, if not spacious, and it was quite well-appointed for their needs. He soon understood her reason, however, for when the time came for her evening ablutions, her earnestly delivered request to the chamber-maid was that her bath be filled almost to over-flowing with fresh, clean, hot water and Geordie could hear her singing happily as she proceeded to soak in the foamy scented liquid.

And, as if to confirm her suspicions about the lack of exercise participated in by the fine ladies of Sydney, Geordie and Betsy found themselves almost solitary visitors when they took a walk in the delightful Domain, a picturesque rocky promontory close to the town, thickly wooded and laid out with fine carriage drives and walks.

A sign at the lodge near the entrance informed them that Lady Macquarie, Governor Lachlan Macquarie's wife, had set out the layout of the Domain from her own plans in 1816. She'd had the walks and drives cut through the rock and undergrowth, carefully allowing the native eucalypt trees to remain unharmed, and had installed seats for the benefit of the anticipated throng of leg-weary wanderers. On the high point of the headland some horizontal slabs of nature's own creation had been engineered into the form of a great seat or throne and an inscription above it provided the information that it was named Lady

Macquarie's Chair in honour of that same lady to whose generosity the city was forever indebted for the development of this lovely spot.

The reason for their almost exclusive use of the Domain was not long in being explained, however, for a young woman approached them along a shady pathway, pushing a baby carriage in which a baby slept peacefully. She bade them an enjoyable afternoon in a friendly manner and in response to Betsy's polite observation about the lack of other people taking exercise, she told them quite frankly why it was so. It was currently unfashionable for the ladies of Sydney to walk or drive in the same place where maid-servants, which *she* was, she happily admitted, retreated to on Sundays to relax in the arms of their sweethearts.

"I thought ye' said there was nae class distinction in Australia, Geordie?" Betsy said wryly when they continued their journey. "There's no' even that kind o' segregation in Hyde Park in London."

Geordie grinned "Yer no' a lady then by the sound o' it Betsy, otherwise ye'd no' be here walking in this terrible park wi' yer own sweetheart."

"Who says *you're* my sweetheart, Geordie Pitkethly?" she giggled. "An' if ye' havn'ae married a lady then it's yer own fault, ye' know." She shook her head in imaginary scorn. "What wi' you being a future minister o' the Church o' Scotland an' all."

They linked arms and wandered along the path, marvelling at the beauty of the white-crested waves washing over the rocks below, and gazing over the countless bays and inlets, small islands and pretty villas and cottages that, however distant, seemed so distinct in the remarkable clearness of the atmosphere.

Whether their wandering in the Domain defined her as a lady or a maid-servant, it was of no concern to her, Betsy declared defiantly. It was not only the perfect way to find her land-legs after the limitations of endless circuits of the ship's deck, but the exquisite views over the town and suburbs, the north shore, and the stunning estuary of Port Jackson, made the excursion worth the risk of her being relegated to a lesser status by the conspicuously absent ladies of Sydney.

6

The sailor was a deeply tanned and weather-beaten young man, broad-shouldered and of average height, and his long black hair was tied back with a leather thong. His black beard and sideburns had been neatly trimmed and he had dressed fittingly for the warm February morning sunshine in full length canvas trousers and a simple cotton shirt. He had taken the time too, to visit one of the public bath-houses that were tucked in amongst the factories and warehouses that lined the streets surrounding the Market Street Wharf at Darling Harbour and now, after a dreary fortnight of compulsory confinement at the North Head quarantine station, having been cleared of carrying any communicable diseases, he was eager to embark on his next assignment.

He had found temporary lodgings at the Seafarers Shelter, an apt name for a billet that was no more than a rough iron-clad shed with wooden bunks stacked three high lining all of the internal walls, and a lean-to attached to it that served as a rudimentary wash-house. It stood near the Sydney Markets and, despite the smell of decaying vegetable matter that wafted in through the high, wooden shuttered window openings, they were left open on all but the coldest and wettest days with the express purpose of ventilating the interior and purging it of the stench of many unwashed seafarers bodies. The habit was not always completely successful, however, and in weather such as Sydney was experiencing now merely resulted in replacing one foul stench with another just as unwholesome.

He sucked in the fresh, salt-laden air as he strode along King Street and he had to admit to being impressed by the extent of commerce and industry evident in the fledgling town that had begun its life as a penal settlement a mere sixty years ago and had only shrugged off that disagreeable label with the end of transportation within the last decade.

The latest designs in iron hulled ships were being assembled in the substantial shipyard and the resounding ring of the metal plates being riveted together could be heard coming from the dry-dock, accompanied by the hiss of steam driven engines wheezing off excess vapour into the air.

A coal-fired gasworks that supplied gas for the various industries as well as the gaslights lining the well laid-out streets belched out black smoke from a towering brick stack that rose above the wool, wheat and tobacco storehouses.

Many of the buildings that were huddled close together in the harbour district to house the common wharf workers had been built in the first twenty years of the colony's existence, gradually replacing the canvas tents and bark huts that had been hurriedly erected for the miserable shelter of the soldiers and prisoners who had arrived with the first fleet. They were of plain brick construction and were in various stages of disrepair, but that was to be expected, a knowledgeable fellow lodger had told him. There had been a lack of good lime for making brick mortar when the colony was in its infancy, and until sufficient quantities had been sent from England and Cape Town in South Africa the enormous middens of shellfish shells that the Aborigines had deposited over thousands of years at Cockle Bay had been crushed to provide the only source of lime available for building.

The young man turned into the main thoroughfare, George Street, which was lined on either side by many grand commercial buildings constructed of massive stone and marble blocks. One of these imposing buildings housed the Merchant Marine Agency and it was to this that the sailor directed his attention.

"James Murrells, eh," the shipping clerk said. He peered into the sailor's face over the top of a pair of horn-rimmed spectacles that were balanced precariously half-way down the slope of a long hooked nose, and then he turned his attention once again to the ledger on his ink-stained desk. "Doesn't seem to be a James Murrells here, lad," he muttered, almost to himself as he again ran a stubby finger down the column of names in front of him.

The sailor scanned the upside-down names on the ledger in confusion. It was a register of unemployed seamen and he had presented himself in the same office, but to a different clerk, as soon as he'd finished his quarantine the previous week, hoping to ship aboard a vessel.

The clerk broke into his thoughts. "You said you asked to be discharged from the schooner, *Terror* from New Zealand bound for London. Is that correct?

The sailor nodded. "Aye sir; it was last week, as soon as I got out of quarantine."

The clerk licked his thumb, used it to turn back to the previous page, and cast his eyes down the column of names with a frown creasing his pallid brow. All of a sudden he grunted as he stabbed a finger at an entry half-way down the page. "Ah, here we are then," he said. "It's no wonder I passed over it. You've been listed under the name Morrill." He read out the entry. "James Morrill, Able Seaman, discharged from the schooner *Terror* on the fourteenth day of February

1846 due to a desire to continue sailing in the Antipodes and not wanting to return to England at this time."

He grinned at the quiet, patient young man who stood clutching his white sailor's cap in both hands. "You're not keen to go home to England lad, eh? Got some skeletons in the cupboard you want to keep locked away from the view of authorities back home, have you?"

The sailor looked at him with a blank expression on his face for several seconds, and then shook his head and laughed, but it had a hollow unconvincing resonance. "Oh no, I've got nothing to hide from the authorities and I was in no trouble at home, I can assure you, sir. I just want to keep adventuring for a while longer. I *might* go back and settle down again at home one day."

"Ah - right then," the clerk said slowly, although he still cast a pleasant, but dubious eye in the young man's direction. "In that case I'll see if we can arrange to get you shipped on a berth that might suit your desire *not* to go home, James, maybe Hong Kong or Singapore, eh? Is it James, – or do you prefer Jimmy?"

"Jimmy's fine, sir."

"Take a seat, lad." The clerk held out his hand. "My name's Clem Ross."

Murrells was surprised by the firmness of the clerk's handshake, for the sallow forehead above bushy grey eyebrows, accentuated by a receding hairline, that he'd presented while he scanned the ledger, had convinced him that the clerk spent too much of his daily routine stooped over in that very same occupation.

"Thank you Mr. Ross," he said. He pulled out the chair and sat down facing the clerk.

"Will it bother you if I leave the spelling of your name as *Morrill*, Jimmy?"

Murrells shook his head, but a frown creased his brow. "It makes no difference to me Mr Ross. I suppose I'll just have to remember *that* when I come back this way next time."

Ross must have noticed his confusion. "It simplifies our records if I don't have to change the *other* clerk's entry from the previous page," he explained, but his long-suffering expression clearly showed his disapproval of his absent colleague's lack of application. "Did he get all your personal details written down for the record, lad?"

Murrells shook his head. "No sir," he said. "He just told me to come back this week, seemed to be in a bit of a fluster."

Ross nodded. "I believe he's got a lot on his mind at the moment." He shoved the ledger to one side, bent down, opened a drawer in his desk and pulled out a contract document, which he laid out on the desk in front of him. "Jimmy Morrill it is then and you can call me Clem if you want to," he said. He dipped a pen in the inkwell. "Any experience you want me to note in our records, Jimmy?"

"I served four years apprenticeship with the Maldon Shipping Company. I sailed in the *Royal Sailor* and the *Duchess of Kent*. Mr Henry May, the shipping agent for the company, gave me two letters of recommendation and presented me with a silver handled tobacco pipe for good conduct, - even though I've never smoked," he added, quite seriously. "Maybe he didn't know me *that* well?"

Ross chuckled. "I've heard of the renowned Mr Henry May and he doesn't give out references to just anybody. If you come with references from him you *must* be a good seaman. You'd have to allow him the blunder with the pipe though, Jimmy. You're probably one in a hundred sailors that doesn't have one hanging out of his mouth. Maldon's in Essex, right?" he said.

"Sure is, Clem. It's on the River Blackwater."

"Yes, I remember it. I shipped there a few times many years ago. The Blackwater River pilot was a friendly natured chap by the name of…" He paused for a moment with the pen poised over the contract. "…Ah, Jim Forman I think. Ever heard of him?"

Murrells stared at him in astonishment. "You mean Jim Firman? I sure *have* heard of him, Clem," he said. "In fact, I know *Captain* Firman well. I was supposed to be working in my father's engineering workshop in Swan Yard at the time, but I wasn't cut out for that sort of work. It felt like I was working in a dungeon and I used to get out as soon as I could and wander down to the Blackwater for the fresh air. Captain Firman was, and still is, one of my father's good friends and he spent a bit of time at our house, so he started taking me along on some of his piloting ventures when the weather was fine. It was on one of those trips that a ship's captain inquired if I would like to become an apprentice on his ship. He must have noticed how keen and interested I was, and when Captain Firman asked me I agreed right away. That's how I've come to be a sailor."

It was Ross's turn to be surprised. "I remember Jim having a young lad with him sometimes." He stared at Murrells over the rim of his spectacles. "Pardon my ignorance, but I thought the lad was a little darker than the usual pasty-faced urchins I'd noticed hanging around the docklands."

"Don't apologise, Clem; that was me, for sure." Murrells said. "I've always been a shade – ah, duskier."

Ross must have decided to let the implication behind the word *duskier* lie. "I could see that *you* were very keen to learn," he said. "It's a small world, Jimmy. I didn't recognise you with the beard, - and you've grown a little bit since then."

Murrells laughed. "I would have been a fresh-faced lad of about fourteen then, but I was big for my age and I managed to get an apprenticeship by saying I was sixteen. My father wasn't too pleased at first when he found out, but I went back to Maldon and made my peace with him when I finished my apprenticeship." He paused and felt his eyes mist over when he thought about that sad time of his life, and his late mother's words echoed in his mind.

'If you can make a change that will grant you true love and happiness you must be determined enough to follow it through.'

Ross was looking at him oddly so he cleared his throat and continued. "My father was happy enough by then, because my uncle had started working for him in his engineering workshop, but he still insisted that it was the safest and most secure prospect for my future well-being. He said he hoped I'd reconsider it when I got over my reckless pursuit of adventure and decided to settle down."

"But you haven't had enough *reckless* adventures to satisfy your wanderlust just yet?" Ross said, eyeing his client with renewed interest.

Murrells shook his head. "The short voyages on the colliers and coastal traders that I shipped on weren't exciting enough for me after a while so I began to think that I would like to get some experience on something a bit bigger and maybe go on a longer voyage. I was fortunate enough, or so I thought at the time, to get on the troop ship *Ramales* as carpenter's mate."

Ross looked at him curiously. "You thought you were lucky at the time, - but not so much now, - I take it from that remark. Wasn't the voyage on the *Ramales* stimulating enough for you either?"

"Oh, it was great to be on the open ocean and the work was easy enough. All troop ships have to carry a double complement of hands, as I'm sure you're aware, and we had fine weather for much of the six month voyage. We shipped a regiment of Infantry bound for Hobart Town and a detachment of Artillery bound for Sydney and then New Zealand, but if I'd known what the Artillery was supposed to do over there I would never have been a part of it."

"You mean the Maori War?" Ross raised his eyebrows.

Murrells nodded. "I left the *Ramales* here in Sydney because they had no more need of half the crew, but I shipped on the *Terror* for New Zealand after that, and I saw first-hand what was going on there."

"You've obviously been troubled by what you saw, lad," the clerk said. Ross's pen was poised over the contract again. "Got any idea what your date of birth is?"

"Yes, it's the twentieth of May 1824."

"Good lad. You'd be surprised how many sailors haven't got a clue when they were born. That makes you twenty-one years old. That's fairly young for an experienced Able Seaman." He dipped the pen in the inkwell, handed it to Murrells and then turned the contract around and shoved it across the desk. "Sign your name or mark your X here, Jimmy. Do you want me to read the agreement to you?"

Murrells shook his head and signed his name.

"Ah, you've had some schooling, I see, lad." Ross looked impressed at the signature.

Murrells nodded. "Five years at Heybridge Village National School."

"I suppose you read the English news sheets whenever you get the opportunity?"

"Yes I do," Murrells agreed.

The clerk looked at him intently for a moment. "I hope you realise that you'll still be within the British Empire if I can get you a berth to Hong Kong, Jimmy?" he said. "It's a British colony now too, so if you want to leave the empire altogether you might have to contact another agent when you get there."

"Yes, I've read about the Treaty of Nanking." Murrells said. "It was the result of hostilities between the British and the Chinese about the opium trade, wasn't it?"

"Sure was, lad," the clerk nodded. "It's another example of our British 'gunboat' diplomacy. The Emperor wouldn't agree to legalise and tax opium in China, because of his alarm at the number of addicts it was producing amongst his subjects, and he actually had his Viceroy confiscate 20,000 chests of the stuff from the British East India Company. We, the Britishers that is, were annoyed of course, and sent in the navy with all guns blazing. It ended with the Chinese having to sign the Treaty of Nanking two years ago and part of the compensation was the cession of Hong Kong to the Empire."

"That's bad enough, but it doesn't affect me as much as the situation with the Maori." Murrells said. "You see, it's not so much the conflict between two nations squabbling over financial deals gone wrong that I detest, but the taking unfair advantage of a nation of innocent people. The Maori don't deserve to have their land seized by crooked merchants who claim that they're entitled to acquire it legally on behalf of the empire."

Ross countersigned the contract document below Murrells' signature. "That all sounds great in principle, Jimmy," he said, "but if you're going to reside in the Australian colonies for any length of time then you'd better get used to the rough treatment that's commonly handed out to the Aborigines."

Murrells face showed his surprise. "It's happening here too?"

Ross sat back in his chair and studied his young client. "Oh yes, it's probably worse than New Zealand in my opinion. It's true that we got off to a good start in our relations and there were a lot of friendly interactions between the British and the local tribes back in the early years of settlement. It went rapidly downhill though, when the Aborigines realised that the weird looking white people, with their strange animals and equipment, were here to stay and had every intention of settling on the land *they* had occupied for countless generations. Some of them turned to aggression to let their feelings be known, but the superior weapons of the invaders made the difference, of course. The boundaries between tribal areas were quite tenuous too and could vary depending on the relationships between neighbouring tribes, so it was quite easy for the British Government to declare the whole continent *Terra Nullius.* I suppose you've heard of the term."

Murrells shook his head.

"It means 'nobody's land' in Latin," Ross said. "It's a concept that's used to describe territory that has never been subject to sovereignty of any kind and therefore can be occupied by whoever discovers it."

Murrells frowned. "But how could the British Government justify the notion that this land was unoccupied when it would have been quite obvious from the beginning that it was?"

"Ah well, you see, it was an ancient Roman concept that was given legal status a thousand years ago to allow the Christian Holy Crusaders to claim land inhabited by non-Christians. I suppose it was quite shrewd as far as the British Government was concerned, to realise that it could be equally applied to justify the seizing of this land from the original inhabitants who, in British principle at least, didn't have possession of it anyway."

Murrells grimaced. "The Aboriginal customs and laws weren't written down on paper, so the British government decided the country had no owners, - is that what you're saying?"

Ross nodded. "Yes, that's how the law was interpreted. The land was empty of anyone who could claim legal ownership of it. I suppose Governor Phillip, with his strict British notion of land ownership wouldn't have been able to understand the concept of people living in the equivalent of small English villages without the necessary chain of authority above them to organise and control every part of their lives."

"But they must have some kind of hierarchy and tribal boundaries." Morrill said

"The government agents couldn't locate provable tribal chiefs similar to the Maori that they could sign treaties with. The strongest Aboriginal men are often leaders of several families and may have as many as four wives, but the laws of the tribe are strictly governed and administered by a respected group of elders."

"It still sounds very much like the Maori land grab." Murrells shook his head in dismay.

"With one major difference," Ross said. "The big problem here is that, unlike the Maori, even the Aborigines don't regard the land as belonging to any one person or group of people." He paused, gathering his thoughts. "You said earlier that you might go back to Maldon and settle down one day, and just like you, most of us Europeans have a nostalgic connection with our birthplace, but the Aborigines have a much deeper connection to the land than that. It would be more accurate to say that they believe their country *owns* them and that when they die, no matter where they are, they will come home to join the spirits of their ancestors who still live in their spiritual home."

"So it's not just their land that's being taken away; it's their sacred home, just like Christians have a place called Heaven to hope for after death." Murrells was stunned. He'd thought that what was happening to the Maori was the fault of a corrupt and backward New Zealand administration supporting the demands of arrogant Sydney traders.

It had reminded him so much of the story his mother had told him of the plantation owners who'd pressured the House of Assembly in Jamaica to resist the anti-slavery laws, citing their dependence on the labour required for the plantation economy. The people didn't matter in either case. It was all about the ongoing accumulation of the wealth of the Empire, but he hadn't dreamt that the corruption was so widespread.

Ross nodded. "You're quite right," he said. "But *we* only have a vague idea of where and what our Heaven means to us. *They* know where theirs is and what it holds for them. A lot of people are starting to think that maybe their culture is just as civilised as ours, but in a different way, and we shouldn't be trying to force them to accept our religious beliefs, but the majority of church clerics and missionaries still believe that they have no spiritual values and need to be saved."

Murrells was impressed. Ross had obviously thought much on the subject. "So the only way to save the *heathens* from eternal damnation is to force them to believe in the same God that they believe in.?"

"Right again, but even those people have had to admit now that the poor heathens *must* have some idea of a life after death. Colonel Collins has reported that he questioned Bennelong, the Aborigine who went to England with Governor Phillip, about their idea of an existence after death and Bennelong said, to quote his own words, - *'when black fella he die, he tumble down a black fella, and he jump up a white one.'* He couldn't get much more out of him except that, - *'The black fella come from the clouds and go back to the clouds, that's all I know.'*

Collins concluded that Bennelong's answer was an indication of their lack of interest in the prospect of a future after death, but I contend, and so do other people, that it could just as easily be due to Bennelong's natural reticence to discuss the subject with *him,* someone that he knew held very different beliefs to his own. The Aborigines generally won't argue with a white person, but will say whatever they think the white person wants to hear, - it's just their way of avoiding conflict."

"I take it Colonel Collins is well known in the colonies?" Murrells said.

Ross laughed. "I forgot you've only just arrived, Jimmy. Colonel Collins is the well-established chronicler of everything that happens in the colony and is sure to be remembered as our first historian, but that doesn't mean that his opinion is always right. I certainly would have regarded Bennelong's answer as proof that his tribe *had* some sense of life after death, - not the opposite, - although probably nothing like Collins' idea of the hereafter."

Murrells mused over Bennelong's answer. *'When black fella he die, he tumble down a black fella, but he jump up a white one.'* "That's an interesting concept Clem," he said. "Do they imagine white people as some kind of – *ghosts of their dead ancestors,* maybe?"

Ross nodded. "They did at first, apparently. When the white strangers arrived they thought they were seeing relatives who had come back from the dead, so there's another reason to believe that they *do* have a sense of the afterlife. You see, their children are born quite pale and get darker as they age and when they burn the bodies of their dear departed on a funeral pyre the burning flesh goes pale, probably a shade of grey, before it's consumed by the flames. That's what I've been told anyway. I've never seen it of course."

"They burn their dead?" Murrells said.

"Some tribes do, others don't. The Aborigines are wise to the fact that we're not ghosts now of course, at least those around Sydney are. I've got no idea if the belief is widespread beyond the Sydney tribes, but there's no doubt in my mind that there will be some tribes we've yet to make contact with who will jump to the same conclusion."

"And be worse off for it," Murrells said with a grimace.

"Unfortunately, yes; I think they will suffer the same fate as the ones who've been *civilised* already," Ross said. "Civilised to the point of having to beg for their very subsistence in a land where they once roamed as free as the uncivilised kangaroos and wallabies they existed amongst."

He pulled a folder from the drawer and placed the document with Murrells details inside it. "Right then Jimmy," he said. "I'll get on to this right away. You can come back next week to find out if I've managed to get you a berth."

They shook hands and wished each other a 'good-day' at the door.

Clem Ross felt a pang of regret as his new client turned to leave, hands thrust deep in his pockets and his shoulders sagging, for he sensed that the young man was carrying a burden on his broad shoulders, *something to do with his family back in England probably*. It had shown on his face when he'd talked about going back to his home in Maldon one day.

He remembered his own youthful ambition to change the world for the betterment of the unfortunates who had got in the way of the expanding empire. And here was someone that he'd previously met at a time in his own life when *he* too was enjoying the freedom of reckless adventure. It was a time that he remembered with nostalgia; a time that he often reminisced on as he sat alone at his desk in this musty building, for in his mind he was still the young swashbuckling sailor that he had been then and not the balding, almost fifty year old has-been his shaving mirror told him he was now. This young man was a link with that exciting past, no matter how brief their encounter had been back then.

It had always irritated him that a severe leg injury, suffered when the merchant ship *Integrity* was wrecked in the Torres Strait in 1841 on a voyage from Sydney to Singapore, had forced him to abandon the most enjoyable experience of his life thus far. It had consigned him to this land based sedentary occupation, although he *was* grateful to the Merchant Marine Authority for looking after his welfare in the aftermath of the misadventure.

On impulse he did something that he'd never contemplated doing before with any client. He called after Murrells. "Where can I contact you if I can get a berth for you sooner, Jimmy?"

Murrells stopped and turned around to face him. "I'm at the Sailors Shelter," he said. "It's down by the Circular Quay."

Ross shook his head and screwed up his nose. "Yes I know where that dump is, and it should never have been allowed to operate." He grinned. "The food's not too bad because the council's sanitary inspectors keep a good watch on it, but I'll bet you're missing a good home cooked dinner?"

"I haven't had a nice pudding and roast vegies since I left Maldon." Murrells laughed, but he looked away quickly and his smile faded.

There it was again, Ross was certain he'd seen a flicker of melancholy pass across the young man's eyes. Something had surfaced in his memory and it had been triggered by the thought of a home-cooked meal. He took his broad-brimmed hat from a hook on the wall. "Let's go and get your baggage, lad. We've got a spare room you can bunk down in, and my Daphne is the best cook in Sydney."

Murrells looked astonished. "That's very kind of you, Clem," he said. "Are you sure Mrs Ross won't mind?"

Ross laughed. "She'll be all right with the arrangement, lad. We don't get many visitors at home. We don't associate much with the upper class in Sydney, - or I should say they don't associate much with us…" As an afterthought he added, "…except for my good friend Sir Maurice O'Connell."

He turned away without another word and started along George Street towards the Circular Quay with Jimmy Murrells falling into step beside him.

7

"Jimmy, there's a barque called the *Peruvian* sailing to Hong Kong with a load of cedar logs for cabinet making. The captain is a Scotsman by the name of George Pitkethly." Clem Ross said. "He hails from Dundee, the home port of the *Peruvian*. I've heard he's a good and fair man and because of that he usually holds the same crew together, but now for one reason or another, he's looking for an extra Able Seaman. What do you think? You could do a lot worse. After Hong Kong the barque's sailing on to England and then back to Dundee, but there should be plenty of opportunities for you to ship on to somewhere else if you still don't want to go home."

Murrells looked pleased. "Sounds like it's just the ticket I'm after. I thought I'd have to wait around in Sydney for a bit longer allowing for the number of idle sailors I've seen, but I suppose I just got lucky, - right, Clem?"

Ross contemplated his young guest for a moment. "Yes," he said at last. "Maybe you *did* get lucky." He produced a contract note, dipped a pen in the inkwell and signed the document with a flourish. He handed the contract to Murrells. "Give this to Captain Pitkethly, Jimmy."

"Thanks for your hospitality, Clem," Jimmy Murrells said sincerely. You and Mrs Ross have made my stay in Sydney very pleasant and I've learned a lot from your local knowledge." He stood up and shook hands with the clerk.

"You've been great company, Jimmy, and I've enjoyed our discussions too. Daphne asked me to give you her best regards and little Eliza Ann is going to miss you." He sighed audibly. "Let's get back to business now though. I'm duty-bound to give you a couple of final words of warning before you go," he said. "It's just to make sure you're under no shadow of doubt about the assignment ahead. Are you superstitious?"

Murrells shook his head. "No Clem, I'm not."

"Ah that's good, because the ship leaves on Friday."

"So?"

"A lot of sailors won't sail on Fridays. They reckon it brings bad luck to the ship and all who sail in her. To be perfectly honest, that's probably one of the reasons it was so easy for me to get you a berth on the *Peruvian*."

Murrells' expression was blank. "I don't care what day of the week we leave, – the sooner the better."

"The other reason may be that the captain has his wife on board," Ross persisted.

Murrells looked at him curiously. "I suppose he has every right to…."

Ross laughed. "…You young *Salts* haven't been at sea long enough to have learned any of the old *Jack-tar's* superstitions, have you?"

"You weren't supposed to take your *wife* with you?" the young sailor asked in bewilderment. "Surely that's the captain's right…?"

"…Tempting providence - and a double dose of bad luck," Ross said. "As I said, it's most likely the other reason why you got the berth so easily."

"Apparently Captain Pitkethly and his crew aren't superstitious either then." Murrells said. "It's *my* good luck then."

They shook hands at the door and the clerk slapped the young sailor's broad back. "I hope it *was* you're good luck, Jimmy, and I hope you have a great voyage with favourable winds. The schooner, *Lucy Ann* has just arrived from New Caledonia with a load of sandalwood and Captain Barr reported excellent weather conditions for the entire passage. Mind you, I hope your captain doesn't have a mind to stop in New Caledonia just because James Cook thought it looked like Pitkethly's homeland and named it for Caledonia in Scotland."

"I wouldn't mind visiting another new port," Murrells said.

"Not *that* port, lad; there are missionaries from the London Missionary Society trying to convert the Kanaks on the main islands," Ross grinned and bared his teeth. "And if that's not enough to put you off your visit, the American cutter, *Promise* was wrecked in a storm last year and the entire crew was captured and eaten by the Pouma clan in the Society Islands."

"Oh, - thanks for the warning, Clem. I'll do my best to persuade the captain not to give in to nostalgia if he decides to visit the New Caledonian cannibals." He chuckled. "I suspect, though, that the only providence we'll be in need of, *is* a good breeze on this voyage, no matter that we're leaving on unlucky Friday and the captain needs his wife to keep him company at night."

8

Jimmy Murrells strode along the Market Street wharf with his worldly possessions stuffed into a duffel bag that he carried slung over his shoulder. He stopped to admire the *Peruvian,* the vessel that was to be his berth for the next month or so, and he smiled inwardly, congratulating himself on his good fortune. It looked like a fine seaworthy ship and it seemed that this was going to be the easiest of assignments. He'd already made up his mind that he would spend some time exploring Hong Kong and then, as Clem Ross had suggested, take another ship to – wherever, only if it wasn't back to his home in England.

The sailor who met him at the foot of the gangway shouted orders to an apprentice on the deck and the lad was tasked with escorting Murrells to the dining room below the foredeck. Captain Pitkethly sat at the far end of the long bench that served as a table, studying some charts that were strewn in front of him. Behind his back was the porthole that provided the only source of light in the cabin and Murrells stood, cap in hand as the captain read through the document provided by Clem Ross. When he had finished he looked Murrells up and down and finally asked him to walk a few paces and then touch his toes and then, apparently satisfied as to his physical condition he studied the document again briefly. "Ye've come tae Sydney on the schooner, *Terror* from New Zealand, eh?"

"Aye sir, I did." Murrells nodded.

"Ye've been through quarantine then, lad?" he said.

"Aye captain – two weeks at the South Head Quarantine Station."

"An' ye've no' been consorting wi' any o' yon lassies down on the wharf since ye've been here?"

Murrells shook his head and grinned. "No captain. They were like a flock of seagulls squawking over a piece of bread, but I managed to get through the gauntlet."

The captain laughed. "Alright then, I'm satisfied ye'll dae the job just fine, lad."

'So that was my medical examination,' Murrells thought wryly. *'No having to bend over in front of a doctor with trousers at my ankles like I had to on boarding the Ramales. The captain is obviously the medical officer too.'*

The captain pushed his chair back and came around the edge of the desk. "Welcome aboard the *Peruvian,* Seaman Morrill," he said.

"I'm Captain Pitkethly. I understand Mr. Ross has furnished ye' wi' all the particulars o' the engagement?"

'I suppose I'm Morrill and not Murrells for the next month at least.'

"Yes sir, Mr. Ross was very thorough," he said.

The captain offered a calloused hand that was hardened enough to suggest immediately to Morrill that he was a hands-on leader who didn't spend all his time in his cabin poring over his charts, and later that day, after signing the final documents for his tenure he realised that there was much more to Captain Pitkethly than met the eye.

He learned from his apprentice attendant, as he helped him stow his gear in the crew's bunk cabin, that the *Peruvian's* captain was also a pious Presbyterian churchman who would recite prayers before the evening meal each day and then lead the crew in a hymn of praise before a single cup was lifted in a toast to good fortune on the voyage ahead. Morrill was amused by the solemn expression on the lad's face as he related this information, but after the first evening of the ritual, as the ship remained tied up at Circular Quay, he was even more amused to hear the crew break into a tuneless melody in unanimous support of the captain's vocal appeal to the Almighty for safe deliverance. It was quite obvious that Clem Ross's observation about the crew's allegiance to Captain Pitkethly was accurate.

'I hope the Lord is listening to our good captain's prayers because He surely wouldn't be impressed with the singing of his crew.'

9

Geordie Pitkethly ordered an apprentice to inform the cook that he was to have another place set for dinner. Later, as he was obligated to do before the ship's departure from each port, he instructed the crew on the various duties attached to each man's particular calling, the watches that they had been assigned for the first three days, and the basic responsibilities expected of each of them during the voyage, particularly with regard to health and cleanliness.

The captain was a great advocate for the consumption of citrus in its various forms for the prevention of scurvy, the cause of the deaths of countless passengers and crew on long distance voyages since it was first described by Hippocrates about 2300 years ago. He was justifiably proud too of the fact that a Scottish surgeon in the Royal Navy, James Lind, had conducted trials and found it to be a successful deterrent to the onset of the disease, - and of course the great James Cook, whom he admired greatly, hadn't lost a single crew member to scurvy in his three year voyage of discovery because of the remedy. Pitkethly made it quite clear that each crew member, as part of his duties, was required to consume the daily ration of lemon juice mixed with sugar that would be provided with the evening meal. Many of the sailors, including his brother Alex, of course, had sailed with the Pitkethly Shipping Line for some years, so there were no objections to the requirement, few questions to be answered at the initial assembly on the fore-deck, and it was simply a matter of introducing Morrill, the last to embark on the *Peruvian*, to the rest of the crew.

Apart from Captain Pitkethly and his brother Alex, the first mate, there were eleven other crew members besides Morrill. The second mate's name was John McDonald. The sailmaker was John Millar. William Harris was the carpenter. Edward McArthur was the cook. Jack Smith, Jim Dicks and Jim Gooley were able seamen and there were four apprentices, led by a particularly strong and mature young man called James Wilson who was close to finishing his apprenticeship.

The *Peruvian* had been laden right up to the load line painted on the hull known as *Lloyds Rule*, the maximum load allowed by the underwriters, Lloyd's of London. After customs clearance, the mail came on board, the moorings were cast off, and the barque sailed through Sydney Heads, the mile and a half wide entrance to Sydney Harbour on the morning of Friday 27th February 1846.

There were seven passengers aboard the *Peruvian*, although that number had to be revised to nine after the first day at sea with the discovery of two stowaways hiding under canvas in the bottom of the lifeboat. They were both of South Asian origin and their eyes, blinking rapidly in the sunlight as they emerged from the darkness, glittered starkly white against their sweating ebony faces when their hideaway was revealed.

Some of the crew, incensed at the impudence of the pair in sneaking on board the usually well-guarded ship without detection, elected to throw them overboard as the coastline was still visible off the port side of the ship, but the captain intervened.

"They're *Lascars*," he said. "They've probably jumped ship from a British East India Merchantman an' are trying tae get home."

His brother Alex glanced at him in surprise. "An' yer going tae let them stay on board? That's surely a breach o' the law, is it no', Geordie?"

"It would be *if* we were still in port," the captain said tersely. "But the breeze is too good fer us tae waste a day going back tae Sydney tae hand them in, an' *I'm* no' going tae face the prospect o' eternal damnation brought down on *me* personally an' maybe the rest o' ye' too, by tossing them into the sea. They'd never make it ashore because, as ye' should all be aware, the sea between us an' yonder landfall is infested wi' sharks." He looked around the crew and then eyeballed his brother. "Dae ye' want the accountability fer that on *your* conscience, Alex?"

"What's a Lascar?" One of the apprentices asked.

The captain was pleased at the diversion. "They're natives o' India, British Somaliland, or sometimes South Asia, recruited as cheap labour tae make up crew numbers by shipping companies like the British East India Company," he said.

"*Why* would they jump ship?" another asked. "I've heard that the company pays well an' a lot of sailors would be happy with a berth."

"They'd pay *you* well, because they'd have tae" the captain said. "It's a different matter altogether wi' the Lascars. Their wages are about one twentieth o' what their fellow white sailors get an' they're usually expected tae work longer hours fer a bowl o' rice or two each day."

"That's just another form of slavery, Captain Pitkethly," Morrill said, his eyes focussed on the two crouching, shivering men.

Geordie looked at him curiously. "It is indeed, Jimmy," he said. "The shipping companies have complete control over these poor creature's lives. They're often kept in squalid conditions fer years on end, ill-treated an' moved from one ship tae another at the whim o' the ship owners, - but I'm glad tae see ye've got some concerns fer the less fortunate among us." He was clearly impressed.

Morrill nodded and pulled himself together, raising his eyes to meet Pitkethly's. "Yes I do," he said quietly. "I'd like to do something eventually to make a difference to the lives of the *Empire's* discards."

Pitkethly studied the younger man's flushed face thoughtfully. He was about to commend him for his sympathetic feelings towards the plight of others, but stopped short, realising that Morrill was already ill at ease with the attention that was concentrated on him at that moment. He felt that the young seaman would have become even more self-conscious at any further words of praise. The inflection in his voice when he'd said the word *Empire* too gave Pitkethly a curious feeling that the young man had issues that he'd probably prefer not to air in public. He turned his attention once more to the general assembly. "Getting help fer these unfortunate wretches is extremely difficult. The Indians are generally treated a wee bit better, because they speak English, but very few of the South Asian Lascars do. That's probably where these two come from an' their ill-treatment usually goes unreported," he said.

"What are ye' going tae do wi' them, Geordie? Put them in chains fer the rest o' the voyage?" Alex said.

The captain looked at the two cowering men. "No' unless I have tae, Alex," he said. "But I need tae get through tae them that if they're willing tae work their passage I can tolerate two more pairs o' hands on deck until the ship reaches Hong Kong. When we get there though, they'll be deposited in the hands o' the authorities who can decide their fate from then on an' my conscience, - an' yours too, - will be clear."

The communication of their ultimate fate was conveyed to the terrified stowaways in sign language and gestures by the First Mate. A natural comic, Alex entertained the crew with his antics, but did succeed in making clear to the men that they *would* be thrown overboard if they refused to scrub the decks or do any of the other unpleasant tasks they were assigned. It was an empty threat, of course, but it had the additional outcome of appeasing the more hot-blooded amongst the crew who began to appreciate that *they* would be excused from performing those meanest of tasks themselves.

And so, with the two men relegated to the status of temporary crewmen, the passengers were again back to seven, including the captain's wife. The others, four adults and two young children, Morrill was told, had joined the ship in Melbourne and had, as a precaution, been confined to the cabins, well clear of the feverish activity that had accompanied the ship's passage through Sydney Heads and into open water.

The *Peruvian*, under a strong leading breeze and with all sails fully rigged, fairly raced up the coast of the Colony of New South Wales, its pointed bow easily piercing the Pacific swell, and the crew, except for McArthur, the cook, and the second mate McDonald who was on watch, with not much labour to occupy their time, began to relax and play deck games on the main-deck to pass the time.

Captain Pitkethly, himself in a relaxed mood, reclined with Betsy and the other passengers on deckchairs on the aft-deck, which was raised about head height above the main-deck.

"What's that game called, Geordie?" Betsy said. She'd been watching intently as the sailors marked out a square in chalk on the deck with sides about three feet long, divided it into nine smaller ones, each about one foot square. They then chalked a number between one and eight in each square at random, except for the centre square which was given the number nine.

"It's called shovel-board," Pitkethly said. "Each player has three *boards*, - being circular pieces o' inch-thick timber about four inches wide. The idea is tae slide them along the deck an' try tae land them on the highest numbers. The next player then tries tae shovel yer board off the square wi' his own an' leave *his* board in the square. The player wi' the highest number wins the game."

A board, shovelled a bit carelessly by one of the boisterous sailors, landed close to the rail that separated the main deck from the aft-deck and Morrill went to fetch it.

"Seaman Morrill," the captain said. "I'm sorry tae disturb yer game, laddie, but I'd like my wee wife an' my guests tae make yer acquaintance as ye've only just joined us in Sydney."

Morrill grinned and glanced towards the pleasant faced little woman who sat by the captain's side, her dark hair with its centre parting visible beneath a coal-scuttle style bonnet. "Aye captain," he said, removing his cap. "Hello Mrs Pitkethly."

"Aye, hello yerself, Jimmy." Betsy smiled back.

"An' here's my other guests," the captain said. "This is Mr. Willmett." He indicated a pale, clean-shaven young man of about twenty-five. He wore a white suit and a grey waistcoat and had been lounging on a deck chair, but quickly got to his feet and leaned over the rail.

"Hello Seaman Morrill," he said with a wide grin.

Morrill took his outstretched hand and grinned back. "It's Jimmy, sir."

"Ah, then you must call me John," Willmett said. "No need for formalities, eh, especially when our very lives may well be in your hands." He winced and pulled his long slender hand away from Morrill's grip, massaging his fingers with the other. "By Jove, and a strong pair they are too, I must say."

He turned to the woman who had been sitting beside him. She was as pale-faced as Willmett, but where his features were pallid her cheeks were pink with the flush of motherhood. She was simply dressed in a plain cream-coloured day frock with a matching wide brimmed sun hat that not only protected her from the sun, but also shielded the exposed face of the sleeping infant that she cradled in her arms wrapped in a white shawl. "This is my wife Emma and the latest addition to our family, John William, six months old and with a voice as powerful as a two year old when he's hungry."

Morrill bowed slightly with his white cap clutched firmly in both hands. "Afternoon, Mrs Willm…."

"It's Emma, if you please, Jimmy," she flashed him a pleasant smile. "As John said, "there's no need to be formal, is there?"

Willmett looked beyond her towards a dark-haired young woman who sat on a blanket playing a game with a baby. "And this is Nora, our nanny, with Frances, our two year old daughter."

Morrill grinned and looked into Nora's deep blue eyes. Unlike the married ladies she wore a white linen cap over her centre-parted dark hair and long curls dangled down towards the front of her simple V-neck cotton day dress. She said in an unmistakably Irish brogue. "Sure, an' it's delighted I am to meet ye', Jimmy."

"Very pretty," Morrill mumbled. He felt his face flush and added quickly, "Ah, little Frances, I mean, - pretty little thing, she is."

A smile played on Nora's lips and she held his gaze for several seconds before the child's shrill demand that the game be resumed drew her attention away from him.

The captain spoke again. "This is Mr. Quarry, Jimmy."

Morrill looked in the man's direction. He too was pale in his complexion with high cheekbones and black hair, and sideburns that poked out from under a tall hat that accentuated his gaunt moustached face. A boldly checked waistcoat covered his thin chest, and the way his legs, encased in long riding boots, hung over the end of the deckchair, Morrill guessed he would have been a bit over six foot tall. That was difficult to gauge, however, for he hadn't bothered to stand and simply eyed Morrill with a laconic smile.

"Jephson Busteed Quarry," he said; the pitch of his voice low and terse. "I'm sure you will find it in your heart to excuse me for not shaking hands, Mr. Morrill, but I noticed that you found it necessary to assert your manly dominance over John, my brother-in-law, and I *would* like to keep all of my fingers intact, if you don't mind."

Morrill laughed, pretending to ignore the man's apparent hostility. "I'm afraid I don't know my own strength, Mr Quarry," he said with a dismissive wave of his hand. He turned back to Willmett. "I'm sorry, John. I can assure you I meant no harm…"

John Willmett seemed unperturbed. "Don't worry about *'Buster'*, Jimmy," he said light-heartedly. "He's trying to overcome a regretful experience so he's a bit despondent at the moment. He'll cheer up soon enough." He turned to look at Quarry. "*Won't* you Buster?"

Morrill couldn't see his face but he knew by the difference in his tone and the way Quarry flinched that Willmett *had* been annoyed by his discourtesy.

The captain, perhaps seeing an awkward situation developing said, "I think the lads are waiting fer ye' tae get back tae the game, Jimmy."

Morrill locked eyes with Quarry and a bewildered frown creased his forehead for a moment as the man regarded him with an arrogant, thin-lipped sneer, but he shrugged his broad shoulders, turned away from Quarry and then acknowledged Willmett's remark with a grin before saluting the captain. "Aye, aye captain," he said.

He turned his back to the group, retrieved the errant board, and went back to re-join the rowdy crew who were indeed calling him to his turn at the shovel, but the feeling of perplexity at the resentment in Quarry's voice remained with him for the rest of the afternoon just the same.

10

Morrill had drawn the first 'dog watch' on the second night out. He secured the wheel, for the ship ran true to course, and then he looked out over the vast darkness of the Pacific Ocean. A half-moon had risen well above the horizon to the east and it cast its feeble reflection across the shimmering sea. Far to his left over the port side rail of the ship he could just discern the indistinct line of the coastline. Was that a light he could see flickering faintly in the distance; a lighthouse maybe, or a tiny community of adventurous settlers clinging to a meagre existence in the wild coastal land of the colony north of Sydney? Or was it something else again?

He'd asked Jack Smith about them at the watch handover and he'd been of the opinion that those mysterious pin-points of light were more likely an indication of a tribal gathering around a campfire; - something Smith said was called a *corroboree*. He'd seen one on the outskirts of Sydney and he'd described the scene to Morrill briefly before wishing him an uneventful watch as he took his leave. Morrill closed his eyes and imagined he was there, sitting cross-legged on the edge of the circle beating time to a dozen pairs of dark feet as they pounded the dust in rhythmic unison.

A voice behind him broke into his reverie. "Well then, *fancy* meeting you here, Jimmy Morrill."

He turned quickly and his heart raced. "Nora?"

"It is, an' all. It's me, Nora O'Meara."

"Are you *supposed* to be out here on your own?" His eyes swept the deck behind her.

"Course I am," she said. "The wee-uns are asleep and so is the missus, Emma. I'm me own woman tonight, - for a little while at least"

She leaned over the rail beside him and she was so close that he became pleasantly aware of her fragrance wafting in the light breeze that fanned her hair, for she wore no bonnet in the cool night air.

"You might catch a chill up here," he said, trying to sound grave and humourless, for he felt ill at ease with the distraction from duty that his visitor represented.

She giggled, ignoring his firm tone. "I'm sure ye' could keep me warm if I get *too* cold. Did ye' really mean what ye' said today?"

"About what?" he said.

She turned towards him and the light from the half-moon caught the profile of her pale face in its feeble glow. "Sure ye' know well enough; ye' said that I was pretty."

Morrill mumbled. "Oh that? - I was talking about the baby, little Frances."

She shook her head. "No ye' were *not* talking about the wee-un at all, Jimmy Morrill."

Morrill scanned the dark ocean ahead of the ship's bow for any tell-tale sign of white breakers. "Well, maybe not, but I shouldn't have said it."

"An' why not, may I ask?"

Morrill could imagine Nora's eyes flashing with indignation in the moonlight, but he avoided her gaze and focussed instead on his examination of the horizon for anything amiss. "I was thinking about my introduction to the other passengers and wondering what I might have done to draw the ire of Mr. Quarry. The only reason I could think of was that you and he, - well I mean…"

Nora laughed. It was a light pleasant laugh, but it had a touch of irony to it. "…Believe me, Jimmy. There's nothing at all between Buster an' myself, although it's not for the want of trying on his part. The man's a boorish dandy who thinks all women are in love with him, - or if they're *not*, they ought to be."

"Well that's a relief to know." Morrill said," but why was he so ratty with me then? I'd only just met him and he behaved like I was his worst enemy."

"You *are* his worst enemy at the moment, Jimmy; every man who he considers a threat to his manly superiority is his enemy; it's all in his own imagination, of course."

Morrill shrugged. "I can't understand how an ordinary seaman like me would be a threat to him. It would more likely be someone like John Willmett. He seemed to have some kind of a hold over him."

"Yes, he has too, Jimmy, - a *big* hold over him."

Morrill was absorbed by their conversation now and the possibility of being thrown in the brig, accused of dereliction of duty, had been banished from his mind. "How did they become related?" he said. "Quarry said he was John's brother-in-law."

"Yes, - an' so he is too," Nora said. She exhaled audibly and shook her head. "The conniving scoundrel managed to get himself ingratiated with Emma Willmett's family because he's such a well-known solicitor an' he handled some legal matters for them. He's considered to be a *'swellish'* man-about-town in Melbourne an' Emma's mam wanted a match that reflected her own social standing in the community. She herself was Elizabeth Bowman, a daughter of the Bowman's who own 'Tarrawingee' station, no less, so she was behind the scene persuading the ever-so-splendid Jephson Busteed Quarry to marry Emma's sister, Helen."

"I see, - so why isn't Helen with him?" Morrill was intrigued.

"Helen was only fourteen at the time." Nora said. "Three months after she was bullied into marrying Buster she took laudanum and put a knife to her wrist." She looked at Morrill through the gloom. "I can't blame the child. Can ye' imagine being married to *that* feeble excuse for a man?"

Morrill had to admit to himself that he couldn't, but he supposed that he shouldn't develop any preconceived ideas about the man due to one brief encounter. He merely shrugged and remained silent while Nora went on talking.

"Helen survived her so-called suicide attempt, though. I don't think she even took enough laudanum to put herself into an afternoon catnap, an' the cut on her wrist was trifling, according to the doctor. He was an honest man, for he said plainly it was nothing more than an expression of dissent against what she'd been forced into doing. Anyway, the next thing that came along to disturb the peace an' keep the tongues wagging was the Willmett affair."

"The Willmett affair?"

"Oh yes, now that *was* a big scandal that rocked our little Melbourne Town to the core. Ye' have to understand that there were only about ten thousand people living there a couple of years ago, an' only a few of those were what I'd call *'toffee noses'* so everybody else knew what was going on, even though they tried to keep it behind closed doors. Quarry sent Helen home to live with John and Emma; it was done *'to try to sort her out'* he said, but it was common knowledge he'd been seeing another woman – or possibly several. Helen didn't waste any time feeling sorry for herself either, because Mr. Willmett – John, that is, caught a man trying to sneak into the house one night to see her. They got into a scuffle an' the man pulled a gun an' shot John in the arm."

"That's pretty serious – even in the colonies." Morrill said.

"It is," Nora agreed. "Buster found a letter from the man to Helen so he knew who he was, an' he challenged him to a duel – just like in the old days, but Melbourne Town's becoming a bit more civilised now an' the authorities put a stop to it. The Separation Association has started a petition for Port Phillip District to become a separate colony from New South Wales in the next five years an' the district administrators needed to show that they were able to keep the population under discipline. That's one of the reasons we're all here on the *Peruvian*. It was strongly suggested that the Willmett's an' Buster Quarry depart from Melbourne for a while to let the scandal die down."

"One of the reasons?" Morrill said. "It sounds like there's more to the man than I first thought."

"There is," she said. "Much more, to be honest with ye'. He smokes opium ye' know. He used to take laudanum for what he calls his *melancholia*, but he got so addicted to it that eventually it wasn't strong enough for him. The Willmett's scullery maids all believe that opium was the real cause of the Willmett affair. Quarry couldn't get enough of it because it wasn't so readily available during the Opium War with China an' he became quite fierce towards Helen at times..."

Morrill's eyes scanned the horizon again, but he saw nothing to cause him any disquiet, and he remembered his conversation with Clem Ross, the shipping agent. *'The Emperor wouldn't agree to legalise and tax opium in China and he had his Viceroy confiscate 20000 chests of it from The British East India Company.'*

"...Buster calls opium his *comforter* an' he thinks none of the scullery hands are clever enough to know when he's been having it, but we all had to admit that his attitude did improve when he could get a hold of it so we just pretended we knew nothing about it."

"That helps to explain his aggression towards me, I suppose." Morrill said. "I guess he has a craving for it now?"

Nora agreed. "Oh, he's got some, but he's got enough of his wits about him to know that he's got to ration it out to himself until he gets to Hong Kong."

'We sent in the navy with all guns blazing and it ended with the Chinese having to sign the Treaty of Nanking two years ago.'

"You seem to know a lot of the Melbourne gossip for someone so young," Morrill said.

"Sure now I'm not at all *that* young; I'm eighteen," Nora said. "Well almost," she added. "John and Buster think I'm just a little Irish scatterbrain who pays them no mind when they're chit-chatting between themselves, but I've got a good pair of ears that are not just for dangling ornaments off. I can read the newspapers a little bit too if the words aren't too big, but most times I don't have to worry about that, because the servants *all* sit around an' talk anyway. You'd be surprised at some of the conversations that go on in the scullery."

Morrill laughed. "The *toffee-noses* have clearly misjudged the little Irish scatterbrain and her scullery friends."

"Buster should know better," she said. "He's from Cork, - that's in the south of Ireland." She looked at Morrill through the gloom and he nodded. "You *know* where it is? Ah, that's good. I'm from the west myself. He's from the Anglo-Irish upper class, an' I mean no offence to you an' your English family Jimmy, but some of them in particular have been the ruination of dear old Erin. He's had a good education an' I haven't been that privileged, like so many in the barren west of our country, but I *am* learning all the time an' in many ways I think I'm more fortunate than he is, because I know my place in the world an' I know where I want to be in the future. Buster has no idea where he wants to be. He only cares about how long he has to wait until John allows him to have his next hit of comforter. The truth is that John would never have got him out of Melbourne if he hadn't told him he'll have all the opium he can smoke when he gets to Hong Kong."

"And where *do* you want to be little scatterbrain?" Morrill teased her.

Nora dug an elbow into his ribs. "I just want to be happy an' contented with my life, Jimmy Morrill," she said. "I want a good man to love me an' some wee-un's of my own. I don't need anything more than that, - just enough food to fill the bellies of my little family an' enough coal for to keep us all warm by our fireside in the cold of the winter evenings."

It could have been the breeze in the rigging, but it seemed to Morrill that she shivered suddenly and an involuntary moan issued from her lips. He instinctively put a comforting arm around her slim shoulders. She leaned against him, and it was then that he realised she was sobbing inaudibly, her small frame heaving with some memory that had surfaced from deep in her thoughts. "There now, Nora," he said quietly. "What's bothering you?"

Her arm slid around his waist and gripped him tightly, as if she thought he might decide to leave her alone at the railing and disappear into the night. "It's my poor unfortunate Da' an' my Mam I'm thinking about; - they only wanted the very same," she sighed, "but their simple desire was never destined to become their grand achievement an' they went to meet the angels without ever fulfilling their dream."

Morrill scanned the horizon again. Away to port he could see the indistinct black silhouette of the top of a mountain range, the firmament behind it dimly illuminated by the residual afterglow of the sun that had dipped below its rim hours ago, but not a single light revealed the presence of any living thing on its steep slopes. Directly ahead the bowsprit rose and fell in the swell with only the faintest of splashes, but the forestay hung loose with no forestay sails rigged, and beyond it, - blackness. To starboard there was nothing to be seen either, for the half-moon had climbed too high for its faint glow to distinguish even a shadowy line to separate sea from sky. It was as if the ship was bobbing up and down in a black pond with nothing to indicate its forward movement but the billowing main-sails above his head and the hissing of the breeze in the rigging.

He hugged the distressed young woman who clung to him. It was a situation *he'd* found himself in before, but at that time in his life it was he who had needed the comforting and now he wasn't quite sure of what he should do or say. Nora was obviously reliving a similar painful memory. "If you want to tell me about it," he said uncertainly. "I'm listening, Nora."

"I *will* tell ye' a bit about my life; it's been bottled up inside me for so long now an' I know ye' won't mind listening, but it's not your pity I'm after needing. I knew ye' were a good man an' one that I could trust the minute I clapped eyes on ye', Jimmy Morrill," she said. "An' I *know* ye' were *not* talking about the wee-un at all when ye' said I was pretty. It came out of your mouth so naturally an' ye' blushed like a love-smitten fourteen year old boy."

"I was embarrassed…"

She put two fingers to his lips. "…now let's not start our friendship with a lie, Jimmy," she said.

Morrill groaned, for the tender touch of her fingers, the sweet fragrance and warmth of her body against his, and the gentle rocking of the ship under a clear night sky with its canopy of twinkling stars had aroused in him a slow burning desire that he had no real understanding of, but what he did know was that this was a singular moment in time that he would remember for the rest of his life. "Ah well then, yes I *was* talking about you, Nora," he managed to mumble.

She sighed. "I *have* been lucky in so many ways, Jimmy, because the Willmett's have been good to me, but they're much too preoccupied with the upsets in their own lives to be listening to any sorrowful tales of mine."

Morrill attended her every word while she spoke, interrupting her only to ask a question or clarify a point, and by the time she'd finished her weeping had subsided and she merely heaved an occasional sigh as if the imparting of the story to a sympathetic ear had lessened the sorrow in her heart. Morrill was thankful for the darkness then, because he knew that his misty eyes would have given away his heartache for her if she had been able to see them, and that would possibly have made her grief even more acute. At last he took a deep breath and composed himself. "It's a sad story, Nora," he said. "I wish I could…"

"Well now, I suppose you couldn't sleep then, Nora?" A voice said out of the darkness.

Nora spun around. "What in God's name are ye' doing creeping about in the dead of night, Buster Quarry?" she cried.

"Oh, I was just doing the same as you obviously are, - taking in the cool night air, Nora." Quarry laughed, but it was a hollow sound with no hint of mirth in it. "I see you're getting to know Able Seaman Morrill a little better."

"That's none of your business, Buster." Nora's voice was at breaking point as she tried to contain her anger.

Morrill stepped forward. "Leave Nora alone, Mr Quarry," he said, his voice quiet but firm. "It's my fault entirely."

The two men faced each other in the darkness. Quarry, about a head taller, but thinner than Jimmy, peered down at him for a tense moment and then he laughed again in his eerily hollow tone. "I'm sure it is, Seaman Morrill. *My* little virtuous Nora wouldn't be at all to blame," he said. "I'm sure she *must* have mentioned that she and I have an undeclared bond between us."

"We have no such thing, Bust..." Nora started, but Morrill was quick to intervene.

"Does your young wife in Melbourne know about this *bond* that you have with Nora, Mr Quarry?" he said.

Quarry drew in a deep breath and then exhaled noisily. "You have me at a disadvantage here on *your* ship, Seaman Morrill," he said. "Perhaps we can discuss this like gentlemen when we disembark at Hong Kong?"

It was Morrill's turn to laugh. "Right then Mr Quarry, if that's what you want," he said, "but do I have to search for you through all the opium dens in Hong Kong in order to have this *discussion*?"

Quarry's head whipped around to look probingly at Nora as she leaned against Morrill's shoulder, but it was too dark for him to see the wry smile on her lips. He turned his back on the couple and walked away into the gloom without another word, bounding down the gangway to the main deck.

Sleep did not come easily to Morrill later as he lay in his hammock in the cramped crew's quarters between decks, and it wasn't the snoring of his shipmates that had him staring wide-eyed at the beam so close above his head that he could touch it. Nora's story of her life had affected him deeply and he recoiled at the thought of the British Empire's role in the terrible circumstances that had resulted in her becoming an orphan in this land so far from her home.

She'd been born in a village somewhere in the mid-west of Ireland where the land was fertile and the grass lush and green, but her family had been forced to leave their cottage and move into a derelict stone hut in the Burren, the most sterile part of Ireland's Atlantic west coast, because the landowner wanted to graze cattle for the lucrative English market.

No vegetable would grow in the desolate Burren in sufficient quantity to feed a family, except for the humble potato; that hardy plant could grow in stony ground and provide just enough nourishment for their daily needs, but to make their circumstances even more dire, the precious potato crop was afflicted by the blight. It was the worst so far of the many outbreaks of the disease that had occurred throughout Ireland's recent history, and the poorest people in the far west were the first to feel its deadly effect. That was three years ago and as far as Nora knew it's still raging now, affecting three-quarters of the population of Ireland and many more in the Scottish Highlands.

Nora's father had joined a peaceful protest in Galway, to try to force the British Government to release stored grain to the starving population, but had been arrested and imprisoned in one of the rotting prison hulks in Galway Bay. He'd been sentenced to seven years transportation to Van Diemen's Land and his faithful wife had pawned almost everything they owned, precious family heirlooms that had belonged to her grandmother and had been intended for Nora's glory box on her betrothal, just to follow him.

The only article that Nora had refused to part with was a tiny gold locket on a gold chain in the shape of an orb. She'd shown it to him by the light from an oil lamp that hung above the door to the passengers' quarters. It wasn't really of much monetary value anyway, she'd said, but when the clasp was undone Morrill was impressed, for it revealed a tiny photo of a young, smiling Nora on one half and opposite it, another of a man with a strong face and a broad grin, obviously taken in much happier times.

"That's my da'," she'd announced proudly. "Is he not the most handsome out of all the men ye've ever seen in your entire life?"

When Nora and her mother had disembarked in Hobart Town, the sentimental value of that tiny locket increased enormously for it was the only photo she was ever destined to have of her da' who, they were told without much compassion, had perished on the voyage and been buried at sea.

Morrill could imagine the desolation that this news must have brought to the mind of a fourteen year old girl, for he'd surely felt a similar devastation when he himself was at the same age, but at least in his case he'd been amongst family and friends. Nora had been abandoned in a strange place with her mother who had so devotedly followed her man to the prison settlement at Port Arthur. With no money and no means of support they'd been removed to the women's workhouse on the Derwent River where, within two months, Nora's mother had succumbed to a relatively minor illness and Nora found herself orphaned.

It was a situation he'd become familiar with. *'Superior force used to take control of a whole population; plunder everything of value and when the victims protest, use even more force to beat them into submission. What was it Clem Ross had called it? Yes, he'd called it Gunboat diplomacy.'*

But from what he'd now learned, it seemed that the taking of their possessions wasn't the vilest act that the Empire had perpetrated on the people it had conquered. It was the wilful and systematic obliteration of their culture; their very way of life, and not least of all it had relegated their humanity to a position less important than that of its own beasts of burden.

The lamp near the doorway sputtered and then went out and Morrill finally found some scant comfort in a troubled sleep that was full of images of forlorn dreams frustrated by circumstances he couldn't control, but through it all the one thing he felt sure about was that he had found that love that his mother had spoken of. He realised that his encounter tonight with Nora had gone far beyond that of two lonely young people seeking comfort in each other's arms. It was not simply the romantic notion of defending a vulnerable girl who had, perhaps, seen him as the means of providing her deliverance from a world in which she could see no other future?

'In the end, love, whether it's love of another human being, or simply love of life, will be what defines your future happiness.'

No, he decided. Nora's love and contentment would be what defined his future and he would care for her and protect her for as long as he lived.

Nothing can separate us now except... He moaned softly and pressed the pillow to his face to stifle the sound... *death itself.*

11

Geordie Pitkethly stood erect at the far end of the long bench that served as a table in the dining room below the fore-deck. Behind his back was the porthole that provided the only source of light in the cabin and was the reason for his choice of position. He held the dog-eared bible that was so dear to him in his right hand and had placed his left on the shoulder of his wife Betsy, who sat at the head of the table next to him. Today was Sunday and, for the moment, he was no longer Captain Pitkethly. Each Sunday he became the Reverend George Pitkethly, and in this capacity he felt it was his obligation to conduct the Sunday service.

He looked around his small congregation. John Willmett sat at the other end of the table near the door, his wife Emma on his right, cradling baby John William in her arms. Opposite Emma was Nora, holding on to a squirming Frances, and standing behind them were the four apprentices, compulsory attendees, and several of the crew including Jimmy Morrill.

"Thank ye' all very much fer yer attendance," Geordie said. "The Lord has seen fit tae bestow on us another fine day fer us tae celebrate the Sabbath." He paused and opened his bible. "It's a great pity Mr. Quarry is unwell *again* an' unable tae join us."

Nora stole a glance towards Morrill. She had whispered to him earlier that Quarry was brooding in his cabin, smoking his comforter and professing his aversion, as an elder of the Church of Ireland, to be preached to by a *Presbyterian*.

By that afternoon the south-westerly breeze had freshened. The First Mate, Alex, was at the helm and he ordered foresails, main-skysails and every other stitch of canvas to be set. The Peruvian responded, slicing through the heavy swell at close to twenty knots and making good headway, but at sunset Geordie came up on deck and ordered all the smaller sails taken in again.

"I don't like the look o' this at all, Alex," he said, a worried frown creasing his brow. "This weather is intensifying by the hour."

"What are ye' worrying about, Geordie?" Alex was bemused. "Dae ye' no' think she can handle it? She went well enough in the North Sea an' rounding the Cape."

"Aye she did, right enough," Geordie said, "but the reports we got in Sydney said the weather was going tae be calm all the way up tae Hong Kong an' it's definitely no' looking calm at all now."

"Is that all ye're fretting about, - a wee bit o' wind?" Alex was still bewildered by his brother's reaction to what he considered to be a moderate change in the weather, but he knew Geordie well enough to realise there was something else adding to his uneasiness.

"It could get a lot worse; the sudden onset o' winds at this time o' year might mean a cyclone is brewing somewhere west o' the Coral Sea, - an' If we dae get one, I hope those cedar logs in the hold are well braced, Alex," he said. "They're stacked a bit too high fer my liking an' it's the first time we've had the *Peruvian* weighted right down tae the Lloyd's Rule mark."

"Well then, that's what the mark's there fer, isn't it Geordie?" Alex shook his head in exasperation as his brother shuffled off to join Betsy in their cabin.

At eight bells on Monday morning all hands were on deck to shorten sail once more as menacing black clouds rolled in from the south-west, and in the early afternoon a fierce storm drenched the watch. The captain called the crew into the dining room for a briefing. His charts had been rolled out and spread across the bench and his nautical almanac, dividers and parallel measuring rule lay on top. When everyone was finally squeezed in he called for silence.

"I called ye' together today because I want ye' tae understand the gravity o' our situation. I know it looks like the storm has passed at the present time, but I want *all* o' ye' tae be prepared fer another sudden change in the weather. It's the tropical monsoon season, ye' see, an' things can change fer the worse very quickly. The barometer's dropping an' I want ye' tae batten down the hatches an' check all stays an' shackles. I've already warned the passengers tae go tae their cabins an' remain there when I give the order an' tae tuck the wee bairns in their cots wi' plenty o' wadding in case we get buffeted around a bit. I'm fair confident we can ride out the weather, but we've got tae take all the precautions we can."

He looked around the group and smiled, and then pointed to a position on the chart in front of him. "By my calculations we're about here," he said. His voice was calm and measured, with no hint of urgency to it. "We're about a hundred miles east o' the most northerly port on the east coast of Australia. It's called Moreton Bay an', fer yer interest, it was a penal colony until about eight years ago when it was opened up tae free settlers."

He ran his finger up the coastline on the chart and around the northern tip of Cape York Peninsula, crossed the vast expanse of the Gulf of Carpentaria and stopped at a point on the northern Australian coast labelled the *Cobourg Peninsula* on the chart. "From Moreton Bay there's no' another port until we get tae the Victoria Settlement at Port

Essington in the Arafura Sea, an' I want tae avoid that hotbed o' fever an' sickness if I can."

He shook his head and looked around at his audience. "How the colonial government ever thought it could establish a port tae rival Singapore fifteen miles up a crocodile infested, land-locked harbour in one o' the most isolated parts o' the continent, I'll never understand..." He paused and returned his attention to his chart. "...but on the other hand, it probably was never meant tae succeed tae any great extent anyway."

One of the apprentices was obviously intrigued by the captain's last offhand remark for he blurted out, "Whatever do you mean, sir, - *It was never meant to succeed?*"

The captain looked up at the boy absent-mindedly, and then around the room, for all eyes were focussed on him and there were questioning looks on most of the other faces. He realised that he'd added the last observation without thinking. "Oh, well, lad...," he said, "...the French were showing a lot o' interest in establishing a trading outpost wi' Asia in the region. The empire had tae establish its own port tae reinforce its ascendancy an' indeed underpin its claim tae ownership o' the whole continent, not just New South Wales. It's nothing more than a military garrison wi' a lot o' sickness an' morale problems amongst the soldiers an' convict settlers who've been sent there from Sydney."

A couple of the apprentices showed some slight apprehension on their faces, but to their credit remained silent, their fears obviously buoyed by the perceived lack of concern on the faces of their captain and shipmates.

"Unfortunately, we have little choice now," the captain continued." We're beyond the point o' no return as far as Moreton Bay is concerned, because *if* we were tae alter course tae westwards an' run fer cover we'd be broadside on tae any approaching storm." He looked pointedly at Alex. "We're a bit low in the water wi' the cargo we've got on board too."

He pointed again at his chart. "On our current bearing an' speed we'll be on the inner side o' the Great Barrier Reef by ten bells Thursday afternoon, where we should get a bit o' relief from the heavy swell, - unless it changes tae a full gale force before that."

He paused again to make certain he had everyone's full attention. "Any questions, lads?"

Another of the apprentices raised his hand. "Is there *nothing at all* between here and Port Essington, sir?" He sounded incredulous.

"That's right; there's nothing in the way o' civilisation fer two thousand nautical miles lad," the captain confirmed. "Ye' might see a few lights, but don't be fooled intae thinking it's a sign o' civilisation, because they'll only be from the Aborigine's campfires."

"But are we going to be entering into uncharted waters, sir?" the boy persisted.

Pitkethly was in his element now. "No lad, certainly not," he said. "This coast has been well an' truly charted. I'm sure ye' all know about the celebrated explorer Lieutenant James Cook, later to be made a captain by the grateful British Government. He passed this way seventy-six years ago an' named many o' the islands and prominences along this coastline. His charts were so accurate, in fact, that when Matthew Flinders circumnavigated the continent in 1803 he was able tae identify all o' Cook's landmarks."

The apprentice wasn't satisfied. "Are we relying on charts that are over *forty* years old, sir?" he said. "Surely the colonial government has done more than *that* to open up this coastline."

Pitkethly was impressed. "Aye lad," he said. "Captain Phillip Parker King filled in the gaps left by the two other great explorers twenty-three years ago, an' I was on board on the last Beagle expedition just six years ago that explored the remaining coastline. That's why I knew about the settlement at Port Essington."

The apprentices, and even Morrill, stared at him in awe. James Wilson broke the silence. "*You* were the famous sailor that came back to Newburgh from that voyage?"

Pitkethly nodded. "Yes lad, I was."

"Then you must know the *whole* coastline very well, Captain Pitkethly." It was Jimmy Morrill who spoke, with a hint of admiration in his voice.

The captain shook his head. "No, Jimmy," he said. "Ye' see, all o' the navigators together charted the whole coastline, but obviously none o' us who came after James Cook went back over his discoveries because, as I've already said, Matthew Flinders found his charts tae be so accurate an' the voyage would have taken too long tae complete. I can easily recognise the parts o' the coast that *we* charted, an' I can rely on the charts o' the previous navigators fer the rest o' it that I've only seen as a distant outline on the horizon. Fer instance, the British Government has, just two weeks ago, given authorisation fer a new colony tae be established called North Australia, an' there have been discussions about establishing its capital port in the harbour that Matthew Flinders discovered an' called Port Curtis. Ye' see, James Cook passed by it at night." He pointed to the relevant point on his chart. "It's about three hundred an' fifty miles north o' Moreton Bay, but it's nothing more than a place name on our chart at the moment."

On Thursday morning the wind increased in intensity and blew with such force that, despite the best efforts of the crew to take them in, all of the fine weather sails were torn apart, leaving only the small storm sails to keep the vessel under some sort of control. The crew scrambled to cut away the tattered canvas, but by that evening the winds had increased again to such gale force that even the rugged storm sails were in danger of stripping. The captain ordered every stitch of sail taken down and the tired crew went to work with a will, but even on bare poles the ship was driven on through the crashing waves.

Friday dawned a little brighter and the occasional shaft of sunlight penetrated the dark clouds that continued to roll in from the south-west. The wind had moderated a little and the crew hoisted a new set of fine weather sails, then, working in two hour shifts, the exhausted men grabbed what little rest they could, knowing that their ordeal was not yet over.

The passengers, on deck for the first time since Monday evening, were aghast at the scene that confronted them and the women and children sat huddled together on the aft deck while John Willmett wandered about, picking his way around torn canvas and tangled rigging.

Nora joined Morrill as he sat with his back against the cabin wall on the aft deck during his designated break.

"That was a bit unexpected, was it not, Jimmy?" she said.

Morrill shrugged as she sat down next to him, pulling her long skirt underneath her legs and stretching her booted feet out in front of her.

"It was for me," he said, "but we've been told by the captain it's quite common for the weather to become unsettled suddenly in tropical regions like the Coral Sea at this time of year. They call it the *monsoon* season in south-east Asia apparently."

"The captain called that *unsettled*, Jimmy?" she said with a chuckle. "Buster Quarry said he was sure it was the end of the world." She screwed up her nose. "Let me think now; he said, *'it's the Lord's way of sending us all to damnation as punishment for that heathen captain's irreverent invocations'*."

Morrill laughed wearily. "Did he now?" he said. "And where is the great prophet of doom now, Nora?"

"He's where he usually is when he's in his troubled frame of mind," she grinned, "smoking his comforter in his cabin, of course." Her voice suddenly became serious. "He says he knows we're not going to get off this ship, Jimmy an' we're all going to the bottom of the ocean with it."

"And you *believe* him?" Morrill said, looking sideways at her.

She shrugged and smiled at him. "I don't know; I'm anxious, for sure," she said, "but I'm not *scared* of dying now, - not anymore." She leaned her head against his shoulder. "If we *are* all going to die, Jimmy Morrill, I can't think of a lovelier man I'd rather die with than yourself."

Early on Saturday morning the sky had cleared enough for Captain Pitkethly to get sights, and with full sail on he ordered an adjustment to the course. His brother, Alex was at the helm. "We need tae make sure we get the ship between the coast an' the Great Barrier Reef tae find calmer waters," he said. "We've been driven much too far tae the north-east during the night an' on our present course we'll finish up in New Caledonia. I don't particularly want tae visit New *Scotland* right at this time, Alex. Change course an' maintain north-west 310°, but warn the watch tae keep a good lookout fer broken water."

"Aye, aye Geordie," Alex said. "What exactly are we looking fer?"

The captain looked worried. "According tae my chart there's a dangerous reef called the Minerva Shoal at the southern end o' the Great Barrier Reef. I think it's still about sixty miles nor'east an' if we keep tae the course I've plotted we should be well tae the west o' it, but I couldn'ae get good enough sights tae be entirely sure o' my bearings. We'll still be in *some* danger until the weather clears up a bit more."

Alex shook his head. "I checked the barometer an hour ago," he said grimly. "It's no' looking too good at all. It's still dropping."

"So did I, an' I'm going tae check it again now," Geordie said. He began to walk away, but paused in his stride and turned once more to face his younger brother. "I know ye've let yer faith slip in recent years, Alex," he said, his face a mask of apprehension, "...but the Pitkethly family have never needed yer prayers more than we need them now."

Alex stared at his back as Geordie walked towards the chart room with his shoulders stooped, looking as though he carried the weight of the world on them. He scowled, for he certainly had lost the faith that his brother continued to adhere to a long time ago, and he held no illusions about their predicament and the futility of getting on his knees to appeal to some unseen being for mercy.

The wind increased in intensity again during Saturday afternoon and the fine weather sails were quickly taken down as a precaution after the harsh lesson learned two days before and it was as well that they were, for by evening it had again become a gale-force nor'easter that howled and whistled through the bare rigging. The *Peruvian* pitched and rolled as the following sea threatened to broach her sideways on, where she might well have capsized, but the storm sails held fast and the barque surged through the heavy swell with the helmsman, James Gooley wrestling the wheel in blinding, driving rain in a desperate effort to keep her on a course that would take her inside the reef.

The storm had abated a little by midnight and a watery moon peeped from behind the dark clouds when Morrill, who was on the second watch, took the wheel from the exhausted helmsman. Gooley made his way along the deck and disappeared down the stairs to the crew's cabin, and Morrill, with Able Seaman Jack Smith keeping lookout, began his own battle to keep the rolling, plunging ship on course.

At 2 o'clock when Morrill gave the wheel to James Wilson, the apprentice, the storm had eased again to some extent. The wind had moderated to a constant moan, the rain had ceased, and the moon cast its feeble rays over the churning, glistening water ahead.

"Nothing to report, Jack?" Morrill said as he climbed up beside Smith on the crow's nest perch above the wheelhouse.

"No Jimmy; nothing at all," Smith said. "I was unsighted for most of my watch though; couldn't see a hundred yards. Are we still on the captain's course?"

"The compass was useless. I just had to keep her to windward and hope for the best," Morrill said. "We could be anywhere."

"Yes, I thought that would be the case," Smith said. He peered out over the bowsprit. "It looks like the squall's easing off again now and there's nothing but clear water ahead, so we've been lucky so far. He squinted up at the mist-shrouded moon that appeared intermittently behind dark scudding clouds. "Next lookout should be here soon; it's the Second Mate, John McDonald, so he can make the decision about waking the captain to take more sights. We should still have twenty miles at least between us and the shoals."

It wasn't long before McDonald's head appeared above the ladder that led down to the wheelhouse and Smith gratefully bid them a safe watch as he climbed down and moved hand over hand along the rail to the crew quarters.

Morrill, with the captain's earlier warning about the shortcomings in the astronomical observations he'd been able to get, coupled with young Wilson's noticeable nervousness, declined to accompany him and continued to keep watch with McDonald, climbing down to the wheelhouse occasionally to check on the young apprentice at the helm.

An hour into McDonalds watch the wind began to intensify again and gust from west to south west. McDonald peered through the spray and then shook his head and wiped his eyes with a wet rag. "My eyes are burning now, Jimmy. I can hardly see out of them," he shouted above the roar of the gale. "I think I'll rouse the captain."

Morrill stared ahead too, clutching the rail and scanning the murky water for any sign of breakers. Suddenly he swivelled and pointed, yelling into McDonald's ear against the wailing tempest. "White water, dead ahead."

McDonald brushed the spray from his eyes again and his face took on a terrified expression. He mouthed a curse, but Morrill didn't hear it, for he'd leapt from the perch and scurried down the ladder with McDonald close behind. Wilson, who was staring awe-struck at the sinister black form with its halo of white foam encircling it that had suddenly loomed out of the darkness turned and gaped open-mouthed at him.

"Rouse the crew," Morrill yelled into McDonald's face. The second mate stared beyond his shoulder in horror and then rushed off to raise the alarm. Morrill grabbed the wheel and he and Wilson strained with all their might to turn the ship to starboard to avert the catastrophe that lay ahead, for they could now see through the spray a massive glistening rock that towered above the churning white water. Despite their desperate efforts to haul her around, however, the barque seemed to have a mind of her own; she surged onward and, with a shuddering, grinding crash, struck the rock and pitched upwards, her bow splintered from bowsprit to below the waterline. Morrill and Wilson were both thrown violently to the floor of the wheelhouse, but managed to hang on to the wheel and to each other, Morrill's superior grip clasping the lad's waist against his own body.

McDonald had pulled furiously on the emergency wire in the stairwell that rang the alarm bells in the captain's cabin and the crew's quarters and he was returning to the deck, making his way along the port rail hand over hand, when the ship struck. He was thrown off balance with the jarring impact, skidded along the deck on his back and collided with the wheelhouse wall, bouncing off it and sliding towards the port lifeboat that hung in its davits two feet above the deck. He would have slithered underneath it and disappeared over the scuppers, but managed to reach up and grasp one of the stay ropes that held the lifeboat in its cradle. He clung on desperately and succeeded in pulling himself up on to the boat, but his success was short-lived, for the violent bobbing of the lifeboat was too much for the restraining shackle and it gave way, coiling the stay rope around his legs and yanking him back down on to the deck. The other shackle, unable to take the full weight, parted too, the boat came loose and toppled sideways and Morrill thought he heard a faint scream over the roar of the wind. He twisted around just in time to glimpse the second mate, his fingers scrabbling on the smooth decking planks, dragged over the gunwale after the boat as it smashed through the deck rail and disappeared into the foaming water.

The captain had emerged from the cabin just in time to see McDonald's misfortune too, and he pulled on his oilskins as he bellowed orders to the rest of the crew who had followed one by one in various stages of dress, some still in their night shirts, having tumbled out of their hammocks from exhausted sleep. No directives from the captain or anyone else could have prevented what happened next, however, and the men could only hold on to the rail and brace themselves as the following sea lifted the *Peruvian* entirely on to the rock where she became wedged, with both her fore and aft ends taking water.

The whole crew remained motionless and mute in utter disbelief as the sickening truth sank in, but the captain, although shocked as much as the others by the realisation that his ship was doomed, managed to present an outward appearance of relative calmness. There was little that could be done in the dark, he decided, and he ordered the crew to ensure that all passengers were accounted for, and then bring them to the chartroom where they would all shelter together until daylight, which was yet several hours away.

Remarkably, an oil lamp still sputtered dimly, casting fitful shadows around the cabin as it swung in crazy circles above the table. They were a sorry looking bunch, Morrill thought, the passengers and crew huddled together in a near silent vigil that was broken only by the occasional whining cries of the babies and moans of despair from their mother, Emma. John Willmett sat on the floor with his arm around his wife trying to comfort her and Nora nestled close beside Morrill with little Frances in her arms.

Morrill looked across at the silhouettes of Captain Pitkethly and his wife Betsy as they hunched together against the opposite wall, each with a bible clutched tightly in their hands and a constant flow of muttered prayer coming from their lips. It was Sunday today, he suddenly remembered, the day of the Sabbath, when Geordie would normally put aside his captain's hat and don that of the preacher, but he knew that the preacher and his wife must both be wondering, even in their steadfast faith, how long it would take for the ship to break up and send them all to meet their Creator.

Jephson Busteed Quarry crouched against the panelled wall with his long legs pulled up under him, staring at some imaginary point of interest on the floor in front of him. He'd been hauled, quite roughly, he'd complained to anyone who cared to listen, from the refuge of his cabin by two burly crew members who didn't seem to care that he was a paying passenger, or give any thought to his fragile state of mind and they'd simply ignored his indignant protests at being manhandled in such a way.

The crew, with the exception of the two stowaways, seemed resigned to their fate. Some, in complete exhaustion, had even gone back to sleep, but the two Asian stowaway's eyes were wide in terror as they listened in silence to the violent gale raging outside the cabin.

Dawn brought with it the full realisation of their bleak situation. No island with tree clad hills and sheltering bays could be seen on the horizon in any direction, the only sign of land a massed legion of half-submerged black rocks that thrust up out of a vast angry ocean as far as the eye could see. The captain's worst fears had been realised, for he was certain that the storm had driven the *Peruvian* directly on to the notorious Minerva Shoal.

"I don't think we've got much time before she breaks up completely, Geordie?" Alex said, peering over the deck railing at the gaping holes in the hull.

Geordie shook his head. "She seems tae be stuck fast, Alex, but we need tae get ready tae abandon ship anyway, - just in case she does go suddenly. Get the crew organised tae have the jolly boat ready fer launching."

The jolly boat still hung from its davits above the stern. It was barely eighteen feet long and was meant for ferrying a maximum of ten passengers and six oarsmen crew between the ship and shore in small harbours where the ship had no direct access to a wharf, and it was to be overloaded with twenty-two people, *'Thankfully two o' them are wee bairns,'* the captain thought grimly.

The crew set about the task willingly. The davits were swung out on the falls and the two men on each of the two hand winches began to lower the boat squarely while other hands kept it from swinging towards the side of the ship with poles and oars.

"Hold it up! Hold it up, lads. Keep it well clear o' the water," the captain yelled, but the order came seconds too late, for the jolly boat had dropped too quickly and it smashed hard on to the rocks close under the stern; the bottom broke out of it and it was swamped immediately. The next sea tore it from the falls and dashed it to pieces against the hull, and the bits of wreckage were flung along the side of the stricken ship and disappeared in the foam. Several members of the crew peered over the railing and shook their heads in disbelief and then turned to the captain, their eyes pleading for some sign of hope.

That hope came in the form of the long-boat that hung on its davits on the starboard side of the ship and the captain ordered it to be prepared for launching over the side, but to be suspended in its tackle just above the deck railing. The crew did manage to get it over the side and into position but a rogue wave swamped it too.

"I've got it Geordie," Alex shouted as he grabbed the tackle rope and climbed up on to the rail.

"No, - *no*! Alex. Come down here laddie…" Geordie's voice was frantic as he realised what his brother's intentions were, but it was too late.

Alex leapt into the longboat and began to bail it out with a bucket, but he had no sooner started than another breaker lifted the boat and then dumped it back down with such force that the stern post was wrenched out and left hanging in the shackle. The boat hung suspended from the fore-tackle for several seconds with Alex hanging on to the gunwale, and then the cleats holding the foretackle gave way too, sending it crashing down into the boiling sea. Lines were quickly thrown down to the captain's hapless brother, who clutched at them gamely, but it was to no avail and the crippled long-boat was carried away from the ship. Alex spread his arms wide, palms upward in a gesture of resignation, yelled his goodbyes and then calmly sat down in the bow of the long-boat to await his fate until it drifted out of sight of the wretched group on the ship.

Morrill turned to the captain, but Geordie was naturally bereft at the sudden loss of his brother and leant over the railing with his hands clasped in front of him, his shoulders heaving and his eyes closed. Betsy stood beside him, her arm thrown around his waist.

The crew had never seen their captain in such a helpless state before and they milled about in near panic, but Morrill's commanding voice spurred them into action. "This is our very last chance," he yelled. "Get the hatch open; we're going to build a raft out of the cedar logs in the hold. Wilson, get the other apprentices and the Lascars down that hatch and start hauling them up on deck. Be careful, the lower hold will be flooded."

The men Morrill had nominated leapt into action and even the terrified Lascars, unable to understand the words, seemed to know instinctively what was required of them.

Morrill spun around. "Jim Gooley and John Millar, release the stays off the main mast and mizzen mast *only* on the starboard side. Leave the port side rigged. Jack Smith and I are going to shorten the pulleys on the port side until the masts topple on that side. With any luck they should bridge over on to the rocks. Now, I think we've got a few hours before high tide to get it ready and I reckon we can float her then."

John Willmett held tightly to Frances, who was delirious with fright and squirming in his arms and Emma clutched baby John Clement to her breast as she clung to John's side. "What should *we* do, Jimmy?" he yelled.

"John, get all the clothing and blankets you can salvage from the cabins and bring them on deck, then shelter in the lee of the cabin with the children." He spun around again and locked eyes with McArthur, the cook. "Eddie, take Nora with you and see what provisions you can bring up from the galley."

The crew, acknowledging that a new leader had taken charge, went to work without hesitation. They knew well enough that this was indeed their only chance. They released the standing rigging that braced the masts on the starboard side and, as Morrill had predicted, the masts fell sideways on to the rocks with a mighty crash, but both remained intact and the cross-spars and tattered sails that had come down with them were strewn about in a tangled clutter. Some of the more daring men climbed out over the fallen timbers and began to drag the mess of ropes into some kind of order while the others toiled to retrieve the logs from the hold and roll them across the deck.

The crew had worked as a team for so long that each man seemed to know instinctively what was required of him and Morrill had to give few orders as the raft began to take shape. The spars and logs were bound with rope between the two masts in a rough rectangle and then more logs were lowered over the side of the ship and hammered into place, creating an uneven platform about thirty feet by twenty. Next, a cabin about ten feet square and six feet high was constructed in the centre with some of the lighter spars, waterproofed with a patch of sail that was thrown over the spars that made up the roof and held down by pieces of the standing rigging that had come down with the main mast.

A privy had also been added outside the cabin and at the far end from the door opening. It was a simple enough frame surrounded by sailcloth for privacy and furnished with a timber seat that had been removed from the wreck. A hole had been cut in the floor below it.

Morrill surveyed the end result of the crew's labours with a feeling of contentment. Given the circumstances, they'd done exceptionally well. The wind had dropped considerably in the previous hour and the men sat about in two's and three's on the cluttered deck, exhausted from their exertions, but elated at the success of the project.

"Dae ye' think she's seaworthy?" Morrill knew the Scottish brogue well. He turned to face the captain who had come up behind him with his wife, Betsy by his side. The tiny woman clutched a small handkerchief and daubed at her swollen eyes and the captain forced a smile, but Morrill could see the pain etched in the man's face.

"Aye, captain," he said. "She should float well enough. The crew have all worked hard at it."

"An' it's all thanks tae *you*, Jimmy," Pitkethly said. "We cann'ae express our gratitude tae ye' enough, but if we ever get out of this predicament wi' our lives, we'll make sure ye' get recognised fer what ye've done here. In the meantime -," he paused and Betsy hugged his arm reassuringly. "I've lost my wee brother – my first mate, in more ways than one, - an' I want ye' tae take his place. Ye've shown us ye' can dae the job very well."

Morrill looked down at his feet, embarrassed. "Thanks Captain Pitkethly, but any of…"

"…I'd like ye' tae call me Geordie, from now on, Jimmy – if ye' don't mind, that is. I don't feel much like a captain o' a ship anymore."

Morrill nodded. He felt wretched for the captain whom he had come to respect a great deal. "Right then, Geordie," he said gently. "You *are* still our captain and if you feel you can take control again the crew are ready for your orders. I had planned on getting us all on to the raft in case the ship breaks up, but I thought after that we'd keep her tied up to the wreck for a few days to see if the weather improves. The lads think we've got enough boat planks aboard to build a decent jolly boat – which might be easier to handle than the raft."

The captain bowed in accord with his reasoning. "That sounds like a good plan, Jimmy an' I'm no' going tae interfere in its execution. Let's see about getting the passengers loaded first then," he said." He pointed to a long wooden box that had been waterproofed with a layer of pitch. "We also need tae make sure this box is safe, Jimmy." he managed a tired grin. "It's got my charts an' sextant an' almanac in it – as well as my bible. We're going tae need *all* o' them tae have any chance o' making it tae shore."

Morrill wasn't sure that the bible would be of any help, but he merely smiled and nodded. "I'll see to it, Geordie," he said.

When everything was in readiness Emma and John Willmett, clutching their screaming, wide-eyed children in their arms, were helped into the harnesses that were usually reserved for the crow's nest watch. A cable had been strung between the ships rail and the makeshift log cabin and the Willmetts scrambled aboard the raft where they were shackled to a running line in the cabin for their safety. Nora was next and Morrill fastened the harness around her slim shoulders. He looked around. "Where's Mr Quarry?"

"Gone back to his cabin, I suspect," Nora said.

"Why, is he smoking his comforter again?"

"I'm sure he is. He said he doesn't want to waste it if he's going to die anyway," she said with a tired smile.

"Strange fellow," Morrill said with a shrug. "I'll send a man to get him."

"Better send two," Nora said gravely. "He'll want to fight them off if he's not finished with it."

The provisions that the cook, Eddie McArthur and Nora had brought up from the galley were next to be loaded, but to the dismay of all it was discovered that the bread that had been stacked in the lee of the foredeck was ruined by salt water spray and much of the preserved meat had been washed overboard, unnoticed in the turmoil. To make matters worse, there was only one keg of water and a small cask of brandy that remained intact, for the fresh water kegs that had been stored in the storeroom below the galley had been destroyed or lost through a gaping hole in the hull. The few tins of preserved meat that were left and the keg of water and cask of brandy were loaded very carefully into the safest part of the raft's cabin.

The tide was now at its highest and the end of the raft that rested on the rocks was almost awash, shifting and grinding ominously with every sea.

Morrill was worried. "I think we'll have to get the raft clear of the ship, Geordie," he said. "I'm not sure if it'll hold together the way it's moving around."

"Aye, yer right, Jimmy," Geordie agreed. "An' if the ship rolls it might take us all wi' it tae the bottom."

A halyard was fastened to the base of the main mast where it rested on the twisted deck rail and a pulley-block was attached high up on the foremast and then to a windlass on the deck. The windlass handle was turned and the weight of the raft slowly lifted off the deck rail. The other end had almost floated free and with some leverage from an oar that had been thrust between it and the rock and coaxing from several pairs of hands, it was pushed far enough adrift to hoist the end that rested on the deck rail clear of the ship. When this was accomplished the windlass was reversed to lower the raft on to the rocks. This was the most crucial part of the task and the raft scraped down the hull of the Peruvian with the harsh grating sound of timber on timber, but to everyone's great relief the creaking mass, supported at the ship's hull only by the pair of straining ropes of the windlass, held together.

For the next two hours the raft tossed and pitched in the churning sea as the occupants cowered in fright inside the makeshift cabin. The Willmett children screamed and cried wretchedly and then passed into an exhausted sleep as John and Emma tried to shield them from the cold spray that drenched them with every sea.

Jimmy Morrill held on tightly to Nora's waist. He knew he had the strength to endure the buffeting and to keep her safe, but he wasn't so sure that the raft was going to withstand the battering it was taking.

Suddenly, the raft lurched and tipped at a steep angle, throwing the hapless people on board into a jumbled pile of bodies against the cabin wall. It crashed down again, but the shock was too much for the ropes that secured it to the ship; they snapped and the raft, with a grating sound that could be heard over the howling wind, was torn off the almost submerged rocks that it had been partially resting on and propelled into the boiling surf.

12

A scorching sun blazed relentlessly from a clear blue sky as the raft drifted on a calm, glassy sea. John Millar, the sailmaker, had rigged up one of the *Peruvian's* storm sails that had come down with the main mast in an attempt to control the raft's course, but it hung limply from its pole. Another storm sail had been attached to the corners of a wall of the cabin and stretched out to form a lean-to shelter and most of the crew lay in its shade, attempting to conserve as much energy as possible. The passengers had been afforded the privilege of a berth in the cabin itself, although the relentless crying of the Willmett's two children made that advantage only a slightly better alternative to the frequent repositioning required by those outside as the sun progressed across the heavens.

Only Geordie Pitkethly and Jimmy Morrill knelt on the edge of the raft in the mid-day heat. Geordie had his chart spread out in front of him. He'd taken some approximate readings on his sextant – imprecise for various reasons, but mainly because the chronometer had been a fixture in the captain's cabin on the *Peruvian* and its removal from the wreck would have been difficult, if not impossible to achieve under the circumstances. Pitkethly had drawn several intersecting lines on his chart and he shook his head and stroked his beard thoughtfully.

"Let's see now, Jimmy; there's where I believe the *Peruvian* was wrecked, - on Minerva Shoals." He pointed to the place on the chart that he'd marked with a large X and paused, and Morrill was sure he detected a subtle rise in the pitch of his voice when he resumed speaking. If the captain *had* felt any anguish or remorse when he reflected on the final resting place of his brother Alex, however, he quickly recovered from it.

"I think we've drifted tae about here, Jimmy," he said.

Morrill's eyes followed the captain's finger as he traced a line from the position of the wreck to an imaginary point in the middle of a vast nothingness. "That seems a long way from the mainland," he said, a frown creasing his brow.

Geordie nodded. "It is Jimmy; the nearest point on the coast is a place James Cook called Cape Capricorn, obviously because it's on the Tropic of Capricorn. It's about two hundred miles west o' our present position if my calculations are right. I believe we've wandered intae the tropics, Jimmy." He paused again, but this time his voice was low and carried an ominous quality when he continued. "It's a much, much worse state o' affairs than just the distance from shore, though. We're well outside the reef an' drifting north wi' the current at about twenty miles a day. Even if we get a favourable wind tae fill that wee sail o' ours, it'll be two – maybe three weeks tae any possible landfall an' before we can achieve *that* we've got tae manoeuvre the raft through a suitable break in the reef tae get intae the channel between it an' the mainland."

Morrill looked at him intently for a moment. "What are our chances of finding a break in the reef, Geordie?" he said.

Pitkethly shrugged. "Oh, there are plenty o' breaks an' some o' them are more than wide enough tae steer a very big ship through. If we were lucky enough tae get close tae one the current would probably drag us intae it, but wi' no steering gear tae help us our chances o' getting through without being grounded an' maybe capsized are no' that good," he said. "Drowning's no' going tae be the first issue we have tae contend wi' though, - our worst challenge tae begin wi' is going tae be thirst an' starvation. If we're going tae have any chance at all, Jimmy, we've got tae conserve the water an' food we've got fer the worst possible circumstances."

"Right, Geordie," Morrill said. "Everyone needs to know what the true scale of the situation is and what we need to do to increase our chances of survival. Let's get the bad news out in the open."

Geordie called for everyone's attention and the gravity of the situation was explained, although it was doubtful that any one of the survivors had expected anything less grim, or was under any illusion that they were likely to survive without some extraordinary turn of fortune or divine intervention.

It was agreed without a word of dissent that the food would be rationed in equal portions for as long as it lasted. One tablespoon of preserved meat was to be served out about mid-day each day to each person, except for Emma who was to have two portions as she was breast-feeding her baby. The water was to be measured out in the neck of a broken glass bottle and dispensed four times a day; one in the morning, two at mid-day, and one in the evening. It was further agreed that, as the most senior member of the party, Captain Pitkethly would preside over the fair distribution of the rations as long as he was able to do so, and in the event of his demise or loss of reasoning a ballot would be held in order to choose another person to act as distributer.

Everyone was resigned to the extreme measures that had been put in place and indeed, if another reminder was needed by anyone, of the dreadful conditions that lay ahead in the coming days and, perhaps even weeks, an additional resolution was put forward and accepted unanimously.

That no lots will be drawn to take each other's lives no matter how critical the degree of starvation, and that no person's body will be cannibalised after they've drawn their last breath, but will be afforded a decent funeral rite with a traditional sermon followed by a committal to the ocean.

The fact that it had been found necessary *at all* to voice such a resolution had horrified the passengers, but most of the crew had heard of cases where exposure to extreme hunger had produced that most dishonourable of all indignities that could be perpetrated on a fellow human.

The days began to slip by monotonously, and Geordie had taken the precaution of hacking a small notch in a beam with an axe each morning to keep track of how many days they'd been drifting. The time was spent in idle chatter or in exercising cramped muscles, although the restricted space on the raft made anything more than bending and stretching a source of irritation for anyone else close by. Tempers flared often and squabbles about positions in the shade or the proximity of someone's foot to someone else's face were common.

Each morning a light breeze would spring up, blow constantly during the daylight hours and then die away at night, but more often than not the small, heavy canvas storm sail would flutter a little and then collapse and no amount of repositioning by John Millar would induce it to billow out fully and carry the raft along in the westerly course that the captain wanted it be taken.

A few tired seabirds were caught by cleverly using snares when they came in to perch and they were plucked and eaten raw. The inedible feet and claws and the gizzards were then used to bait a hook on a line. The fishing lines were attended to eagerly and in a spirit of competition by the sailors, and their successes were greeted with great jubilation and merriment, while any prolonged failure to land a fish was met with shouts of derision and cries of, "you're hopeless; give someone else a turn now." Several fine fish were caught in this way each day and the fillets cut up and served out in equal portions, but even with that extra nourishment the meagre rations of food and water were simply not sufficient to sustain vitality and the whole company became weaker and more lethargic with each passing day.

On the sixth day it rained, and every adult on board took advantage of the break in the weather with delight, some scrubbing their hands through their matted hair and washing the salt out of their pores while others lay on their backs with their mouths open and arms spread wide, revelling in the drenching. Clothes were washed and changed and the two children thoroughly groomed by their refreshed mother.

A piece of sailcloth was spread out to catch the water, but it was soon found that the salt had to be strained out of it before the water was fresh enough to drink. Fortunately the rain continued for several days and the water supply was replenished in the keg and the empty brandy cask while everyone on board drank to the point of bursting, but after that the weather became fine again and the same old squabbles were renewed, although with much less vigour than before.

The raft had been drifting for eighteen days according to the captain's notches in the log when John Millar, who'd struggled to his feet to again try to adjust the sail, gave a feeble cry. "A sail; look there, lads, - on the horizon."

Morrill and several other seamen clambered to their feet, but most had already had their expectations of rescue crushed and remained where they were, contemplating the sailmaker cynically through half-opened bleary eyes. Morrill strained his eyes in the direction that Millar's outstretched arm was pointed and joined his hoarse cry of frustration. "They're too far away and we're too low in the water. We can see them, but they can't see us." The ship came no closer, bearing south towards civilisation, and the tantalising sight remained in view for another three hours before it finally disappeared over the horizon, leaving those on the raft more despondent than ever.

Jephson Busteed Quarry lay on his makeshift bed in the cabin. He was so emaciated that his tall frame seemed to have shrunk into itself. It was the morning of the twenty-second day on the raft and he had been deteriorating steadily since the beginning, for he had found the raw flesh of the birds and fish difficult to keep down. His skin, which had been pale to begin with, looked pasty and more yellowed as the days passed, and black spots had formed on his face and arms – the classic signs of advanced scurvy. He had been mumbling incoherently for much of the preceding night, but went ominously silent before dawn, and so the manner of his passing was unremarkable, but his burial at sea left those who witnessed it in retching convulsions.

The captain prayed for the salvation in death of the man who, ironically, had refused *any* of his ministrations in life, for Quarry had not only refused to participate in his religious service; he'd also refused point blank to take Pitkethly's daily ration of lemon juice and sugar, claiming that it made him ill. After the ceremony the women retreated to the cabin while Quarry's outer garments were removed, for it had been previously agreed that the clothes of the dead were of no further use to them and would be saved for those who might be in need of them in the future.

The men watched in silence as Quarry was consigned to the ocean. The body floated away from the raft face down, some looking on impassively and others perhaps with a touch of regret, for it remained to be seen when their own turn would come and how much they would have to suffer before the same blessed relief overtook them.

A black fin sliced through the calm water, leaving a tiny wake as it made for the body. Another came from a different direction and it was followed by several more. The corpse jerked and was pulled under and then it resurfaced head first amid a threshing mass of sleek black bodies that churned the red stained water around it in a sustained feeding frenzy. Some of the men turned away from the gory spectacle, retching in disgust, while others appeared fascinated by Quarry's dead eyes that were wide open and seemed to stare accusingly at them.

"My God," someone cried out. "We're all going to end up like *that, -* in the belly of a shark."

Another, whose hoarse tone of voice belied his muted laugh, chimed in. "Don't worry, matey. You won't feel a thing. Just as well to finish up in the belly of a shark as to be eaten by worms inside a wooden box, eh?"

The sharks hardly left the vicinity of the raft after that and there were several near misses when people dipped rags in the sea in an effort to wash themselves clean.

Several days later Geordie was called on to conduct his second and third committal sermons.

"...Suffer the little children to come unto me, and forbid them not, for such is the kingdom of Heaven..."

Both of the Willmett children had died within minutes of each other in their mother's arms. Nora had confided to Morrill the previous day that she believed they were close to the end and was surprised at how long they had lasted. "I'm sure Emma has no more milk to give John William, though she keeps trying," she'd whispered. "And little Frances has been lying there languid beside her mother for days now. Her eyes are open and she's stopped crying, but she's not responding to her mother at all. Emma won't let me touch them and just rocks back and forth holding them to her breast."

Morrill was still shocked at the suddenness of the double tragedy and even more so at Emma's calm and serene expression when she hugged their little bodies for the last time before handing them over to her distraught husband.

The children received the same ghastly treatment from the ocean predators, but neither of their parents witnessed the desecration of their emaciated little bodies. At the urging of the captain, John Willmett took his wife by the shoulders and led her to the cabin, but just before she entered it she turned to Betsy with an anxious frown.

"I had to… God forgive me." she started. "*You* understand, don't you?"

Betsy nodded. "God *will* forgive ye', Emma; I'm certain o' it. Yer poor wee bairns are no' having tae suffer any more, love."

Emma smiled gratefully and John followed her into the cabin. She laid her head down on a makeshift pillow in the darkest corner and turned her face to the wall.

"I know it's not much consolation for John and Emma, Nora, but at least their babies have gone to heaven together," Morrill whispered gently. "I think they would have wanted that."

Nora's eyes were downcast. "Yes, she knew the end was near for herself and the wee-un's, Jimmy."

"You think she'll be next?" Morrill said.

She nodded. "I'm sure of it Jimmy, and don't ye' think she made the terrible decision herself that no mother should ever have to make?"

Morrill looked at her sharply. "You think that Emma…?"

"…She asked for God's forgiveness, didn't she?" Nora's face reflected the ache in her heart that she felt for the young mother whose companionship she had grown to love during her term as her babies' nanny. "It's been happening in Ireland too, Jimmy. There's only *so* much suffering that a mother can watch her children go through before she will risk eternal damnation in the fires of Hell to relieve them of it."

Nora was right. Emma Willmett never raised her head again.

After Geordie's sermon, John bade her a tearful goodbye and then retired to the cabin again to endure his grief in private, while Nora and Betsy commenced the awful task of partially undressing Emma's withered body. The captain and the other men, in respect for her dignity, turned their backs, and thus they remained until several minutes had elapsed after the faint splash told them that the consignment of her body had been completed. Thankfully for the grieving John Willmett, in a small way at least, the sharks didn't attack her remains immediately and Emma's body had floated away in the current for quite some distance before the inevitable agitation of the water could be discerned from the raft.

The Lascars went together too. They appeared to have made a pact, for it happened quite suddenly. They had been talking quietly in their own language for most of the morning as they rested, side by side, against the back of the cabin and occasionally cast wary glances in the direction of the other castaways. The captain had been unable to convey to them the resolution that had been accepted by the others, - *that no lots will be drawn to take each other's lives no matter how critical the degree of starvation may be.*

Despite repeated attempts at cordiality it was obvious that their perception of the pleasantries offered them was that it was trickery intended to keep them ignorant of the real intention, which was to reduce the number of mouths that needed to be fed as well as perhaps to provide extra nourishment for those who were left.

The situation had indeed become critical, for the last remaining length of fishing line had been lost two days before and the captain had laid out the only remaining portions of dried fish for cutting and distribution. As was his custom, he closed his eyes and intoned a prayer for deliverance from their plight, but a cry from Morrill made him look around in confusion. The two Lascars had risen unsteadily to their feet and, arm in arm, were standing on the edge of the raft.

"*No*, no! Don't *do* that, lads," he cried out in a voice full of anguish, realising instantly what their intentions were, but the terrified men stared at him wide-eyed for a moment as he advanced towards them, arms widespread and holding the axe, and then, as if on a signal, they both turned their backs on him and jumped feet-first into the water. Death, in the shape of half-a-dozen black fins, wasn't long in arriving, but neither man uttered a sound as their gaunt and shrunken bodies were jerked and tugged from side to side in the centre of the widening red-stained pool that surrounded them. Finally, they were dragged under, still in a brotherly hug, and Geordie sank to his knees and clasped his hands together, and it was only then that he realised, to his horror, that he'd been wielding the axe as if he'd been about to use it on the unfortunate men.

The cook, Edward McArthur was next, and the captain read the sermon as usual, but the corpse was not immediately consigned to the ocean. Instead Geordie asked everyone to turn their backs as he picked up the axe and held it loosely in his hand.

"What are ye' doing Geordie," Betsy was horrified. "Didn't we agree…?"

"Turn yer back, woman," he said curtly. "I have tae dae this an' it's no' very pleasant fer me either."

Betsy obediently complied; her heart was cold as ice, and she clapped her hands over her ears when she heard the chopping sound behind her.

"Right lads," the captain said. "Heave him over." And to Betsy he added, "Don't look around love. Take Nora with ye' an' get intae the cabin."

Morrill was impressed. The captain had obviously put some thought into this. He'd made a running noose with a strong length of halyard rope and tied it to the end of an oar. Another oar had the severed leg of the cook attached to it. They were both dangled out just above the water in such a way that a shark would have to pass through the noose to reach the bait. It worked admirably. Morrill and young Wilson tightened the noose as the shark struggled fiercely and the captain brained it with the axe as it was drawn in. The same method was used successfully three days later. The cook's foot had been cut into strips and dried and it still proved quite effective as bait, but although the fish were filleted and the contents of the stomachs carefully avoided, the survivors were acutely aware of the possibility that those stomachs may have contained parts of the remains of someone who had been alive on the raft quite recently.

Two of the able seamen, James Dicks and Jack Smith, had steadfastly refused to have anything to do with eating the sharks, professing a conviction common amongst mariners that it was a form of sacrilege to consume an animal that had devoured a human being. *They* were the next to die of starvation and be consumed by the sharks, but they were, as the captain said at their homily, honourable men who were true to their principles right to the very end, and they would undoubtedly be welcomed into the arms of their Saviour.

There were thirty-two notches on the captain's calendar beam when the first of the apprentices died. He was followed within a few days by two others, leaving only James Wilson, the eldest of the four to endure his misery without their company. Robust young fellows at the beginning of the voyage, they'd become skeletal and looked like wizened old men as their organs gradually shut down with malnutrition. The lads had all been close friends and after the first passed away the others seemed to lose the will to live. James Wilson became withdrawn and almost comatose after that, refusing or unable to communicate except for the occasional nod of his head.

William Harris, the carpenter, was the thirteenth person to die on the raft. He'd been showing the same severe signs of scurvy that Jephson Quarry had presented before *his* demise and the poor man knew his death was imminent when the black spots on his face, arms and legs began to suppurate. His teeth were falling out from his bleeding gums and he grumpily pleaded with the captain not to pray anymore for his return to health, but for a quick release from his suffering.

Thirty-four days into their ordeal Morrill and Geordie Pitkethly examined the distant western horizon. There seemed to be white water gleaming in the early morning sun and the raft was being driven towards it by a strong current.

"The Great Barrier Reef." Geordie announced, and Betsy and Nora came out of the cabin and stood beside the two men. It was a grand sight, they all agreed, as the raft drifted ever closer, with the muted roar of mighty white breakers crashing over bleached coral reefs.

"Grand indeed," Geordie said, "but remember what I said about it being highly dangerous too. We need tae be vigilant or we'll be dashed tae pieces on those sharp reefs. I just hope there's a decent enough channel between them fer us tae get the raft through. We need tae grab the oars an' try tae push off the reef wi' them if the raft gets too close."

"I'll try and raise young Wilson to help," Morrill said. "I don't know about Jim Gooley and John Millar. They might be too far gone."

"We're here." A hoarse voice croaked from within the cabin. Both men staggered out into the sunlight. They looked skeletal and the rags they wore hung off their stooped shoulders, but their eyes were bright with hope.

"Get through the reef and we might be right, eh?" Millar rasped.

The apprentice, James Wilson came out from behind the cabin. He said nothing, but he too looked as if he had gathered all of his remaining strength just to be involved.

The captain grinned, but it was more of a grimace as he looked at the last living members of his crew who had all been so healthy a few weeks before. "Aye John," he said. "If we *can* find a wide enough channel the current should take us through."

"I can help too." It was John Willmett who had hardly left his bed since the death of his wife and children and looked to Morrill as if he would soon follow them.

"Take it easy, John," Morrill said gently. "You're going to…"

"…kill myself with the strain?" Willmett cried. There were no tears left in his vacant, swollen eyes, but his voice cracked with raw emotion. "Oh dear God, how I wish I *could* die with the strain. Why am *I* still alive when I craved for it to be *me* instead of *them*; - my poor wife, my babies, all gone." He sank to his knees, cupped his hands over his face and wailed. "I'm sorry, - so sorry, but I have nothing to live for now, Jimmy."

Nora and Betsy both went to him and his thin shoulders sagged as each hugged him, one on either side. Nothing was said and it was plain to the others that nothing had to be, for he sighed deeply and pulled himself to his feet, perhaps appreciating once again that they all shared his grief and were trying to reduce his personal burden. That could never be fully achieved, of course, but his wretched attempt to force a smile told them that it had comforted him a little that they cared.

Brightly coloured corals with schools of tiny fish darting amongst their waving fronds and tentacles could be seen just below the surface of the crystal clear water as the raft scraped over the reef, and the wasted muscles of the exhausted men were strained almost to rupturing point as they struggled to keep it free of the jagged outcrops that would have arrested its surge and perhaps even capsized it. Their luck held out, however, and their efforts were rewarded, for the raft was safely into deep water by the late afternoon and the survivors rested, completely drained, but elated at their success.

Nora O'Meara lay with her head in the crook of Morrill's arm in the darkness of the cabin. Morrill could hear the regular breathing of the Pitkethly's who lay together against the opposite wall, and the snoring of some of the men who were distributed in various places outside in the lee of the cabin walls. He could feel Nora's frail body stir against his own, her head resting on his chest, and he suspected that she was awake, but he lay there contemplating their future together *if* they should survive this journey.

Nora must have known that he was awake too for she raised her head slightly. "What are ye' thinking about, Jimmy Morrill?" she whispered.

"I was thinking about *us*, Nora," he said. "I was thinking about how we're going to survive now that we've made it this far. We'll be rescued soon and I'll take you back home so that we can get married and then spend the rest of our lives together."

"Are ye' proposing to me now, Jimmy?" She tried to laugh, but it came out as a dry crackle in her throat. "I accept your proposal, sir, but we'd better make the wedding quick because the rest of our lives together might not be too long in the unfolding, my darling. Let's just say the words together right now," she said.

"What words? Morrill said.

"Well, our marriage vows, of course.

"I...I don't know how," Morrill stammered. "And it won't be a lawful..."

"...It will be lawful to us an' that's all that matters, doesn't it? Come on now before I change my mind and abandon ye' at the altar."

She took his hand in hers. "I hereby solemnly take ye', Jimmy Morrill to be my lawfully wedded husband. Do ye' solemnly take me, Nora O'Meara to be your lawfully wedded wife?"

Morrill's voice trembled with emotion. "I *do*, Nora," he said.

She sighed deeply. "Ye've made me a very happy woman, Jimmy. Here's to Mrs Nora Morrill, an' ye' may now kiss the bride, Mr Morrill, for I'm thinking it won't be long now - *till death do us part.*"

Morrill bent down and kissed her dry cracked lips, and she didn't flinch although he was certain that it must have caused her some agony. He rocked gently as he held her close in his arms. "Try to rest Nora," he said. "Now that we're inside the reef we'll likely be rescued by a passing ship or, if that doesn't happen straight away, we'll reach land soon and be able to send a smoke signal to the passing ships to tell them we're there, waiting to be saved. When we get back to Ireland we'll have a big wedding ceremony, the like of which they've never seen before." His words tumbled over each other in his eagerness to bring her out of her melancholy mood, but she seemed not to respond directly to his reassurance and simply reached up again and kissed him briefly.

"Ye' *are* my first an' only love, I swear to ye', Jimmy Morrill, an' ye'll be my last too, but I want ye' to promise me that ye'll not grieve over me if I don't survive, - well, not for too long anyway, for I'll be blissfully conversing with my da' in our watery home on the very day it happens."

"Don't speak like that, Nora." Morrill chided her gently.

"An' tell me why not?" she said, her soft brogue becoming more faint with each strained word. "I shouldn't have said ye' were my first an' only love, Jimmy, for ye' know I love my da' too, but in a different way of course." Her fingers went to the tiny locket that she always wore around her neck and she kissed it gently. "I used to watch him going about his daily chores when I was a wee-un'. It was his little ways, - ye' know, like winding the clock on the mantelpiece above the hearth as soon as he heard the angelus bells being rung at Saint Mary's church in the village every Sunday. He'd say, *'I'm winding the clock for ye' Nora, my darling so ye'll always know when it's time to say your prayers.'* I've dreamed of watching ye' wind the clock for me in our own little cottage, Jimmy. Would ye' think of me when ye' do that, like my da' did all his life…"

Morrill's voice was hoarse as he choked back the tears that threatened to engulf him. *Such a simple request, but from a lifetime that seemed so long ago and much too far away to even dream about.* "I promise I will do that Nora," he said, and I'll tell our own wee-un what your da' told you while *you* sit and watch me wind the clock." He wasn't sure that she'd heard his promise for she'd already sighed wearily and settled back in his arms, as if she'd submitted to the inevitable and fully expected death to come upon her swiftly and silently and without further warning.

Her words seemed prophetic, and sleep eluded Morrill for many hours. He took some comfort though, from the fact that her breathing was regular and he could feel her heartbeat, strong and firm against his chest as she slept in his arms.

Sometime during the early morning hours he fell into a troubled sleep and dreamt that he was back home in his bed in Maldon. Nora stood at the end of his bed. She was smiling cheerfully at him and her face had that radiantly cheeky grin that he'd noticed when he first saw her on the foredeck of the *Peruvian*, but her eyes showed a hint of sadness. She held up the gold locket that contained her father's photo, and when she spoke her voice sounded faint, as if she was a long way off.

"Ye' must not spend your life grieving for me, Jimmy Morrill. You're going to be the one who will live to let the world know what happened to the rest of us after the wreck of the Peruvian. Take this locket to remember me by, Jimmy, but don't grieve for me, for I won't be needing it anymore. I'm in a better place now with my da' an' my mam. You truly were my first love and my last love, Jimmy Morrill..."

Nora's voice seemed to fade away into nothingness and with it Morrill woke up in a cold sweat. It was first light and she still lay in his arms, but her frail body was unmoving, and she was cold – too cold. He shook her gently. "Nora?" he moaned. "I love you, Nora. Don't leave me now. We've got our whole lives to live together; just us and the wee-un's..."

Betsy had woken and she came over and put her arm around his shoulders. She knew immediately what had happened, of course. It had happened so many times before in the last few weeks. "She's in God's hands now, Jimmy," she said.

Morrill hugged Nora's frail body. Tears streamed down his face and his shoulders heaved as the full comprehension of his loss hit him. There was to be no future with his little Irish scatterbrain now; only the sweet remembrance of their brief encounter on the *Peruvian* and the painful memory of their shared misery on the hellish journey on this raft.

Geordie had joined them. "Stay here, Jimmy. We'll take care o' her now," he said gently.

Morrill sat against the wall inside the cabin with his knees drawn up under his chin. He heard Geordie read the sermon as usual, but his thoughts were far away in a little village on the other side of the world.

'I just want to be happy and contented with my life, Jimmy Morrill. I want a good man to love me and some wee-un's of my own. I don't need anything more than that – just enough food to fill the bellies of my little family and enough coal for to keep us warm by the fireside in the cold of the winter evenings.'

Geordie, his verses from the bible completed, appeared in the doorway holding the book to his chest. "Betsy's going to do the committal, Jimmy," he said. "The men have turned their backs in respect for Nora's dignity." He sat down next to Morrill. "She was a bonnie lassie, Jimmy, an' her young life is over much too soon."

Morrill could only nod in agreement. He heard the all too familiar splash and clapped his hands over his ears to block out any possible sound of threshing water.

Betsy joined them in the cabin a short time later. She knelt in front of Morrill and handed him a tiny locket on a gold chain. "Here, Jimmy," she said. "I believe Nora would hae wanted ye' tae keep this safe."

Morrill took the locket in his trembling hands and opened it. Nora smiled at him from one half and her father seemed to nod approvingly at him from the other, as if he was thanking him for taking care of his daughter in their short time together.

'Don't grieve for me Jimmy Morrill for I'll be blissfully conversing with my da' in our watery home on the very day it happens.'

"Thanks Betsy," he managed to mumble through his tears. "Nora's safe now."

13

Clem Ross was distraught. The shipping agent sat alone in his office in the Merchant Marine Agency building with the *Sydney Herald* news sheet in front of him. He read the text again for perhaps the sixth time.

'The mystery of the fate of the lost barque, Peruvian has been solved. By the arrival in Sydney Town of the American whaler Pleiades, we have been placed in possession of the exact position of the wreck of this unfortunate vessel. Captain Russell states that he boarded her on the 28th of May last, when she was high and dry on a reef in lat. 21° 40' S., long. 159° 68' E. Her hull had been much stove in the bottom forward, through which the water rushed at high tide; her mainmast and mizenmast were gone, but the foremast and fore-topmast were standing, with the topsail and foresail hanging from the yards. A search was made to endeavour to obtain some document of the particulars of the wreck, and also the means resorted to for leaving the vessel, but none was found.

The various papers saved were secured by Captain Russell, who has brought them on to Sydney and delivered them up to her agents, Messrs. Thacker and Co. The cabins were strewn with female daytime apparel, and everything gave indication that those on board had left shortly after the vessel struck, quite probably during the hours of darkness. It was the general opinion of those who visited the wreck that the lifeboats had all been dashed to pieces when they were being hastily launched as pieces of them were found still hanging from their shackles, and as no spare spars were on board, that a raft had been hastily constructed, upon which the crew and passengers had taken refuge. It is manifest, however, considering the distance from the east coast, and the remoteness of the wreck from any port of call, that all passengers and crew must surely have been lost at sea. Fearing that some other vessels would be led into danger by the wreck, Captain Russell thought it prudent, to set fire to her.

Sydney Herald of 8 Aug 1846'

The *Peruvian* had been found. He remembered the final chat he'd had with the young Able Seaman, James Morrill, when he'd signed him on. *'The ship leaves on Friday,'* he'd said. *'A lot of sailors won't sail on Fridays. They reckon it brings the ship bad luck.'*

Morrill had laughed. *'I don't care what day we leave - the sooner the better.'*

He hadn't been at sea long enough to have learned any of the old *Jack-tar's* superstitions, - if they *were* superstitions, that is. He felt a wave of regret sweep over him. Perhaps he should have been more forceful in warning him of the danger of tempting providence.

He couldn't have prevented the catastrophe from happening to the captain, his wife and the other crew members and passengers, a couple of children amongst them. Why on earth those passengers had taken passage on a *cargo* ship was anybody's guess, but that *was* out of his control and it was a peril all sailors and their passengers took for granted as soon as they ventured out of port and on to the high seas.

He'd not only met Morrill, however, he'd realised on that first meeting that Jimmy reminded him of how his own noble principles had driven him during his first years at sea, standing up for the underdog and believing he could change the world for the better. He'd enjoyed the boy's company immensely and appreciated their stimulating conversations so much, in fact, that both he and Daphne continued to think of him as a newly acquired young acquaintance and had looked forward to his return to Sydney.

He had, he remembered, joked that the captain was flirting with fate twice over by leaving on a Friday and taking his wife on a voyage, but as it turned out his prophecy had come true. The first stroke of bad luck was obviously the storm that had smashed the ship, but the second was the decision to leave the wreck. The sea hadn't broken her up, according to the Herald report, and if they'd stayed on board, perhaps most of them would have been saved.

He tossed the Herald to one side and opened his ledger. The book fell open at the page with James Morrill's name on it and he shuddered. He took his quill, dipped it in the inkwell and wrote *deceased, lost at sea,* across the entry.

14

Forty-one days after the raft began its journey the one woman and six men on board were all but finished. Betsy lay in the cabin, unable to stand any longer. James Wilson cried out occasionally from the agony of the open sores on his swollen legs, but otherwise showed little sign of life, and John Millar rambled incoherently in his sleep. John Willmett lay against the cabin wall sobbing quietly and James Gooley was comatose. Only Geordie Pitkethly and Jimmy Morrill were, in any sense, capable of conversation, - and that only with some considerable effort.

They'd caught another shark the day before and the remaining fillets of its flesh were drying on the roof of the cabin, but there had been no more water since a brief shower of rain two days ago had put a little into the bottom of the keg.

Morrill, suddenly animated, grasped the captain's arm with one hand and pointed with the other. "Geordie, is that *land* I can see above the horizon?" he rasped, squinting into the distance.

The captain hurried into the cabin and came back with his spy-glass. He trained it in the direction of Morrill's outstretched arm and adjusted its focal length with unsteady fingers. A thin cry escaped from his lips and his voice rose in shocked delight. "It *is* land alright, Jimmy," he croaked. "Let's get my charts."

Morrill spread the chart out and held it while Geordie took sights and then pored over it, drawing some intersecting lines. "Jimmy, I think that's Cape Upstart," he said. "I remember it from the Beagle voyage, because we all thought James Cook had named it sae well. It seems tae jump right up out o' the water because o' the low land around it. We anchored in the bay on the western side. If it is, an' I'm almost certain o' it, then it's one o' the places where we made landing an' found fresh water." He tried to laugh, but the sound that escaped from his throat was a sputtering cackle. "The current's taking us towards the shore. We're going tae be saved after all, lad, by the grace o' God," he said. "I'll have tae get Betsy out here tae witness this grand sight an' then we can all get on our knees tae pray in thanksgiving fer our deliverance."

Morrill didn't laugh with him, for he had reservations which he kept to himself. *Saved for what?* There were no communities between Moreton Bay and this desolate spot on the north-east coast, and despite his made-up guarantee to Nora that they did; he doubted that any ships ever passed this way. "I think it's a bit premature for prayers and I don't think it's wise to try to get the others up and about just yet, Geordie," he said. "We're close, but we're not there yet and it could be several hours before we make landfall, - if in fact we do." He pointed to the place on Geordie's chart where the two lines intersected. "According to your map the coastline bends westwards north of here so we could be driven parallel to it for a long way."

Pitkethly looked crestfallen, but he reluctantly agreed. "Aye, I see what ye' mean, Jimmy," he said. "We're sae close tae fresh clean water that I can almost smell it, but we could still die o' thirst within the very sight o' land. That would be a cruel end tae our miserable voyage after all we've been through. God wouldn'ae dae that tae us, - would He?"

His once proud captain cut such a pathetic figure as he looked to Morrill for reassurance that Morrill's cracked lips parted in a forced smile and he shook his head. "No Geordie, I don't believe God would do that to us," he said. He cringed at his own words, hoping that he hadn't sounded patronising. Geordie had been, to his mind, the strongest member of their little group, but he felt that he'd just seen the first crack appear in the armour of Geordie's hitherto unconditional belief in the mercy of his God.

The raft drifted in a north-westerly direction, approaching tantalizingly close to another headland with a long sandy spit that curved outwards to form its own enclosed bay and then, having rounded that, the mountain range that they'd glimpsed behind it came into full view. Its lower slopes rose upwards in a long easy grade that climbed gradually from the coastal headland to level out in a series of high ridges that terminated in an even higher peak at its northern extremity. Pitkethly, after consulting his chart, was now certain that it was called the Mount Elliot Range.

"That high peak is Mount Elliot itself," Geordie said.

A single rising wisp of grey smoke curled in lazy spirals from the mountain's forested slopes until it slowly vanished into the blue of the sky.

"We're not alone," Morrill said. "I don't suppose it could be a land expedition from Port Curtis, Geordie?"

Pitkethly shook his head. "There's no chance o' that, Jimmy; we're too far north. It'll be a native campfire fer sure."

"Aye, well then, I hope they're friendly." Betsy had crept out of the cabin unnoticed and rose to her knees, holding on to the doorway for support.

"I didnae hear ye' coming out, my love," Geordie said. He helped her to her feet and she leaned against him and stared at the tiny rollers breaking mildly on the rock strewn sandy shore no more than half a mile away.

"My, oh my, but isn't that the most beautiful sight ye' could ever wish tae see? It looks like we could get off the raft an' wade ashore from here, Geordie," she said, with a trace of elation creeping into her voice.

Geordie managed a weak grin, although the effort caused another bloodied crack to appear in his dry, parched lips. "We'll have tae bide our time just a wee bit longer, Betsy," he said. "I've tested it wi' an oar an' I cannae touch bottom yet, an' I'm no' going tae even stick my big toe in that water until I'm certain the sharks aren't still following us."

The raft was being driven further north by the strong current. It swept past the headland and another stretch of sandy coastline came into view. Pitkethly reckoned that they were now in the vicinity of a place James Cook had named Cleveland Bay, and away to the north a mountainous island reared up from the calm sea, an island that gave him ever increasing confidence that his bearing was correct, for he recognised it as Cook's Magnetical Isle.

A strong land breeze took them further out to sea during the afternoon, and the cheerful spirits of the group began to diminish as the green hills receded into the distance, but the wind changed again after sunset and they were driven back inshore, and then, sometime around midnight, the raft grounded itself on a sandy beach on the southern side of the point of Cape Cleveland.

There was no great celebration amongst those of the survivors who were able to comprehend that their ordeal - on the ocean, at least, - was finally over; just a sense of overwhelming relief that affected each of them in different ways. Betsy cried and laughed at the same time. Jack Millar and James Wilson managed a grin and a weak slap of each other's shoulder, but James Gooley simply stared at them with vacant eyes. John Willmett still lay in a moribund state in the cabin, unwilling to accept that fickle destiny had decreed he might have to endure his miserable existence for some time yet. Morrill and Pitkethly staggered into knee deep water and blindly fought their way to the beach where they collapsed onto the cool sand and lay revelling in the feeling of solid land beneath their bodies.

"We've made it, Jimmy," the captain said, slowly hauling himself to his knees. "This is a grand achievement, ye' know. It's the equal o' Captain Bligh beating the odds tae get tae Kupang after being set adrift by Fletcher Christian an' the other *Bounty* mutineers."

Morrill was not so sure. He got to his feet awkwardly and peered into the darkness beyond the sand. "It's not Kupang or Batavia, Geordie," he said. "We're not out of danger yet, - not by a long way."

"But we're on land, Jimmy, - an' it's probably only about seven hundred miles tae Moreton," Geordie's voice was tired but euphoric. "I *know* there's fresh water around here, an' we'll find enough food tae make us strong enough tae build a boat that'll get us *back* tae civilisation."

The remaining five survivors were taken off the raft. John Willmett and James Gooley were so weak that neither could stand without assistance and Morrill dragged each ashore in turn and laid them down on the sand clear of the high water mark. The captain, although barely able to walk himself, tenderly picked up Betsy and carried her bodily to the beach. Jack Millar and the apprentice, James Wilson made their own way, but both collapsed on the sand at the water's edge. Morrill, grunting with the effort, pulled them up onto their knees and persuaded them to crawl further on up the slight incline of the sand. Geordie then returned to the raft and retrieved his bible, his box of charts and survey instruments.

"We'll have tae be patient an' wait fer morning light before we assess the situation, Jimmy," he said. "We'll get lost too easily if we try tae dae anything now." He lay down beside Betsy, and Morrill, too drained to reply, sank onto the sand a few yards away and almost immediately fell into a sleep of exhaustion.

It rained during the early morning hours and at sunrise they were elated to see that the depressions in the rocks were filled with fresh water. With Geordie's arm around her waist Betsy managed to stumble to the nearest of them and they both drank lustily. Geordie laughed suddenly. "My wee Betsy," he said. "Where are yer manners lass? Ye've been slurping the water like a pig at a trough. It's no' very lady-like, ye' know."

Betsy wiped her mouth with the back of her hand and splashed some of the cool clear liquid over her face. "Oh Geordie," she cried. "I cann'ae believe that water tastes sae good out o' a rock hollow." She turned to face him and slipped her thin arms around his waist. "Ye' were quite right back in Sydney though, I'm no' so much o' a lady as I once thought…."

She looked up into Geordie's red-rimmed eyes and for a moment he saw the mischievous smile that he'd seen so many times in the past begin to form, but then it just as quickly disappeared and she looked pensively over his shoulder at the ocean beyond. Droplets of the water that she'd splashed on her face ran down her haggard cheeks and he gently brushed them away, not sure if they were mingled with tears that had welled up in her sunken eyes. The reality of their current circumstances had surely closed in on her mind, for he too recalled their pleasant stroll through Sydney's Domain and it seemed almost a lifetime away. There were two things he was certain of though; the first was that *he* alone must shoulder the blame for getting his beautiful Betsy into this unbearable situation, and the second, that he must do everything in his power to get her out of it and back to civilisation.

Morrill and Wilson had also slaked their thirsts directly from the stone hollows until they were satiated and could take no more, but Gooley and Willmett remained where Morrill had laid them in the sand during the night. Morrill managed to crawl to their few possessions that had been unloaded from the raft and fill an empty preserved meat tin with water. He held it to the cracked lips of each man in turn and they gulped down the precious liquid.

When the sun was high enough in the sky Geordie took a piece of rag and some twigs, and using the lens from the spy-glass as a magnifying glass, started a fire. He then cut some pieces of the dried shark and boiled it in a preserved meat tin and thus provided breakfast, washed down with fresh clean water.

The tide had turned and at low water Geordie, the most mobile of the group, set out along the beach on unsteady legs to conduct an initial exploratory survey of their surroundings. His excursion was short and painful, but it yielded a find that brought about sobs of joy from the others. "There are rock oysters here, lads; plenty o' them too, sticking tae the rocks in great clusters."

Morrill picked up the axe and joined him.

"These are great fer getting rid o' scurvy, Jimmy," the captain said. "Make sure that young Wilson eats some even if he doesn't like the taste o' them."

"I don't think he'll complain," Morrill said.

They gathered up as many oysters as they could carry and shared them out amongst the others, but although John Willmett managed to chew on those that were put to his lips, for James Gooley the landing had come just hours too late. Pitkethly and Morrill together dragged his lifeless body a respectable distance from the temporary camp and laid him to rest beneath the sand.

The raft had drifted offshore with the outgoing tide and Morrill supposed that it was a poignant time for the captain. It was the final link with his doomed ship, and Pitkethly confirmed his suspicions when he sighed deeply as he watched it carried away to the north by the current. "We must have been set down here fer a purpose, Jimmy," he said. "I cann'ae believe God would land us here wi' plenty o' food an' water all about us an' then simply abandon us in this foreign land?"

Morrill continued to stare across the bay. "I hope you're right, Geordie." I don't believe much in dreams coming true, but I *did* have a strange dream the night Nora died." He turned his gaze from the raft as it disappeared from sight around the promontory of Cape Cleveland. "She told me in my dream that the world would one day know what happened to us." He didn't mention that Nora's apparition had specifically said that he was the *one* who would survive, and he hoped that it was just his grief that was to blame for a flawed recollection of the actual words uttered by the wraith.

'You're going to be the one who will live to let the world know what happened to the rest of us after the wreck of the Peruvian.'

15

Bunginna sat cross-legged on the rock ledge high above the ocean on the mountain known to the *Wulgurukaba* tribe as *Cutheringa*. Over her shoulder she could see the old warrior, *Werboonburra*, his full round, wrinkled face still visible just above the horizon of the distant mountains. He would soon plunge to earth somewhere behind those mountains, up in the high country of the *Warungu*, but she knew that those warriors would catch him to save him from injuring himself and then another tribe would throw him gently back up to his home in the sky again as they always did. The elders said it was a game he enjoyed playing and he would then partly hide his face with his dark hands and even turn away altogether to show his black hair as he laughed at their concern for his safety. But then he would mock them by showing his full face again and the game would begin anew. *Werboonburra* was so regular, in fact, that the tribe had always been able to measure the time between wet seasons by counting the number of his games on all of the fingers of both hands.

The first golden rays of *Injin*, the ball of fire that rose up from the ocean in front of her, had already begun to warm the yellow-pink rock beneath her bare skin, although in this, the first of *Werboonburra's* games of the dry season, the rock hardly ever cooled down to an uncomfortable temperature. She straightened her long brown legs and stretched them out luxuriantly, almost to the edge of the ledge, admiring their gleaming silkiness as the new light reflected off them.

Below the ledge the ground fell away steeply and then flattened out near the shore of the bay that was itself shaped like the half-round face of *Werboonburra* as he played his hiding game. Out from the bay the rocky island *Yunbenun* lay brooding, partly in the shadow of its own mountain.

Yunbenun was where the elders said the head of the great creation snake, *Gabul*, that was the *Wulgurukaba* tribe's totem, had rested as it slithered along the coast carving out the valleys as it went. Beyond the headland that was called *Pallarenda* and out in the ocean, its great body had pushed up the small islands called *Dhanu-mira* that now lay shrouded in the morning mist. Along the coast further on than *Pallarenda* where the *Wulgurukaba* country ended was the *Warakami* and *Nawagi* country and beyond that again was the mountain island of the Bandjin tribe who called their island home *Muddamuddanahmy*. It was told by the elders that there, in the channel between *Muddamuddanahmy* and the mainland, was the place where *Gabul's* great body had rested, but that was where her own awareness of country ended.

Bunginna's earth-mother had been a *muju* of the Wulgurukaba, but her earth-father was a warrior of the mountain people, the *Bindal*, whose main camp was on the slopes of *Mandilgun*, the imposing mountain that rose high above the surrounding plains. She was not a *nunga* of the Bindal anymore though, for she had reached the age where she could soon be taken as a *muju* of one of the young warriors of another tribe. Every wet season since she had fallen out of her earth-mother's belly, a notch had been cut in her life stick. She held up both hands in front of her face with her fingers extended. Now she could put five fingers to the notches with one hand and then another five with the other, and after that, four more with the first hand again.

A great initiation *corroboree* was due to take place on *Mandilgun* after the next wet season when the rivers and swamps were passable and there was plenty of food for all the tribes. The *boree* was, of course the ceremony where young men were made into warriors. It was only held about every three or four wet seasons and there would be many tribes coming together from far and wide for the three days of the initiation.

After the initiated warriors were made she would be invited to join with the other women in the great corroboree and one of the newly initiated warriors *might* take her as his own muju. Until then she was not allowed to go anywhere on her own in case she should accidently meet one of the uninitiated men and tempt him to do things that were forbidden to both of them. The elders needn't have worried about that though for *she* knew she wasn't ready to become someone's *muju* just yet, - not after what had already happened to her dreams.

She looked over at *Obungella*, her long-time friend, who was now her sister, because she had been chosen at the last corroboree by *Bindjuk*, Bunginna's older earth-brother, and even though she had been offered no choice but to have Obungella as her constant companion, she couldn't have been happier, because she enjoyed her sister's company so much.

Obungella sat with her eyes closed and her back against the rock that rose up almost vertically behind her. They'd come to this place on Cutheringa, one of their favourite spots, to gather *malboon*, the soft moist root that grew so well in the foothills and was a much favoured delicacy with the tribes.

Obungella was slightly darker than Bunginna and her breasts were bigger and her hips wider, although that was to be expected because her life stick had three more notches than Bunginna's, but bigger breasts meant a plentiful supply of milk and wider hips meant more of a chance of survival for her and any *nunga* she might bear, so it was no surprise that she was taken quickly at the corroboree by Bindjuk, one of the strongest of the newly initiated warriors at that time.

Bunginna had often dreamt of the great *Bindal* warrior Karkinjib Wombil Moonie in the past, although she knew that most of the other untaken women had probably dreamt of him too, but in *her* dreams he had selected her ahead of all the more beautiful women at the corroboree. Her dreams and the dreams of all the other women had been dashed to pieces, however, for the *Warungu* had come from beyond the mountains with a raiding party to steal some women for their *mujus*. That was nothing new of course, because it happened often enough, and the hostilities frequently ended when both groups of tribal warriors got tired of the posturing and menacing and the Warungu went back to their own country, usually with several Bindal women happily tagging along.

This time though, things had taken a serious turn and the belligerent posturing had boiled over into sudden and unexpected violence. To the dismay of the Bindal and even some of the Warungu who knew him well, Karkinjib had been felled by a blow from behind as he tried to calm the rival warriors in the short encounter that followed. It had been a bitter time for the tribe because Karkinjib had been so popular amongst the men as well as the women and everyone had agreed that he was destined to become a great tribal leader one day.

She sighed and shook her head in disappointment. There was no point in daydreaming about him now, for Karkinjib was gone, probably forever, - although the elders had insisted that he might return one day.

'How is that possible?' She looked out again across the bay and shook her head as she considered the likelihood of such an event, but she knew well enough that she would never know the answer unless it actually happened and Karkinjib appeared in their midst. The elders were the most ancient and wisest men in the tribe and they knew things that she would never be able to understand, even if they were explained to her. *'I must not question the wisdom of the elders. If they say it could happen then it must be true.'*

Her eyes narrowed against the glare of the sparkling water below and then she sat bolt upright with a startled cry. *'Obungella look there.'*

'Yes, what is it Bunginna.' Her friend spoke without opening her eyes.

'Down there, canoe on the water!'

Obungella opened one eye and looked sideways at her. *'Always canoe's on the water,'* she said with a hint of scorn in her voice. *'I am Wulgurukaba – we are canoe people, right?'*

Bunginna ignored her mockery. *'Not like that one. Look!'*

Obungella sat up reluctantly and narrowed her eyes to squint across the shimmering stretch of sea that lay between Cutheringa and Yunbenun, following Bunginna's outstretched arm. Three canoes bobbed gently on the calm water, their single fishermen standing up holding nets ready to cast, but they too were looking at something that slowly floated towards them on the current.

Obungella gasped in awe. *'Big canoe, that one, Bunginna! Not bark canoe like Wulgurukaba for sure - made from floating trees I think.'*

Bunginna agreed. *'Not Wulgurukaba canoe for sure, that one!'*

16

John Willmett gave a great cry of anguish that seemed to echo along the headland that rose up behind the beach. James Gooley had been buried two days ago and Willmett was still unable to move from the position he had occupied since the landing. Only he and Betsy remained at the landing place, for the water that had gathered in the rock hollows from the showers on the first night had almost dried up and the other men had gone their separate ways in a bid to locate a permanent stream.

Jack Millar, the sailmaker, had gone south along the beach. James Wilson had set out north, but he acknowledged before he left that the painful boils on his legs would prevent him from going too far. Geordie and Jimmy went up over the headland, intending to split and head in different directions once they'd got an idea of the layout of the country.

"Lord, just let me die; *please, just let me die.*" Willmett's voice trailed off and Betsy mopped his brow with a rag which she'd soaked in water. Willmett's rheumy dark-circled eyes opened wide, and he slowly turned his head towards her, but his stare was vacant. "Emma, is it *you?*" He lifted a thin, frail arm and touched her cheek with the back of his hand. "*Emma?*" His tone became more urgent and appealing and his arm began to shake, and Betsy took his cold, skeletal hand in hers and held it against her face, but said nothing.

"Ah! It *is* you, Emma my love. It's so wonderful to see you again, and our beautiful children too." His voice became soft and pleading despite the dry crackle of his throat. "Have they been behaving as they should? Ah! Little Frances has grown so much since I've been away, and our baby little John William; he looks so contented in your arms." His emaciated face seemed to split as his cracked lips spread into a grimace that revealed yellowed teeth and pale bloodless gums and he laughed, a hollow echo that rose up from deep in his chest cavity and became a harsh, discordant cackle. "It's good to be home again, Emma; so good to be home…"

Willmett's claw-like fingers clenched and then went limp, and Betsy placed his hand over his heart as a long, drawn-out sigh escaped from his lips. She avoided looking into the wide-open empty eyes that bulged out of their sunken sockets. She'd stared death in the face too many times already.

'How long will it be before we all join him? Will I be the last to die on this lonely beach, only for my bones to be picked over and scattered by crabs and birds and wild animals?'

She picked up Geordie's bible absent-mindedly, intending to say a prayer of thanksgiving that John had achieved his wish and was now at peace, reunited with Emma and their children.

'Will my bones be found by someone in the future, who will give me a decent Christian burial? And does it really matter in the end? What kind of God would make his loyal servants suffer like this?'

She placed the bible back in its box unopened, for praying to such an unkind God seemed meaningless at this particular time.

'If I've lost my faith now I've nothing left but courage tae keep going, - an' I haven't got much o' that either.' She sat on the sand, pulled her knees up under her and cried bitterly.

Jimmy Morrill was feeling much better after four days on the beach. He'd found a trickle of water coming from a spring near the top of the headland and followed it down until it entered the bay half-a-mile south of their landing place. He'd met up with Jack Millar and the two of them had found a cave in the cliff face that was elevated above the beach enough to be clear of the highest tide. On closer inspection they found that it was about twenty feet deep and higher than a man's head and seemed quite suitable as a temporary refuge.

Geordie had found a native canoe. It was constructed of bark with the ends securely lashed together and sealed with a yellow resin and was big enough to hold two people. In it were two small paddles, several fishing spears, each with a double spike bound to the end and barbed with fish-bone, a couple of water bags made from closely woven reeds and sealed with resin, and the lines and nets of a fishing party. It was more evidence that this part of the coast was inhabited by someone other than themselves, and judging by the elaborate sealing and fastening of the canoe and the intricately woven nets, someone with a particular skill in fishing.

That afternoon, and after the burial of John Willmett, the little band of survivors gathered their meagre possessions together and made their way further south to the cave. They lit a fire and boiled the fish that Morrill had caught off the beach with a line and oyster-shell hook from the native canoe and as dusk fell the captain concluded his thanks to God for the hearty meal they'd enjoyed. The discussion then turned to what their plans might be for the immediate future.

Jack Millar was adamant. "I'm not staying here to die slowly or be eaten by cannibals," he said. "I'm going to find out how far away civilisation is." He looked around the group. "I'm guessing ye'll stay wi' Mrs Pitkethly, Captain, 'cause there's only room fer two in the canoe, but what about you Jimmy, or young James. Either *one* of ye' coming wi' me, lads?"

Morrill and Wilson both shook their heads.

Geordie stared at him sceptically. "Yer no' going tae get very far in that wee thing, Jack. It's only meant tae be used fer fishing around the bay here, I'd wager, – an' even then only in good, calm weather. Just look at how flimsy it is, will ye'? An' I've already told ye' civilisation's a long, long way from here."

The others agreed. "When we're all strong enough we'll build a proper seaworthy boat to get us back to Moreton Bay, Jack," Morrill said.

Millar wouldn't be put off. "What are ye' going to use to build it wi', Jimmy, - that little axe Geordie's got?" He shook his head. "I'm not intending to go out to sea in it, lads, - just hug the coast all the way down to, - what's that place ye' said, captain? Port Curtis wasn't it?"

"I'm glad ye' were listening tae me at the time, Jack," Geordie said, "but if ye' can remember *that* then ye'll also remember that I said it was only a name on a map at the moment. It's doubtful the New South Wales Government would've been able tae organise an' then get a settlement underway in the two months we've been adrift, sae there'd still be no community between here an' Moreton Bay right now."

"But ye' said the British Government had approved a whole new colony called North Australia so there might be a few pilgrims who've jumped the gun an' got a head start already, - or if not, they might be arriving soon." Millar said.

Geordie shrugged. "Aye, an' it might also be ten years or more before the New South Wales Government complies wi' the British Government's orders, – if they *ever* do. Are ye' going tae search every bay an' river estuary between here an' Moreton in hope o' finding the campsite o' some foolhardy coloniser who might even be worse off than yerself? I think yer taking too big a risk, Jack."

Millar stood up. "Maybe so, but I still think it's my best chance o' survival. There's nothing left to be said so I'll say goodnight to ye' all then because I'll be leaving first thing in the morning. I hope ye' don't object to me taking a couple of those fishing lines an' one o' them water bags that was in the canoe? Ye'll probably find more o' them anyway, - unless the owners find ye' first."

"We cann'ae stop ye' from doing what ye' want, Jack," Geordie said. "An' yer welcome tae the fishing lines an' the water bag. Good luck, lad. I think yer going tae need it."

Millar grinned. "Pardon my insolence, but I think *you're* going to need good luck more than I will, Captain Pitkethly." He looked around the group, his eyes gleaming in the firelight, until they finally rested on

James Wilson. "If ye', - any one o' ye' that is, - changes yer mind during the night, yer welcome to join me."

James Wilson stared into Millar's probing eyes for a moment and then shook his head. He looked towards Geordie, but the captain said nothing and merely nodded his head in approval.

Morrill poked at the fire with a stick absent-mindedly. "Goodnight Jack; best of luck on your journey," he said, before he too turned to look at the captain as if in confirmation of his decision.

Millar shrugged. "Right then it's settled; I'll send a rescue party to pick ye' up when I get back to Moreton Bay."

Betsy had been staring into the campfire in a subdued silence giving no hint as to whether or not she'd been listening to the conversation, but she stirred at Millar's mention of sending a rescue party. "I hope ye' dae make it that far, Jack," she said, "An' I'm sure we'll *all* be eternally grateful tae ye' if ye' can send a boat tae pick us up." She managed a weary grin, but it soon faded with Millar's parting comment.

"I'll do that, Mrs. Pitkethly, but I hope the cannibals don't eat ye' all in the meantime," he said cheerfully.

He left alone early the next morning.

17

The mourning period was well past, but Karkinjib's earth-mother, Maneba still couldn't contain her grief and she could be seen and heard around the camp or in the surrounding forest, wringing her hands and wailing his name to the stars, as if she expected him to fall to earth from high above, like Werboonburra did every morning.

And it was not only Maneba who suspected Karkinjib might appear magically in their midst, for there were some elders who swore to the council that it had happened before and that the greatest warriors sometimes returned as pale ghost-men to avenge their own deaths.

As testimony to what he declared to be a fact, an old Bindal elder told of an incident that had happened long ago when he was a young warrior. The Bindal and Wulgurukaba tribes had combined their forces in a raid against the Bandjin tribe of Muddamuddanahmy, he said, and a fierce battle took place in which the leader of the Bandjin was killed by a spear thrown by a Wulgurukaba warrior. The victorious tribes had returned to their country and had gathered for a corroboree to celebrate their success and share out the spoils of war when a sentinel higher up on the slopes of Cutheringa called out a warning. *'That big one canoe, - come from Bandjin country along there,'* He pointed with his spear in the direction that the canoe had come from.

The warriors had armed themselves and gathered at the highest point on the sand at the end of the beach, gawking at the spectacle, for a great canoe had rounded Pallarenda headland with white sails as big as the clouds in the sky billowing in the breeze, and nobody had ever seen a canoe of such great proportions before.

They watched in astonishment as the white sails were gathered in and the great canoe stopped midway in the channel that separated them from the mountainous island of Yunbenun. A smaller canoe was lowered out of the great one and moved towards the shore with four figures sitting in it, the one at the front facing forward and the other three with their backs to him, each plying a pair of oars.

'Four warriors only, - maybe come to avenge death of Bandjin leader,' someone said with a touch of scorn in his voice.

Many of the assembled warriors laughed and slapped their thighs in anticipation as the small canoe grounded on the sand, but one, perhaps with more acute eyesight than the others had noticed something different about the appearance of the intruders. *'Might be Bandjin warrior come to avenge own death?'* he said, and he looked nervously on as the oarsmen set down the oars and leapt out of the canoe. All three carried long sticks that gleamed and flashed like the reflection of the great yellow ball, Injin, in the water.

The men hauled the canoe a little further on to the beach and the other man, who seemed to be their leader, stood up imposingly and stepped on to the sand without getting his feet wet. And what a strange leader he proved to be. He wore what appeared to be a piece of bark on his head in the same fashion that the women sometimes did in the wet season, but his was painted with black ochre. The cloak that hung over his shoulders was not made of wallaby skin and was as red as the blood of their enemies; a covering around his loins was whiter than the coral sand of the beach and his legs were hidden beneath shiny black skins, - but the strangest thing of all and that which made some of the younger warriors recoil in alarm was his *face*. The other three men, at least what could be seen of them, for they too were covered in odd-looking cloaks, were almost the colour of the Bandjin, but their leader had *white skin* like the skin of a new-born nunga. Or worse still, as they had learned around the campfires when they themselves were nungas, - *like the skin of a dead warrior returning to avenge his own death.*

A shout went up from several in the mob. – *'The Bandjin leader has returned as a ghost-man.'*

The Wulgurukaba warrior who had killed the Bandjin leader stepped forward and walked towards the ghost-man. He strolled calmly, with his oval, red and white daubed hardwood shield strapped to his left arm and the two long barbed spears that he carried in his right hand pointed towards the ground in a display of peace. *'Come no further, ghost-man,'* he said. *'The battle is over and I will not harm you again if you and your Bandjin warriors leave now in peace.'*

The ghost-man raised his arm and the mob could see that he was pointing what appeared to be a small hollow bone at the warrior's chest. He turned to his companions and said something in a language that the mob didn't understand, but could tell from its sharp tone that it was a command. The men raised their strange sticks until all were pointed at the Wulgurukaba warrior, who quickly transferred one of his spears to his left hand and crouched in combat posture, brandishing the other above his head.

A puff of white smoke appeared from the end of a stick held by one of the oarsmen, immediately followed by a loud sharp crack. The warrior's body jerked upright and spun partly around, and the mob could clearly see the look of astonishment that came over his face as the spear dropped from his grasp. He sank to his knees, where he lingered for a moment, and then fell face down on to the sand.

The ghost-man leader turned to the man whose stick still smoked and barked another sharp angry command and the man lowered his stick. The others, with their sticks now pointed at the stunned mob, backed towards the canoe, the ghost-man leader stepped in and the others pushed it into the water until it floated. They then scrambled aboard, quickly working the oars until it sliced through the calm water towards its great mother canoe.

And so, the old Bindal warrior said, the Bandjin ghost-warrior avenged his own death simply by pointing a smoking fire-stick at his enemy.

Each of the elders at the council nodded their heads in solemn agreement. Karkinjib Wombil Moonie could quite easily return to do the same to the Warungu if he wanted to avenge his own death.

It was the still grieving Maneba who saw it first, a shower of lights that streaked across the night sky like the sparks that shot up from the campfire when a log was thrown on to it. The mob had been sitting around the fire while the elders took turns at recounting the dreamtime stories that had been handed down for generations, and many caught a glimpse of the spectacle when Maneba screamed and pointed in delight.

'Karkinjib, Karkinjib, my son, you have returned to your earth mother,' she wailed.

Those who had missed the first shower were not disappointed either, because no sooner had Maneba called to her son than a second shower descended, falling in a great arc towards the ocean as if to confirm that it was indeed a sign from the great warrior himself.

The shooting star was the totem of the Bindal and it had always been accepted as undeniable fact that it was Werboonburra's means of warning that an enemy tribe was lurking in the direction that the star descended to earth. The elders agreed now that Karkinjib was as great a warrior as Werboonburra and a whole shower of stars could mean that Karkinjib was angry. This was his way of letting the tribe know of his intention to return to avenge his own death.

But Werboonburra, great as *he* was, needed assistance to be thrown back up into the sky after he fell to earth and the old Bindal warrior also said that the Bandjin ghost-man had three warriors to attend him when he returned to avenge his death. The council decided that Karkinjib would possibly need such an escort to attend him also and accordingly three of the tribe's finest warriors, led by Bindjuk Werrewa, were chosen to accomplish the task.

When Injin, the great ball of fire, had just begun to cast its light across the slopes of Mandilgun the warriors set off towards the coast in the direction in which the stars had fallen, and Injin was high in the sky when the warriors first sighted the ocean from the headland, but that was of little consequence to them for they had discovered something of far greater interest and mystery.

From the time they were nungas the warriors had learned to detect the passage of any living thing by the faintest of toe prints, a small upturned stone on bare ground, or a recently broken twig or bent blade of grass. In this case, however, no such fine skills had been necessary for it could be easily seen that a single traveller had passed this way, - but not a Bindal or Wulgurukaba warrior or even a lone Bandjin warrior passing through. No, this was different to anything they'd seen before, a creature whose tracks were flat pads with no toe marks or round heel indentations.

The creature had gone down towards the ocean and they followed it cautiously, noting that it seemed to be dragging one leg slightly as it walked, perhaps a sign that it was injured in some way, and as they came closer to the beach they were alarmed to see numerous footprints of the same type criss-crossing the sand in many directions. The three warriors crept to the edge of a high sand dune that rose from behind the shoreline and lay flat on their stomachs, scanning the beach for any movement.

'There! Look over there.' Bindjuk said in a hushed voice. He pointed towards the mouth of a cave about a spear throw along the sand from which a figure had emerged a moment before, and the warriors could tell from the way it dragged one leg that it was the creature they'd been tracking. It used a long stick for support, digging it into the sand with each step as it hobbled along. It was soon followed by another and each of the warriors gasped in disbelief, for brave as they were, none had ever seen such a sight in their lives. The body of the first creature, the one with the injury, appeared to be wrapped in an animal skin, but from what animal it came was impossible to tell for it was a dirty white colour and hung off the creature in shreds, much like the thin bark of a river tree that the women stripped off to lay over the body of a dead warrior before parts of it were ceremonially consumed.

The other creature was wrapped too, but in a flowing cloak that covered its body from the neck down to where its feet should have been, and even from the distance that separated them the warriors could see that the skin of their faces reflected the whiteness of the sand beneath them.

Bindjuk slid down behind the sand dune and the other two warriors followed. Both men looked at him expectantly.

'Ghost-men for sure, - not Karkinjib Wombil Moonie, - those two.' One of the warriors said.

'Should we attack?' the other said uncertainly.

Bindjuk thought about it for a moment, remembering what the old Bindal elder had said about the Bandjin ghost-men killing the Wulgurukaba warrior by pointing a stick at him, and one of these ghost-men had such a stick. He made a decision. *'Many tracks, - maybe could be more ghost-men. Might be that Karkinjib sleeping in cave right now? Go back to camp, - bring others. I will stay here and watch for Karkinjib.'*

The next afternoon about twenty warriors gathered behind the sand dunes, some carrying several spears and others with wooden clubs and stone-headed hatchets. They squatted in a semi-circle and Bindjuk faced them, his voice controlled, but with a tinge of excitement in it as he recited what he'd observed during the previous evening vigil. *'I have seen Karkinjib Wombil Moonie,'* he said.

Several of the newly arrived warriors stared at him sceptically, for even though none of them would ever have publicly stated any doubts they harboured about the infallibility of the elders teachings, the return of a warrior to avenge his own death was just a little too difficult for some to comprehend.

Bindjuk was oblivious to their incredulity, however, and he continued to relate what he'd seen as if it had been a routine event. He held up three fingers. *'Karkinjib has this many attendants, - all ghost-men, just like Bandjin ghost-men. Only one left at camp right now. Karkinjib and the others gone, maybe find food and water.'*

'Ghost-men need food and water?' Again some of the warriors seemed unconvinced.

Bindjuk nodded. *'Eat and drink just like Bindal, - make fire too, but not like Bindal.'* He pointed at the sun. *'Ghost-men bring Injin down to water, - make fire.'*

He motioned to them to be silent and the whole mob crept to the lip of the sand dune and peered over. What they saw made some of them cringe and several, unable to contain themselves, yelped and whistled in dismay, for there, standing on the sand and looking in their direction, was the lone ghost-man, its white sail-like cloak billowing in the sea breeze.

18

Fourteen days had passed since the raft grounded itself on the sandy cove at Cleveland Bay, and the four survivors had settled into the daily ritual of foraging for enough of the necessities of life to sustain their meagre existence. Their attempts at fishing weren't always successful and they were painfully aware that unless they could obtain sufficient nourishment to regain a reasonable degree of health, any hope they might have of being able to build a suitable boat to take them back to civilisation was out of the question.

The captain and Morrill had got into the routine of setting out early each morning in their efforts to discover edible plants or game that could be easily caught. They had quickly realised that the small thick-legged wallabies that seemed to be abundant were most active before the heat of the day forced them into their hiding places amongst the rocks. No matter what action they took, however, they found that the animals were too quick and agile to be caught in snares or felled by rocks and the few edible looking fruits they found were bitter to the taste. More often than not they returned to the cave-camp with just a few rock-oysters that were added to the infrequent supply of fish caught off the beach. Geordie would then use the lens from the spy-glass to start a fire and they would huddle over it and cook whatever paltry fare they had managed to gather between them.

James Wilson had been brave in his attempts at assuming his own role in the continual search for food, but the last few days had seen him deteriorate quickly. He'd had to spend the night before last more than a mile from the camp because of the reduced mobility that was the result of the boils that had again festered on his legs. The other three had been worried by his absence, but had decided it would be foolish to attempt to locate him in the dark, and they could only pray that he had found shelter and then wait impatiently for his safe return. When he did arrive, tired but unharmed the next morning, he was ordered to remain in camp until further notice, a consequence he understood, but only grudgingly agreed to.

Betsy was only a little better off than James, Geordie told Morrill when they were alone together. He felt that, physically she was coping, perhaps even better than *he* was, but mentally the pressure showed in her thin face, her slumped shoulders, the fatigued and listless response to attempted conversation and the constant wretchedness that issued from her hollow eyes. Her melancholy was his misery too, he admitted, but he felt powerless to break down the emotional barrier that she seemed to have put up between herself and her three companions.

Her efforts to preserve her modesty were becoming futile too as the fabric of the few rags of clothing she was forced to regularly wear deteriorated, and he could only stand by with his heart aching as she disengaged herself from the male company that surrounded her. She retreated into her own isolated female domain and took every opportunity to wander alone along the sand and to go about the demands of her femininity as discreetly as possible.

Morrill stood at the entrance to the cave and peered into the semi-darkness inside. James Wilson lay on his back on a makeshift bed of straw and Betsy sat near him on the dirt floor with her chin resting on her drawn up knees and her arms clasped around them.

"Hello Jimmy. How was the food hunting today?" She tried hard to sound cheerful, but Morrill could tell instinctively that something had happened while he was away, for her voice had a strange timbre to it that immediately alarmed him.

He spread his arms and shrugged. "Not much good again, Betsy," he said. "I saw quite a few wallabies and some big lizards, but I'm too slow and weak now to catch anything. I'm going to see if I can bag a fish later, but I'll have to wait for the tide to turn." He studied her face carefully and then turned his attention to Wilson, who hadn't moved. "Is young James all right?"

She stood up and joined him at the cave entrance. "He's been suffering, poor lad; rambling away in his dreams, but he's fallen intae a deep sleep now," she said. "It's an awful thing tae say, but I don't think he's going tae last much longer, Jimmy."

Morrill shook his head. "Maybe none of us are, Betsy," he said. *'There's no point in pretending; we're all in dire straits now.'*

"Dae ye' think Jack Millar was right, Jimmy, - about the cannibals, I mean?" Betsy looked into his eyes gravely as if she craved confirmation that Millar's parting comment was nothing more than a macabre joke.

"Maybe Betsy - I don't *really* know," he said honestly. "But Jack wouldn't have known either so don't pay any heed to what he said." He noticed that her hands were trembling as she clasped and unclasped them and then put one up to her mouth to stifle a sharp intake of breath at his reply. "*Something's* got you frightened hasn't it?"

"I *heard* them, Jimmy," she said.

Morrill stared at her, bemused. "You heard what, - cannibals?"

"I heard *someone*." She pointed along the beach towards the sand dunes. "Up there; near where we buried John Willmett an' James Gooley."

"There are some strange birds in this country, Betsy," Morrill said. "I've heard them too, squawking and whistling and making a racket."

Geordie came up behind them. "What's up, Betsy?" He said. "Why are ye' both standing out here looking along the beach?"

Betsy turned and her hands shook as she grasped his arm. "Geordie, there's been a lot o' jabbering an' whistling over there, amongst the sand dunes."

Geordie looked over her shoulder at Morrill and grimaced. "Come on inside, Betsy," he said, his voice soothing. "Yer getting yerself all worked up."

He put his arm around her shoulders and Betsy allowed him to lead her inside the cave. She sat down on a low ledge that projected from the back wall, still shaking visibly. "Jimmy's probably right," she said. "He thinks it was just birds I heard."

Geordie sat next to her and stroked her hair. "Aye, Jimmy an' I have heard them too…" He stopped mid-sentence and froze, for they all clearly heard a peculiar whistling followed by several caw-caw sounds.

"That's *no'* a bird." Betsy said. She struggled to her feet and pushed past Morrill who had turned and walked towards the cave entrance. Geordie and Morrill hurried out to join her and the three of them stood side by side gazing in awe at the spectacle that greeted them. A mob of about twenty naked warriors, their brown bodies painted with stripes of white and red ochre, had gathered in full view on a low ridge about seventy yards away. The whistling and bird sounds had ceased as soon as the trio emerged from the cave and now the mob stood silent and motionless. All were armed, some holding wicked looking clubs across their shoulders, while others held small round wooden shields in front of them and carried several long spears with the barbs pointed upwards in their free hands.

"I told ye' so Geordie," Betsy cried. "We've come tae our last now. Oh my, but there's such a lot o' them an' they look sae wild. Jack was right; we're all going tae be killed and eaten."

Morrill was intrigued. "I don't know about that, Betsy," he said. "They've obviously been watching us for quite some time. They could have rushed in and killed us all before now if that was their intention."

Betsy wasn't convinced. "Aye, ye' might be right, Jimmy," she said. "But maybe they've just no' been very hungry until now."

Morrill stifled a laugh at her unintended humour. "I don't think they're cannibals Betsy. I'd say they're just as frightened of us as we are of them," he said.

Geordie looked at him sharply. "How did ye' work *that* out, Jimmy?"

Morrill had recalled what Clem Ross told him back in Sydney. He shrugged. "I've heard that if they've never seen a white person before they may see us as some kind of – *ghosts*. Maybe they won't harm *us* if we let them know we're not going to harm *them*."

"How can we let them know that, Jimmy?" Geordie said. "I'm sure they don't speak our language."

Morrill thought for a moment. "Let's just walk towards them nice and slow and put our arms out in front of us, palms upward, to show we have no weapons and we come in peace," he said.

Betsy shivered. "But *they're* all holding weapons," she said.

Geordie sighed. "It might work." He looked at Betsy. "We've got nae choice my love. We must put our faith in the Good Lord tae protect us. Are ye' ready?"

Betsy drew her small frame erect and took a deep breath. "Aye, Geordie," she said. "I'm as ready as I'll ever be."

They began to shuffle along the sand with Betsy and Geordie praying quietly and earnestly, their arms outstretched in front of them.

They'd only gone twenty yards when Morrill chuckled. "Well now, that seems to have worked out all right."

Both of the Pitkethly's gaped wide-eyed in astonishment, for the warriors were, one by one, laying down their weapons and holding their arms out, palms upward.

Three of the warriors leapt down from the ridge and shuffled slowly along the sand side by side, arms outstretched and mimicking the gait of the advancing trio. When they were about five yards apart both parties stopped and regarded each other in silence for several seconds, Morrill and the Pitkethly's with apprehension and the warriors with evident curiosity. The impasse was broken when Morrill grinned, dropped his hands to his sides and stepped forward. His opposite number did the same and when he was within arm's length he reached out and tentatively touched Morrill's forehead. A grin then spread across his face too and he ran his hand over Morrill's face and beard and then over his shaggy long hair, apparently satisfied that he was indeed human.

'*Wadda mooli,*' he said, slapping Morrill's shoulder. The other two warriors stepped forward too and the three of them began a minute inspection of Morrill's body. They tugged at his ragged clothes and walked around him, and he remained passive and smiling as they gently prodded him from head to foot with their fingers. One of them even rubbed Morrill's arm with the heel of his hand, evidently to find out if he was dark underneath, and when he discovered that it wasn't ochre he chattered to the others excitedly.

"I don't know what *wadda mooli* means, Jimmy," Geordie said, "but he looks happy tae see that yer really skin an' bone."

"A greeting maybe?" Morrill said. "I don't think he wants to eat us, Betsy."

The rest of the mob, having observed the leading warriors interact with the ghost-men without any dreadful consequences, strolled over the sand unarmed and Betsy cringed and clung to Geordie's side as several eyed her up and down inquisitively.

"I believe they're just curious about us, Jimmy," Geordie maintained his grin and spoke without looking at Morrill.

The warrior in front of him cocked his head to one side and looked at him intently. *'Anda gugaya?'* he asked, sweeping his arm in a circle above his head.

Geordie took a guess. "I think he wants to know where we've come from." He turned towards the ocean and waved his own arm in that direction. "Long way from here; across the sea."

The warrior seemed to understand for he grinned and pointed to the water, then to Geordie and made a waving motion with his hand. *'Yiay.'*

Geordie made the same wave like action and nodded in agreement. *'Yiay.'*

The warrior who had first approached them placed a hand on his own chest. *'Bindjuk,'* he said. He then placed the same hand on Morrill's chest and looked at him expectantly. *'Karkinjib?'*

"I've already learned their word for 'Yes' I think, but you can work that one out, Jimmy." Geordie quipped.

"I think he wants to know my name," Morrill said. He placed his hand on his chest over the top of the warrior's. "Jimmy Morrill."

'Jemmy Morl?'

Morrill nodded. *'Yiay.'*

Bindjuk pointed at Geordie. *'Ngan-du?'*

"Geordie." Morrill said, hopefully.

'Jordee?' Binjuk repeated.

'Yiay,' Morrill nodded again and pointed to Betsy, who still clung to Geordie's arm with her head resting on his shoulder. "Betsy," he said.

'Betsee?' Bindjuk said. He looked at her questioningly for a moment and then turned back to Morrill. *'Mujumuju?'* He placed his hand on his lower belly and pointed towards Betsy's torn dress.

'Yiay,' Morrill said and turned to the Pitkethly's. "I think he understands you're a couple, but you'd better be prepared for him to check, Betsy."

Betsy cringed and uttered a small moan and then buried her face in Geordie's shoulder. "It's all right, lass," he reassured her. "They're all naked my love an' I'm sure all the women in their tribe will be too. Close yer eyes an' just let him see that yer' a woman an' I'm sure they'll no' bother us after that. Please turn yer back on her, Jimmy. It'll make it easier tae put up wi' if ye' dae."

Morrill obliged and waited with his back turned while Bindjuk walked over and lifted the hem of Betsy's dress.

'Yiay, - Mujumuju,' he said, satisfied with his inspection. He turned to the other warriors and pointed to Geordie and Betsy. *'Nangga Jordee. Betsee muju.'* It was said in a curt tone of authority and several who had been standing close to the couple moved away a respectable distance.

"Once again we've got tae thank ye' Jimmy," Geordie said, with relief in his voice. "I'm no' sure Betsy an' I would have been able tae understand what their intentions were. Ye' seem tae have a knack fer communicating wi' them, laddie."

"Aye, Jimmy," Betsy said, her voice trembling. "Thank ye' very much."

Morrill smiled in satisfaction, for there was no question his confidence was growing all the time. "I hope you're right Geordie. And it looks like they understand that you and Betsy are a couple. I don't think you've got anything to worry about in that sense."

The sky was beginning to darken as the sun crept down behind Mount Elliot and Bindjuk turned again to Morrill, whom he seemed to regard as the leader of the group. *'Jemmy Morl yuga?'* He pointed towards the cave.

Morrill frowned and shook his head.

'Yuga?' Bindjuk insisted. He placed both hands on the side of his head and tilted it to one side, closing his eyes.

"Ah, you want to know if we sleep in the cave." Morrill said. He beckoned to Bindjuk to follow him and the whole party made its way back along the beach. Most of the warriors remained outside while Bindjuk and the two other warriors who had made up the initial exploratory party in the search for Karkinjib Wombil Moonie entered the cave.

'Gandu muji?' Bindjuk said when he saw Wilson lying asleep on his makeshift cot. He made a coughing sound and held his hand to his mouth, pointing to the boy with the other.

Morrill nodded. "*Yiay*, he's not well," and directed Bindjuk's attention to the festering boils on Wilson's legs.

Bindjuk responded by walking a few paces dragging one leg behind him before pointing to the boy again.

"He's seen James before now by the look o' it." Geordie said, bemused. "An' I'll wager they've followed him back here from when he spent the night out."

"Have they been watching us *that* long?" Betsy groaned.

Bindjuk rubbed his belly and made a chewing sound, pointing to Morrill's mouth. '*Wunda-na?*'

Morrill spread his hands wide. "Jemmy, no eat," he said.

Bindjuk walked to the cave entrance and called to one of the warriors outside and after the space of five minutes or so the man returned with an armful of roots, which he unceremoniously dumped in the middle of the floor before leaving the cave to re-join his friends outside.

 Bindjuk picked up one of the roots and prised the outer layer open to reveal a white nut about the size of a marble. He held it up and popped it into his mouth and then offered one to Morrill who did the same.

"Ah, good," Morrill said, rubbing his belly and laughing, which seemed to make the three warriors very happy.

Bindjuk distributed them evenly and sat watching as they ate, and then, satisfied that they'd had enough, he and the other two warriors lay down and within a few minutes were snoring in peaceful harmony.

Geordie laughed softly and shook his head in wonder. "The Lord has provided fer his starving believers once again, Jimmy. Here we were, no' far from our final days on earth, but wi' the help o' the most humble o' His creatures we've received His providence once again."

"Yes, Geordie," Morrill said, but he was relieved that his companions couldn't see his face, for he was thinking of it in what he considered to be more rational terms. '*We weren't far from our final days on earth simply because we didn't know that food was buried just beneath our feet all the time.*' As the morning sun filtered through the dust particles that hung suspended in the dank air of the cave, Geordie woke up to a grim discovery.

"All my instruments an' charts are missing," he said bleakly. "They must have stolen them during the night." But what devastated him even more was that his precious bible, his prayer book and his hymn book had been stolen too, as well as every spare coil of rope and piece of canvas that had been salvaged from the raft.

"Where's the axe?" Morrill said.

Geordie stared at him oddly, as if it was the wrong question to ask at that particular time when he was lamenting his lost treasures. "I don't know, Jimmy," he said. "We don't need it now, but my *bible*? I *dae* need my bible."

Morrill ignored the captain's grumbles. "We've convinced them that we're harmless," he said. "I'm worried that they'll think we've deceived them."

"I've hidden it." James Wilson said. He'd propped himself up on one elbow and was grinning through his pain. "It's buried just under the sand floor next to me."

Morrill laughed. "Good work, James."

Bindjuk, through signs, told them that he and the two warriors who had spent the night in the cave were making preparations to leave and if they came with them they would be provided with sufficient food and drink to fill their bellies. It seemed like a cordial enough offer, but the other two warriors had already helped Wilson to his feet and, supporting him between them, began to carry him out of the cave.

"I don't think we've really got any choice, Jimmy. They might get a wee bit annoyed if we don't go wi' them," Geordie said.

"It's our only hope anyway," Morrill said without looking at him. He grinned at Bindjuk and rubbed his own belly. *'Yiay, Bindjuk.'*

Outside the cave, a great commotion greeted them. A quarrel had erupted between two opposing sets of warriors, and they were lined up opposite each other jabbering and making threatening gestures. It became apparent immediately that the cause of the disturbance was the distribution of the scraps of clothing and the other items that had been stolen from the cave during the night. When the four survivors emerged into the sunlight the posturing ceased immediately and all eyes were turned on them.

"Oh, no," Geordie said. He'd seen the leather covers of his bible and prayer book lying on the sand, the torn out pages scattered and fluttering in the light breeze, but his distress at the destruction of his precious books was forgotten immediately, for the warriors who had been unable to secure their share of the spoils from the cave eyed them up and down with obvious intent.

James Wilson, whose arms were still thrown over the shoulders of the warriors who had helped him from the cave, wailed in a most piteous manner as the first two to reach him pulled on his trousers. A tugging match then took place between them when they finally succeeded in ripping them from his legs. Geordie offered no resistance to his assailants, perhaps hoping that they would be satisfied with his garments and leave Betsy alone, and he was completely stripped, but that was not to be, for the warriors were just as keen to remove the rags that she wore.

Betsy, although terrified, stood resolute and held on to the hem of her dress as a warrior tried to lift it over her head, and two more tried to claim Wilson's shirt and sou'wester, but the lad pointed to the sun too and made signs that it would kill him. It wasn't their desperate pleas, however, that abruptly halted the proceedings. Morrill had received the same attention and when his shirt was torn off the warriors who were arguing over it stopped suddenly and cried out, pointing at the shining thing hanging around his neck that reflected the rays of the sun into their astonished faces.

Morrill had noticed that until that moment Bindjuk had shown no interest in the melee, obviously unconcerned by the distribution of their clothes, but now he took a step backwards and gestured to the others to move away. Morrill calmly undid the clasp on the gold chain and held it out at arm's length, lightly moving it back and forth so that it sparkled and glinted in the sun and Bindjuk stared at it with a look of either admiration or incredulity, Morrill wasn't sure which. He let the locket drop into his other hand and then, with a theatrical flourish, opened it to reveal the tiny images in either half.

Morrill was playing for time, hoping that the diversion would be enough to stop the warriors from pursuing any further interest in their clothes, but Bindjuk's reaction was totally unexpected. His expression of alarm changed gradually to one of astonishment as he examined the locket in Morrill's hand closely, refusing to touch it, but glancing at it from one angle and then another, as if he was trying to see what else was in the room behind the portraits. He pointed to it and then up at the sun *'Injin?'* he said.

Geordie laughed. "I think he believes you've got someone alive in there, Jimmy," he said. "An' ye've done us another good turn wi' yer performance. Why dae ye' think he pointed at the sun?"

Morrill grinned. "I'm not sure; he might think it's a little sun I've got in my hand, but I *am* certain he's noticed that Nora and her da' have got clothes on in it," he said.

Bindjuk had barked an order to the warriors and, one by one, they returned the items of clothing they had taken and then wandered over and sat together in a circle on the sand, chattering and glancing back at Morrill in wonder.

Bindjuk explained to Morrill in sign language that they were welcome to join the warriors in some kind of a ritual.

'Corroboree', he said several times.

"What…" Geordie was shocked. "…The natives in an' around Sydney call *their* tribal dance a corroboree too," he said. "That's heartening, Jimmy. There must be *some* contact between them all if they've got the same name fer their celebrations, don't ye' think?"

"Yes, I've heard that word before too," he said. "You're right; we might *still* have a chance of getting back to Moreton Bay overland, although as you've said before, it's a very long way."

The elation was still evident in Geordie's voice. "The major corroboree's always have tribes coming from a large area around Sydney, hundreds o' miles sometimes, but who would've thought that the same kind o' festivity could stretch as far as here?"

Morrill grinned at Bindjuk, but shook his head. He pointed to the boils on Wilson's legs and to his own thin and emaciated muscles and Bindjuk seemed to understand that they couldn't join in the celebration.

'Didana,' he said, pointing to the ground. They all sat down cross-legged in the sand, for they supposed that was his intention, and he nodded his approval. Some of the younger warriors were then directed to form a circle and the corroboree began with Bindjuk facing them and beating a rhythm on his thigh as if he was leading an orchestra

'Balmbur,' he said, and the warriors who were seated began to beat the regular tempo on their thighs too.

Two warriors leapt into the circle. One crouched and pointed towards Mount Elliot and then traced an arc across the sky with his outstretched arm, stamping his foot in the sand in time to the beat. The other warrior had dropped to his knees and held his head in his hands, but raised himself up and staggered in the direction that the first man pointed before falling to his knees once more. The first man then sprang out of the circle and Bindjuk and the same two warriors who had been the first to advance along the sand with outstretched arms bounded into it, each of them drumming the sand with their left and then right foot alternately in short staccato actions and shading their eyes with their hands as if they were searching for something in the distance. The three of them crouched, pointing to the man on his knees and then the other two warriors jumped out of the circle leaving Bindjuk on his own, backing away, but with his eyes fixed on the prostrate figure.

Morrill was enthralled. He felt as one with the seated warriors and was caught up in the intensity of the throbbing beat that seemed to render the dancers into an almost trance-like state.

Two more warriors leapt into the circle next to the prostrate figure and helped him to his feet, and two more gathered behind Bindjuk opposite. The two groups then advanced towards each other, all stamping their feet in time to the beat and holding their arms outstretched, palms upward.

Morrill suddenly realised what it was the dancers were doing. "They're telling *our* story, Geordie," he whispered in wonder.

"I was told that the Sydney tribes don't have a written language, Jimmy, an' it must be the same here," Geordie said. "They tell about important historical events an' repeat them over and over in the corroboree until they're embedded in the memories o' their children; that way the stories get handed down through their future generations wi' a fair amount o' accuracy, an' of course if it's something really big that might affect a lot o' tribes it gets top billing when they all get together."

When the corroboree was over, the seated warriors remained still, all of them regarding the four survivors in silence.

"I think they're expecting us to respond in some way," Morrill said.

"Aye, we need tae dae something," Geordie said. "Let's show our appreciation by singing a hymn o' praise." They all rose unsteadily to their feet and at Geordie's count of three broke into a hearty rendition of a hymn that they were well used to from the captain's ministrations on the *Peruvian*.

'God moves in mysterious ways.
His wonders to perform...'

When the hymn was finished the warriors gathered round them and laughed excitedly, slapping their own thighs in what was obviously a show of appreciation.

The preparations for the journey began. James Wilson was too weak to walk and one of the warriors, a powerful man, hoisted him on his shoulders and carried him. Morrill and the Pitkethly's, although able to make their own way slowly, were also supported by many pairs of willing hands, but before the whole group set off in happy spirits towards Mount Elliot, he made one final visit to the cave. When he emerged after only a few minutes and joined the group, Geordie edged over to him.

"Why did ye' dae that, Jimmy?" he said. "Were ye' afraid one o' the natives might take it from ye', or ye' might have lost it?"

Morrill looked back towards the cave. "Yes, something like that, Geordie," he said quietly, but his purpose in leaving the locket hidden in the cave was much more complex than simply ensuring it wasn't stolen. It was obvious from the way Bindjuk had gazed at the open locket that he didn't understand, but readily accepted that Nora and her Da' were alive and living blissfully in their home in the little golden sun. And was that notion very much different to his own belief, - or to Nora's for that matter?

Geordie had expressed his surprise at the innocent gullibility of such a simple savage, and any other Britisher too, on opening the locket, would have dismissed the images as just another pair of meaningless, long-dead faces enclosed in a frame. Yet Geordie and his kind accepted without reservation the concept of an all-encompassing invisible being; a powerful being who controlled *their* whole lives and whose teachings, contained in Geordies destroyed bible, must be followed to the letter.

When he'd looked at the locket that morning he'd tried to imagine it in the way that Bindjuk had understood it and what he'd seen in his mind's eye was an uncomplicated world within the little sun where everyone was happy and contented. He knew that Nora and her Da' were there, of course, but his own mother was too, and all oppressed people, no matter what faith they were born into or what colour they were, all of them living side by side in harmony. It appealed to him as a precious alternative to Geordies harsh and demanding beliefs, and he had closed it for perhaps the last time knowing that it wasn't just a memento to remember Nora by now, but a window into that unsophisticated and happy place where he might eventually be admitted to himself one day.

He'd buried the little sun reverently, knowing that he didn't need to carry it around with him to absorb its wisdom, unlike Geordie's bible that taught him the rules about entry into *his* invisible heaven. The little sun's wisdom was simple enough, and it would always be there under the sand, waiting for him to return if ever he felt he needed to look into its world and see Nora's happy smile. But there was another reason for his resolve to remove it from view too. He'd decided that nobody else would ever be permitted to gaze in curiosity at his beautiful Nora and her Da', for until he could join them in their happy place, along with Bindjuk and the Maori, and all the other outcasts of the Empire, it was *his* memory and his alone.

19

Bindjuk was pleased. He'd fulfilled the task that the elders had set him without the loss of a single warrior. It was just another step on his way to becoming a future leader of the tribe and eventually, a respected elder. Every warrior aspired to becoming one of those wise men who could read the signs that foretold the future and who were entrusted with the custody of the oral traditions of the tribe, but although a leader at any particular time was always the strongest warrior in the tribe, he was not always the wisest man. Those who had strength and wisdom had every prospect of becoming a respected elder, but those with no wisdom seldom survived long as leader once their strength diminished, and they were eventually relegated to the lowest level of tribal outsiders, where they existed on the fringe of country.

He *was* confused though, because he had serious misgivings about who these ghost-people really were. He'd known Karkinjib Wombil Moonie quite well, for they'd gone through their initiations at the same time, and both had excelled in the tests of strength and endurance that had been set for the initiates. It was unfortunate that he'd been killed before he could truly prove himself, because he would have been a worthy opponent in the mock skirmishes that were conducted to keep the warriors in good shape for the protection of the tribe during any raids by the Warungu or the Bandjin.

The elders had said Karkinjib's ghost would be found in the place where the shooting stars fell from the sky and that had been proven to be true, as he expected it would, but had death robbed him of the ability to speak and understand Bindal? And why was he so emaciated? This ghost-warrior who called himself Jemmy Morl certainly looked like he supposed some warriors might *after* death, pale and bloodless, with dark-rimmed eyes staring out from behind sunken cheeks. That would certainly be the case if a warrior had become sick from snakebite or had foolishly looked into the light radiating from the eyes of a *clever-man*, the *Wingirii,* but Karkinjib had died in the prime of his youth. He still looked so powerful after death that Bindjuk had been happy to share in the ritual partaking of his flesh, an honour that was only conferred on the strongest warriors who had died in battle.

Perhaps it was the funeral pyre that had caused his sturdy body to waste away, but why had his assistants not provided him with food? – in fact, they were *all* starving. Had Karkinjib even forgotten how to dig for the *manoon* nuts that were plentiful here on *Guliman*? And who *were* these who attended him, the ghost-man called Jordee and the small ghost-muju Betsee? Jordee was feeble and unarmed, and of what use was a tiny ghost-muju likely to be in a battle? If Karkinjib had returned to avenge his death against the Wurunga he had certainly chosen some unlikely assistants who were nothing like the strong warriors the elders had expected would accompany him on his mission.

He smiled when he remembered that he'd been worried at first that the stick he'd seen the injured one, Jems carrying was like the one the elder said the Bandjin ghost-warrior used to avenge his death, but no, - that's all it was, - a stick. He'd examined it closely and it had no magical properties that could be used to kill a warrior merely by pointing it at him that he could see. It was nothing but a branch broken from a tree to help the injured Jems to walk, and there were no other weapons anywhere in their camp either.

The elders had told of great corroboree's in the past where warriors from distant tribes traded strange objects that were said to have been bartered from tribes who's country was even further away; objects whose original purpose was unknown, but made excellent axes and spear points when hammered into shape. Some of the objects retrieved from the cave looked like they could be pounded into useful shapes, and others, like the one that could bring Injin down to make fire, were definitely beyond anything that the elders had ever spoken about, but in their present condition they were useless as weapons.

Wasn't it more likely that these supposed ghost-people were just ordinary people from a remote tribe and had lost their way? He'd first started to suspect that Jemmy Morl was not Karkinjib when he opened the shiny little Injin and showed him the people who lived in it, but if he could carry the little Injin around with him then why couldn't he find his way back to his tribe? And now it seemed that the little Injin had escaped from him and had probably found its own way home like the big Injin in the sky did every night. That was a pity, for it would have made his triumph even greater to be able to prove that there *were* people living in it, something that the elders had debated about the big Injin for countless wet seasons.

So many questions were yet to be answered about these strange ghost-people, but he was confident that, in time, the facts would come out, for the elders were wise, - much wiser than he was at this stage of his life. They would be able to sit in state at the inner circle and meditate to find the truth. In the end, what might happen to the ghost-people when they reached the Bindal camp on Mandilgun was not his decision to make. If they were judged to be *not* Karkinjib and his attendants, as he suspected, it would be the verdict of the elders in council that would determine whether they lived or died.

20

"There's a small party coming towards us, Jimmy," Geordie said. He was being helped along the well-worn track with just Bindjuk and his two attendant warriors leading the way, and was slightly in front of Betsy and James Wilson, with Morrill behind them and the rest of the warriors trailing along at the rear.

Morrill strained his neck to see past the people in front, but was only able to make out that a warrior had been despatched to meet the party by Bindjuk.

"He must have told them tae go back," Geordie continued. "They've turned around now an' gone back the way they came. Maybe he wants tae save the big surprise back at the camp fer himself."

The scrub thinned out and was replaced by a grassy plain with a few stunted trees scattered here and there, and in its centre wisps of smoke from a small campfire drifted lazily into the blue cloudless sky. As they drew closer they could see that, seated around it, were the same three warriors that Geordie had sighted earlier. The whole party came to a stop and sat down in a big circle with the campfire in the centre.

Morrill watched the strangers with apprehension, for they sat rigidly upright and hadn't moved a muscle since the mob's arrival, not even acknowledging Bindjuk. *Are they the chiefs who will have us cooked and eaten?* He looked at the campfire. It was a small affair that looked like it was working hard to stay alight on little criss-crossed twigs and there were no visible signs of any weapons. He began to relax. *'Ceremonial fire only, I suspect.'*

The men appeared to be still in some kind of a trance and two warriors took hold of James Wilson's arms and lifted him to his feet.

"Oh no! God save me, - these cannibals are going to cook me alive," the boy howled, resisting weakly as he was led into the circle.

"Wheest lad," Geordie said. "I'm sure that's no' their intention at all."

"James, look at that fire," Morrill said. "It wouldn't even singe your beard."

Wilson's eyes were wide with fright and he glanced at Morrill and then at the fire, but whether it was resignation to his fate or Morrill's words of reassurance that persuaded him, he stopped struggling then and allowed himself to be placed on the ground in front of the strangers, but he continued to shake with terror.

A few minutes later and as if on some unseen signal each of the strangers became animated. All three stood up at the same time and approached him, with the cowering boy's eyes following their every move, his mouth gaping in abject fear, but they warmed their hands at the little fire and placed them on his face and over his body to reassure him that they meant no harm. When he'd stopped shaking they proceeded to inspect him minutely from head to foot as Bindjuk and the other two warriors had examined Morrill on the beach.

Morrill and Geordie then underwent the same inspection and when it came to Betsy's turn, Morrill noted that both Geordie and Betsy seemed resigned to this further invasion of her privacy, for as she was led forward, with her thin shoulders sagging, which made her look even smaller than usual, the tiny woman's face was a mask of grim acceptance of her lot.

'Like a lamb being led to the slaughter.' Morrill couldn't help but reflect on the analogy as decency made him turn away from the examination of her frail body and he locked eyes with Geordie's, but the anguish that showed in the captain's expression told him clearly and without uttering a word that the humiliation that Betsy was being forced to suffer once more was affecting him greatly.

When the strangers had finished their inspection a circle was made, the four weary castaways were seated in its centre, and a corroboree was soon underway. The dancers gyrated and stamped their feet to the chanting and thigh-slapping of the spectators and occasionally pointed to the little group of ghost-people before whirling away in feigned fear. Bindjuk and his attendants leapt into the circle and slowly advanced towards them, arms held out and palms upward.

"It's the same as on the beach," Geordie said. "They're telling them the whole story again about how they found us."

Betsy sighed and stifled a groan with a thin bony hand to her lips, her eyes downcast. "How many more times dae ye' think we'll have tae go through these indignities before they're satisfied, Geordie?" she pleaded.

The captain took her free hand in his, but he said nothing and stared at the ground in front of him, shaking his head.

Morrill could feel his pain. *'His poor wife's suffering, but there's absolutely nothing he can say that will make it any easier for her.'*

Geordie looked up at Morrill in surprise as he struggled to his feet. "What are ye' doing, Jimmy?"

Morrill held his arms out, palms upward and shuffled forward towards the advancing warriors. "Joining in," he said.

"Maybe yer no' supposed tae…" Betsy said.

Morrill was fascinated by the ease with which the story of their appearance on the beach and their peaceful interaction with Bindjuk and his two attendants was being communicated to these new arrivals, and it struck him as significant that even if they spoke an entirely different language the story was essentially the same. "…We're part of the story, Betsy," he said.

Bindjuk's eyes lit up and he stopped a couple of yards away as he'd done on the sand at their first meeting, but this time it was he who smiled first. Morrill grinned too, dropped his hands to his sides, and stepped forward. Bindjuk stepped forward at the same time and when he was within arm's length he reached out and touched Morrill's forehead. They clasped each other's shoulders and, in that moment, Morrill felt a genuine bond had been created with the powerful brown warrior who looked so fierce from a distance, but whose face, close up, radiated such a subtle intelligence.

When the dance was over the march resumed, but the three strangers took a different path and disappeared into the scrub.

"They're heading north-west, Jimmy. They could be from a different tribe, maybe," Geordie said.

Morrill looked along the path they'd taken. "I think you're right about that, Geordie," he said. "We've been travelling generally south-west towards Mount Elliot so I suppose we're heading straight for Bindjuk's camp."

Bindjuk had overheard their conversation and looked at Morrill curiously, and as if he'd read his mind, he pointed towards Mount Elliot and then placed his hand on his own chest and said *'Bindal'*. He then pointed in the direction the men had taken. *'Wulgurukaba,'* he said.

The well-trodden track had left the flat plain behind and had entered the dense eucalypt forest that covered the lower slopes of Mount Elliot.

"How far dae ye think we've come, Jimmy?" Geordie said.

"About six miles, I think," Morrill said. "I saw some smoke just before we got into the woods. I don't think we've got far to go to their camp now."

His speculation turned out to be accurate as the track came to the edge of a shallow, meandering, stream that was about thirty feet between its fern covered banks and, instead of crossing it, the party turned and made their way upstream.

"I can hear voices ahead," Betsy said suddenly.

"Aye, yer right, my love; I can too," Geordie said. "Shrill voices – like bairns at play."

Without warning the warriors stopped and those who had been assisting them gently lowered the exhausted group to the ground. Several warriors then gathered branches that they'd broken from low scrubby trees and began to stack them around in a rough circle.

“What now?” Betsy said, alarmed.

“It’s all part of the surprise, I’d wager,” Morrill said. “They’re probably going to keep us hidden until they’re ready to show us to the rest of the tribe. I’d say they’re going to dance another corroboree and then we’ll be brought out as the final act.”

Betsy sighed, but said nothing, and her pallid face took on that steely air of resolve that Morrill had noted at the previous corroboree, as she prepared herself for more humiliation.

“Aye, we’re celebrities all right,” Geordie grinned at Morrill. “At least we’re safe fer the time being.” His voice seemed to radiate optimism as he clasped Betsy and gently squeezed her trembling shoulders, but there was no possibility of disguising the pain that Morrill could still see in his eyes.

21

Bindjuk had sent several warriors on ahead to prepare the elders for their return, which he estimated would be around the time when Injin dropped behind Mandilgun, due to the weakened state and slow progress of the ghost-people. The messengers were told to arrange for a grand corroboree to be held to announce the success of the expedition, but they were warned, however, not to tell the story before it could be depicted as it should be to the elders in dance. That was the only way this historic event could be described exactly as it had unfolded so that it could be recited over and over again to satisfy the curiosity of, not only the Bindal, but also the many other tribes who would show great interest in it. And as time went by and the actual event faded from the recollections of ordinary warriors the story would then remain in the memories of the elders so that future generations would know of it too.

When the party reached the outskirts of the camp, which consisted of a collection of gunyah's in a large clearing next to a shallow, crystal-clear river on the lower slopes of Mandilgun, they laid the ghost-people down and covered them with dried grass and tree branches. The warriors then marched triumphantly into camp, and were greeted by a mob of squealing nunga's and chattering muju's who gathered around them excitedly.

The elders were already seated and Bindjuk called for the mob, which by then numbered more than all the fingers of five warriors together, to join them and form a great circle, and they began to tell the story of their meeting with Karkinjib Wombil Moonie and his attendant ghost-people.

At first there were some whispers of disbelief, but the strange pieces of coloured animal skins that the performers wore, supposedly taken from the ghost-people themselves, convinced most of the captivated spectators that the warriors had indeed witnessed a momentous event in the long history of the Bindal tribe. And as the dance progressed, even the most resolute cynics amongst them conceded that there *must* be at least some truth to the events that were being described.

Bindjuk extended his arms and made fists of his hands with his thumbs pointing down in a traditional gesture that was an order for all to remain seated, and he and his two companions leapt out of the circle and disappeared amongst the trees. When they reappeared a few minutes later a great commotion followed as people panicked and ran in every direction at the strange sight, for they had brought with them the only evidence that was required to validate their claims.

Between them, watching the small fearful crowd that remained rooted to the ground, were four pairs of red-rimmed, cadaverous eyes, surrounded by ghastly, pale features that did nothing to dispel the corpse-like appearance of their gaunt features. *Karkinjib Wombil Moonie and his three attendants had returned to avenge his death.*

Bindjuk laughed and slapped his thigh with an open hand and his fellow warriors did the same, mimicking the cries of the mujus and squeals of the nungas who peeped from behind trees, with great merriment. Even the ghost who called himself Jemmy Morl had grinned, he noticed, but the other two ghost-warriors stood passively watching the scene and the tiny muju trembled in fear, holding on to Jordee's arm.

The circumstances still troubled him though; this was not as it should be. The great warrior Karkinjib was supposed to return in triumph to seek his revenge, - not be brought in to the Bindal camp near to exhaustion and death for a second time suffering from the effects of starvation. Perhaps something *had* gone wrong. The stars that had transported them back to earth might have landed too hard, or set down a long way off from where they were supposed to. *'They did say through sign language that they'd come from over the sea, after all.'*

One by one the frightened mujus returned, their faces still masks of astonishment, and their nungas crept close behind them following their mothers encouraging chatter. Bindjuk too, called out his reassurance from the circle and placed his hand on Morrill's chest to show that he was flesh and blood. Gradually order was restored and the elders, who had remained seated throughout the uproar, rose and stepped slowly forward.

It was immediately apparent to Bindjuk that their main interest was in the ghost of Karkinjib, *or Jemmy Morl as he knew him*, for they surrounded him and began to examine him minutely, rubbing his bare skin and feeling the texture of the strange animal hides that covered parts of his pale, thin body.

One of the oldest and most revered, an ancient, grey-bearded warrior whose name was *Ada Wumira*, stood directly in front of the ghost-warrior. His spine was curved and his bony knees protruded from thin bent legs that looked like they could barely support his delicate frame. He'd once been a tall, proud warrior, Bindjuk thought, but after all his wet seasons, - possibly as much as all the fingers of four warriors together, - his wrinkled, balding head was level with the ghost-man's chin. He slowly traced an imaginary line with a claw-like finger across the ghost-man's gaunt chest and then looked up into his sunken eyes with an intense stare that contradicted his own rheumy, glazed orbs.

'Karkinjib Wombil Moonie?'

The ghost-man turned his head towards Bindjuk and frowned in evident confusion.

'Not Bindal speak – Abaya' Bindjuk said.

Ada Wumira continued his inspection, shaking his head gravely and stroking his beard. *'Not Bindal – speak?'* He repeated. *'Not Karkinjib Wombil Moonie, - Karkinjib initiated warrior, - this one not initiated.'*

Ada Wumira had confirmed Bindjuk's worst fears. It was a pity really for he'd developed an unlikely bond of friendship with Jemmy Morl and didn't wish to see any further injury come to him, - or the others, - who all seemed harmless too. *'Funeral pyre burn initiation marks, maybe, Abaya?'* he said hopefully.

Ada Wumira glanced towards him, his bushy grey eyebrows drawn together, in a frown that reflected the doubt in his mind, but Bindjuk's interest had been drawn to a commotion amongst the onlookers on the far side of the circle. Suddenly people were pushed aside as a large and very old muju burst through and rushed into the circle, her pendulous breasts swinging underneath her outstretched arms and her long white hair fluttering in unruly wisps about her lined face.

'Karkinjib,' she wailed. *'My son, my nunga – you came back to Maneba, - your earth-mother. The stars foretold it; they said, - Karkinjib will return to you, Maneba.'* She threw her arms around the stunned Morrill's neck and buried her face in his matted beard.

Ada Wumira was almost knocked over and the ancient warrior stumbled to one side. Morrill too was almost bowled over, such was the old woman's excitement, and, in an effort to prevent himself from falling backwards, he involuntarily clasped her around her ample waist. This had the effect of increasing Maneba's delight and the old muju pranced around with Morrill pinioned by the shoulders.

Several elders helped Ada Wumira to steady himself. This was highly unusual; muju's were not usually allowed into the circle of a corroboree, - and to frolic around in a strange dance that appeared not to have any story for future generations to recall was surely against tribal law. They stood in shocked silence until the old muju, exhausted by her exertions, stopped cavorting and looked up at Morrill's gaunt face breathlessly. *'Karkinjib, - my earth-son. I almost did not know you, - I must feed you. I will gather roots and berries, - make you well.'*

Some of the other muju's, seeing Maneba within the circle and not being punished for it, joined her. *'We help, – Maneba, - feed great warrior, Karkinjib, - make well again.'*

They laughed and giggled and some even shyly touched his arms and body, rubbing his skin delicately to see if it was painted and if he was dark underneath it.

Ada Wumira quickly regained his composure. *'Yiay, it is the great warrior, Karkinjib. His earth-mother has recognised him. We must make him healthy so that he can avenge his death on the Warungu.'* He patted Maneba's shoulder and he and the other elders shuffled away in single file to their customary places in front of the large gunyah where they went into a huddle to discuss the day's historic events.

Bindjuk called to several of the younger women, among them his sister Bunginna. *'Take Karkinjib and his attendants to the gunyah and go with Maneba to gather food and arrange drink for them,'* he said.

22

The camp was still. Maneba and her willing helpers had brought roots and berries and a kind of green tea that smelled strongly of eucalyptus, but the comings and goings had gradually diminished as people drifted off to their sleeping mats. Maneba had sat in front of Morrill, dutifully watching as he ate until he couldn't fit any more in, and then, after he had shown by gestures that he was tired and needed to sleep, she clapped her hands together and ushered the remaining mujus, who had satisfied the needs of the other three ghost-people, out of the gunyah.

Jimmy Morrill was surprised, to say the least. It seemed that the old woman who had rushed at him believed he was her son who had returned to her, and he couldn't help thinking that they had all been fortunate that she did, for the questioning look in the old man's eyes and the scowl on his face had given him a feeling of dread that sent a shiver down his spine.

The faint sound of heavy breathing arose from the spot where he knew young James lay close against the flimsy, broad-leaf covered wall of the gunyah. Betsy lay in Geordie's arms and he could hear her little snorts and the irregular breaths that suggested she too had lapsed into a restless sleep.

As if Geordie had read his thoughts, he spoke softly to him out of the gloom. "Are ye' awake, Jimmy?"

"Yes Geordie," he said.

"What dae ye' make o' that business today? I mean wi' the auld lady grabbing ye' like ye' were her long lost son."

"I believe that's *exactly* what she was doing, Geordie," he said. "Yes, that old lady thinks I'm her son; I'm sure of it, - and her son's name was *Karka-neb* or something similar."

"*Karka-nib?* Wasn't that what Bindjuk said tae ye' on the sand before ye' told him yer name?" Geordie's voice was still muted, but intense enough to convey his surprise.

Morrill didn't answer right away as he gathered his thoughts. *'Bindjuk was asking me if my name was Karka-neb!'* "You're right, Geordie," he said finally. He paused again before adding; "so maybe the whole tribe was expecting to find the old lady's son, but they came upon us instead."

"Aye, an' that would explain why they were down at that part o' the beach wi' all their war paint an' spears," Geordie said. "Bindjuk must have been sent tae get Karka-nib an' bring him back tae their camp. *That's* probably why the auld men were all waiting fer us tae arrive an' Karka-nib's mam got so excited."

"Phew! I think we've been very lucky she did." Morrill said, exhaling loudly. "That old man who came right up to me; I suppose he was one of their leaders, didn't look too convinced about who or *what* I was. If the old woman thought I was her son, then he was just as certain that I wasn't." He chuckled in the dark. "I'm sure he was making his final inspection to see if I was even an initiated warrior when she almost knocked him flat on his back. It seems to me that he was too stunned to argue with her in the end."

"Aye, maybe they're no' all that different tae us Scots after all," Geordie sniggered. "I noticed that he an' his cronies went intae a wee huddle o' their own after it an' started pointing at us an' jabbering tae each other."

"Karka-neb's mam might have saved our lives, Geordie, - for now anyway." Morrill became subdued as he thought about the implications of being discovered by the tribe to be a stranger pretending he was the son of the old lady, - probably a great warrior that they thought had come back from the dead.

"Ye'll have tae try tae keep yer distance from the auld men, Jimmy," Geordie whispered. "An' *we'll* have tae dae the same. I don't know what they think o' the rest o' us; maybe we're supposed tae be yer servants or something."

"Yes, I will keep away from them, but I don't know how long I can fool my new mother and the rest of the tribe. I suppose it would be in our best interests if we *all* try to just blend in, Geordie," Morrill said. "I don't think we'll come to any harm if we can convince them that we're not any kind of a threat to them."

"I'm no' sure that I *can* dae that, Jimmy; I mean mixing in wi' the tribe an' all that. Betsy's suffering, as I'm sure yer aware, an' I don't think she can take any more o' these inspections an' all the prodding an' poking an' stuff. It's no' decent fer a Christian woman tae have tae go through all that."

"Yes, I know what you and Betsy are going through, Geordie, but getting out of here *soon* doesn't seem to be a very likely option at the moment."

"I pray tae God that yer wrong, Jimmy an' that He can deliver us out o' our misery before *too* long."

"I see it in your eyes every day that you're suffering, Geordie, and I know your main concern is for Betsy, but we might have to get used to their hospitality..." His voice became hoarse, for he remembered again Nora's fateful words, *'You're going to be the one who will live to let the world know what happened to the rest of us after the wreck of the Peruvian, Jimmy Morrill.'* He cleared his throat and added almost inaudibly, "…for a while yet, anyway."

Pitkethly didn't answer, but a muffled groan and a sharp intake of breath that ended in a quiet sob reminded Morrill that his former captain, once confident and self-assured, with his trust in God so strong at the beginning of the voyage from Sydney, was now spiritually confused, - and it was most likely that he would remain in that mentally shattered condition until his God delivered he and Betsy from their anticipated short term of captivity, - *in one way or another.*

Morrill and his companions slowly gathered strength, thanks to the ongoing care provided by Maneba and the other mujus. The various members of the tribe went about their daily tasks as they always had, leaving their nungas in the custody of the older mujus while they set off from the camp early each morning to replenish their stock of seeds, berries and roots, or to hunt and fish, and when they returned each afternoon they immediately set about preparing their evening meal.

On most afternoons they were accompanied by other groups that had evidently been invited for the sole purpose of seeing first-hand the ghost-people they'd all heard about and so, when the evening meal was over, another corroboree would be performed to tell the story of how the strangers were rescued. As on the first day, the ghost people would be paraded in the circle for maximum effect.

"There cann'ae be many more in this neighbourhood that haven'ae seen us, Jimmy." Geordie said after the sixth or seventh evening. He said it offhandedly, but there was no hiding the tension in his voice.

Betsy had resumed her air of resigned acceptance and merely stood like a disinterested spectator as the new arrivals walked around her, cautiously touching her arm or examining the hem of her shabby white dress. Only when one or another tried to go a little further out of curiosity and invade her privacy did she object, but Bindjuk was always nearby with a stern directive, *'Ngaw – Betsee muju - Jordee,'* to prevent any such occurrence from happening.

Morrill too was weary of the attention, and he was worried about James. Wilson had not improved much at all physically despite the care and attention being lavished on him by some of the young mujus, who seemed to have taken a great interest in him. The boils on his legs had not healed up fully and for such a big, strapping lad as he had been at the start of the voyage he was now a mere shadow of his former self. His mental state seemed to be no better, and he either sat on a log with his head down and his arms folded across his knees, or walked about in a kind of a trance, simply following any directives that he was given with total indifference.

To the great relief of Geordie and Betsy in particular, however, the visitations stopped after a couple of weeks as the novelty of the presence of the ghost-people wore thin amongst the nearer tribes, and they were often left to their own devices. They were still prevented from participating in the tribe's daily activities, it being judged by Maneba that they were still not strong enough to forage for food for themselves. The days then passed slowly and monotonously until Maneba's ban was lifted and they were free to join the tribe to undertake the daily tasks.

As he had done on the raft Geordie had continued to keep count of the days, mainly so that he and Betsy could observe the Sabbath with a day of prayer, and even though he readily admitted that he may have missed a day here and there, by his reckoning it was now the afternoon of Monday the fifth of July 1846, a little over eighteen weeks since the Peruvian had left the safety of Sydney Harbour.

He and Morrill were sitting on a log in the shade at the edge of the camp clearing while they rolled thin strands of stringy bark between their palms to make a strong twine that would be used as fishing line or to make snares to catch wild ducks, geese and other water fowl.

Morrill had quickly learned the art of knotting the strings together to fashion fishing nets much in the same manner as he'd often watched the fishermen use in his childhood excursions to the wharves in Maldon, and he felt justifiably proud that his nets were much sought after, as his technique was considered by many of the fishermen in the tribe to be much better than that of any other net-maker.

"Yer new mam seems tae be still looking after ye' well enough, Jimmy." Geordie said with a sly grin.

Betsy had gone down to the creek to bathe in the cool water. It was one of the few times in the day when she left Geordie's side now. She still went about the demands of her femininity discreetly, of course, but where in the past Geordie had been worried that she had disengaged herself from his company, now she smothered him in constant suffocating contact.

"Yes, she is, Geordie." Morrill hadn't looked up from his work, knowing that the captain was merely teasing him. It *was* remarkable, though, how much Geordie's mood changed when poor Betsy was briefly out of his sight and he was temporarily released from the absolute depression that he was confronted with in his every other waking moment.

It seemed to Morrill that the mental burden of his failure to protect her that he had imposed upon himself was forced to the back of his mind and he was able to make use of the short separation to regather his emotional strength. "Thank God Maneba hasn't realised I'm not her *dhula*, although I'm sure everyone else has by now," he said.

"Dhula? That means her son, I suppose?" Pitkethly frowned. "An' doesn't it worry ye' at all that the others might suspect we're no' who they thought we were?"

"Not anymore, Geordie." Morrill shook his head. "The elders seem to have got used to the fact that I'm *not* Karkinjib and I think they're too worried about the repercussions from the mujus if they were to order us killed. Young James has become a bit of a favourite with the younger mujus too since his health has improved a bit."

"Aye, I'd noticed that; an' ye' seem tae be doing fine wi' the young ones yerself. There's a wee lassie that seems tae have taken a shine tae ye' as well."

Morrill grinned and glanced at him coyly. "Bunginna?" he said. "She's been teaching me a lot of their words, Geordie. I'm sure she'd be happy to teach you too."

Pitkethly shook his head and glanced cautiously in the direction of the creek. "I've got my hands full with Betsy as ye' know all too well, Jimmy. I've already mentioned tae her that we should make the effort tae mix a bit more wi' the tribe an' learn about their ways, but she says there's no point, *because we're going tae be rescued soon.* She's sure Jack Millar would've made it tae Port Curtis or Moreton Bay by now and the government would've sent a ship tae find us. She wants us tae go down tae the head o' Cleveland Bay an' build a big bonfire so we can light it tae guide the ship in when the time comes, just in case Jack has forgotten the exact spot where we landed."

Morrill stopped what he was doing and stared at him in surprise. "I *told* you a week ago that some of the fishermen found Millar – or what was left of him and the canoe, washed up on the beach in the next bay south of the landing, Geordie. We were right; that's as far as he got on his journey south. There's nobody coming to rescue us - *nobody.*"

"I know, Jimmy; I know." Geordie held up a fist to his brow and tapped it in self-recrimination. "I just haven't had it in me tae tell Betsy about that yet. I think it would surely be the last straw fer her the way she's feeling at the moment, an' if I start learning more o' their words than I've picked up already she'll think I've given up on being rescued an' expect tae be here fer a long time."

Morrill looked again to his assignment. "You'll need to tell her eventually, Geordie, and the longer you put it off the harder it will be."

His voice softened. "But, I do understand your predicament and I wouldn't like to be in your position when you do have to come out with the truth."

Several months passed. By Geordie's reckoning it was the beginning of October and seasonal storm clouds were beginning to develop on the horizon, although the monsoon hadn't broken yet. Morrill's lessons from Bunginna, who he had learned was Bindjuk's *earth-sister*, had paid off, because he was beginning to communicate quite well and understand some of the small-talk amongst the tribe. He was able to explain to the others that an earth-sister or *abari* meant that Bindjuk and Bunginna had the same mother, as opposed to someone else who was also called a sister, but who might, to a Britisher, be a cousin or even a sister-in-law.

Morrill also explained that Bunginna had told him the wet season would arrive soon after *werboonburra next showed his full round face in his endless hiding game.* In other words, it would start shortly after the next full moon.

"She thinks she knows when the wet season will arrive?" Geordie was sceptical and Betsy, apart from the occasional shifting of her position against Geordie's side, showed little interest in the conversation.

Young James grinned. "I think she's either teasing you or you've picked up a wrong meaning," he said.

"They *all* know when the monsoon rains will come," Morrill said, his face expressionless. "They're so much in harmony with nature that they notice things you and I would never see; they take note of when the crocodiles lay their eggs, and that happened ten days before the last full moon. It takes six weeks for the eggs to hatch and when they do it *always* signals the start of the wet season."

Geordie shook his head. "You've certainly learned a lot about their ways already, Jimmy," he said bemused. "You're becoming more like them than some o' their own warriors are, I think."

"I'm working on it, Geordie," Morrill said. "The more we learn about how to do things their way, the more likely it will be that we can survive, but here's something else I've learned that could be interesting. Bunginna told me there's going to be a really big corroboree that'll be held in about four or five round moons – so that would be after the wet season, maybe around March next year."

Geordie frowned. "Why should *that* interest any of *us*, Jimmy? That just means more inspections, doesn't it?"

Betsy groaned.

"Probably," Morrill agreed, "but it also means tribes will be coming from far away and Bunginna told me they come from much further than the *Mall-mall*, the river that always flows. She said it's a good round moon and a half in that direction." He pointed south.

"The river that always flows?" Geordie said. "Surely that would *have* tae be the one Captain Wickham discovered when we anchored in the lee o' Cape Upstart in the Beagle. He called it after himself, - the Wickham River. That's certainly a lot closer tae civilisation than we are at the moment, Jimmy."

Morrill nodded. "And if some of the tribes are from even further south *again,* they might know of a settlement of ghost-men being founded along the coast. The way news seems to travel between the tribes I'd imagine that, if there *is* a settlement some of them would surely have heard of it, - or maybe even seen it. If they have, they'll most certainly share it with everyone else at the corroboree, - just like the Bindal has shared the story of our rescue. It will give us a better chance of making contact in some way. The dialects of all the tribes that are coming to the corroboree are similar in many ways; enough words are common anyway for them to be able to communicate easily with each other, - and with us if we can learn to understand them."

Betsy had suddenly emerged from her moribund state and become animated. "Oh, Geordie, maybe we could go wi' them when they go back home," she whispered.

Geordie glanced at Morrill and then at his wife, and Morrill saw once more the suffering in his sunken eyes. "I don't know about that, Betsy," he said gently. "It's an awful long way an' we're in no condition tae…"

"No condition tae dae what, Geordie?" Betsy said, her tone rising. "Do ye' want us tae just sit here an' slowly get weaker an' weaker until we're no' able tae walk at all?"

Morrill looked at her with compassion. "There's a chance that *one* of us might be able to go and bring back help, Betsy."

"Aye, just like Jack Millar did." She was crying now. "All that waiting an' wondering when he was going tae come back wi' a rescue party an' it *never* happened."

Geordie wiped away a tear, but he refused to meet Morrill's searching gaze.

He still hasn't told her yet about Millar's body being found.

"I don't want tae go through all that waiting an' wondering again, Jimmy," Betsy's shoulders were slumped. "If we can get the opportunity tae go, we should all go together."

Morrill relented. "It might be possible, - if our tribe will let us leave, Betsy," he said.

"*Our* tribe, Jimmy, - *our tribe*? It might be *your* tribe, but it's definitely no' mine. I just want tae get back tae *my* tribe, an' they're the Britishers in Scotland who don't describe their cousins or other kinsfolk as their sisters an' brothers." Betsy's voice was high with emotion and the passion in it was uncompromising. "I know *you're* getting quite used tae all that, Jimmy, an' I can see that, apart from a new mother tae give ye' lots o' attention, an' a lot o' new brothers an' sisters yer learning from, ye've decided tae dispense wi' most o' yer clothes as well." She looked away momentarily, a little embarrassed at having to confess that she'd noticed his near nakedness, but she gathered her hostile spirit again quickly. "Let me ask ye' this though; are ye' really learning all about them sae it might be useful in getting us out o' here, as you say, or are ye' becoming more like one o' them than even their own warriors are, as Geordie seems tae think?"

Morrill flinched at her direct questioning of his motives, for he felt unable to answer honestly at that point. Geordie looked away in embarrassment, but Betsy was not to be denied and she continued her outburst.

"It's *no'* our way o' life that we're living at the present time, Jimmy; we're just existing on the edge o' somebody else's. No, it's definitely no' *my* way o' life, or Geordies, or young James' either. She stabbed a bony index finger in his direction. "An' furthermore, it's no' *your* way o' life either. Your life is wi' us, an' wi' the morals an' standards o' our society. It's no' even about whether ye' like it or ye' don't; it's what ye' were born intae, - ye' cann'ae just throw away all the things ye've learned an' throw away yer clothes as well tae go frolicking around *naked* wi' these people."

She held up a trembling hand to avert any possible response, although each of the men were listening to her tirade in wretched silence and immersed in their own thoughts. "I know they rescued us when we were in trouble, an' I *am* eternally grateful fer their kindness, but we're no' like them an' ye' need tae consider that ye've got yer *real* family back home. They're the ones suffering because they surely think ye're dead an' buried at sea."

Morrill looked down at his fidgeting hands as a means of escaping the little woman's wrath that he felt was directed squarely at him only. "I'm sorry Betsy. I didn't want to give you any false hope...," he began.

Geordie cut in. "...but ye' *have* given us hope, Jimmy. It's the *only* hope we've got left now." He hugged Betsy and she sighed deeply and leant against him, the tears streaming down her face and the fire gone from her eyes.

She looked much older than her years, Morrill thought; a small shrivelled, worn-out woman who, eight months before, had been a respectable and strong young captain's wife on the journey of a lifetime.

'How things have changed in such a short space of time, but not only for Betsy, - for all of us.'

He remembered Clem Ross's prophetic words in Sydney. *'The captain has his wife on board and you're leaving on a Friday, but you young Salts haven't been at sea long enough to have learned any of the old Jack-tar's superstitions, - tempting providence, - and a double dose of bad luck.'*

And his own youthful observation. *'The only providence we'll need is a good breeze, no matter that we're leaving on unlucky Friday and the captain needs his wife to keep him company at night.'*

Geordie took a deep breath and Morrill could see that he was trying, with great difficulty, to appear composed for Betsy's sake, as he always did. He looked at Morrill and then at young James. "I'm going tae make a better effort tae learn their language now," he said. Betsy squirmed in his arms, but was too exhausted to protest further. "But *that* will only be sae that we can talk tae the tribes who might be able tae help us get as far south as possible."

Young James was enthused. "Me too," he said, with more vigour in his voice than Morrill had heard for a long time.

Geordie looked meaningfully at Morrill. It was a look that said, *'thanks again for your understanding, Jimmy.'*

Morrill acknowledged it with a slight nod of his head. "Let's all agree to learn whatever we can of their language over the next few months then," he said. It was said in a tone that lacked conviction, but he hoped that it sounded genuine to them, and to the little woman in particular, whose expectations for the future largely depended on its self-assurance. "We need to get ourselves fit and well, physically and mentally, so that we can have the best chance of leaving with the tribe that can take us the furthest south."

His voice faltered, and the words seemed to stick in his throat, for he recalled his reasons for wanting to embark on the particular journey that had brought him to this place, and not home to the family that Betsy had so indefensibly reminded him of. "Maybe, if we're lucky they'll lead us right back to *our* kind of Britisher society."

23

'Jemmy, - muga wulguru.' Bunginna was excited, for she thought what she had seen would please her companion. They were on the slopes of Mandilgun gathering *mugurdah,* for the breadfruit plants that grew on the higher slopes were always sweeter, and they'd wandered a short distance away from the rest of the tribe, - at least Jimmy had, and naturally she had followed him.

Morrill was behind an outcrop of rock and out of her sight for only a moment when she first saw it in the distance, - a very large canoe with its white sails billowing like the clouds in the sky. It rounded the Pallarenda headland and glided through the blue water in the inner channel between Cutheringa and Yunbenun, the mountain island. She called again more urgently, *'Jemmy, Jemmy, ngurany – muga wulguru.'*

Morrill was in the act of cutting the stem of a fine looking specimen of breadfruit when he heard the shrill voice from twenty yards away. It only took him a moment to register its meaning, - *'Jimmy, Jimmy, come quickly – big canoe.'* He bounded through the long grass and over the rocks like one of the long tailed rock-wallabies that were common on this part of Mount Elliot, and when he rounded the outcrop he followed Bunginna's outstretched arm as she jumped up and down in delight.

A three masted schooner sliced through the calm waters of the inner channel between Magnetical Isle and the mainland. It was a grand sight, but Morrill's initial elation at the spectacle of the full-rigged ship running down-wind in a light breeze was quickly dampened when he realised from its sail arrangement that the crew had no intention of heaving-to in search of a fresh water stream. The ship was merely passing through, probably hugging the coast because of contrary winds out closer to the reef. He gazed longingly at it and Bunginna joined him as he sat down heavily on a rock with his shoulders slumped forward and his arms resting on his knees.

'Ula minga wulguru – balina, Jemmy,' she said, throwing an arm around his neck.

'Yiay, Bunginna,' he agreed, shaking his head sadly. *'Too far that one canoe - running away.'*

Morrill wondered if Geordie and Betsy had seen the ship, for they had left the Bindal camp weeks before to join the Wulgurukaba, whose main camp was on the banks of a fresh water stream at the foot of Cutheringa, a good twenty miles closer to that part of the coast than the Bindal camp was at Mount Elliot.

It was Betsy who'd insisted on their transfer to the Wulgurukaba camp of course, and Morrill had put the proposal to the tribal elders through Bindjuk, but instead of the frank refusal to allow them to leave that he had expected, the elders had shown little interest. They had, in fact, aided their passage by readily providing several warriors to act as guides, and then sent messengers to inform the neighbouring tribe of the impending resettlement. It seemed that the presence of these two constantly unhappy ghost-people in the Bindal camp had worn their tolerance thin and they were happy to be rid of them. Bindjuk was pleased to relate that he and Jems, on the other hand, were not to go with them, for their skill in making fishing nets and weaving baskets had made them too highly valued for the Bindal to part with them so easily. The Wulgurukaba had been receptive to the idea too, as only a few of their elders had actually sighted the ghost-people, and the constant reports from Bindal warriors travelling through had made them naturally curious about the disposition of the strangers. Morrill wondered, with a sense of detachment how the pair, and in particular, Betsy, had handled the subsequent round of inspections that the move would inevitably have demanded?

The decision to move to the Wulgurukaba camp had been made for the very purpose of being within hailing distance of any ship that might be sent by the government to rescue them. *'I'm certain that Geordie still hasn't told her about Millar being found,'* or indeed, in the event of *any* ship passing through the channel, as had just now occurred. If they hadn't seen it, perhaps because they were gathering roots on the western slopes of Cutheringa, they would be told of its passage by the Wulgurukaba mujus who'd been on the shore or on the eastern side of Cutheringa. That would be hard enough to accept, but if they had watched its swift and steady passage from some impossibly distant position, as he had, until its disappearance from their view beyond the headland of Cleveland Bay, they would by now be in a state of utter desolation.

He turned and looked into Bunginna's big, innocent brown eyes as she regarded him with a worried expression. *'Come Bunginna, we gather mugurdah more.'* He picked up his basket and managed a weak smile and she returned it with a wide grin that lit up her young face.

'Jemmy sad not anymore?' She took up her own basket and linked arms with him.

'Ngaw - not unhappy for Jemmy,' he said. *'Jemmy have Bunginna, and Bindjuk my brother for clan. Jemmy unhappy for Jordee and Betsee,- clan too far away, – no hope get back to tribe.'*

24

Maurice O'Connell was younger than his good friend Clem Ross by more than a decade, but Maurice had been well-educated in Edinburgh, Dublin and Paris and had gathered such a wealth of experience and knowledge in various theatres of war that any trace of lingering youth had been extinguished long ago and had been replaced by a maturity that extended well beyond his years. He was a son of Sir Maurice Charles O'Connell and Mary, a daughter of Governor William Bligh. Despite his connections to the elite of the colony, though, he had been elected to the office of Member of the New South Wales Legislative Council for the electoral district of Port Phillip in August 1845 solely on his own considerable popularity.

He, like his father, was in fact 'Sir' Maurice, having earned the title in the British Auxiliary Legion as a reward for his services to the Spanish Queen against the Carlists, but to Clem Ross and his other close group of old friends he was simply Maurie, the larrikin who loved to catch up with all of them whenever he was back in Sydney from his far south electorate.

Clem Ross pushed open the ornate glass entrance door to the Australian Hotel and looked around the half-empty lounge. Maurice O'Connell hailed him from their usual table.

"Hello, Maurie," he said, "Only the two of us today?"

O'Connell grinned. "It seems that most of my friends have deserted me." He studied Ross's face closely. "What's the matter Rossie?" he said. "You look like your cat died overnight, old man."

Ross sat down heavily on the soft cushioned wicker chair that a waiter had pulled out for him. "I wish that was what it amounted to," he said. "You've heard the news about the *Peruvian,* I suppose?"

O'Connell nodded and looked at his friend curiously. "Yes I heard they'd found the wreck; bad luck to the poor souls who sailed in her, but what's that got to do with you, Rossie? Did you have someone close to you on board?"

Another waiter appeared from behind a screen pushing an ornate trolley and proceeded to lay out a coffee cup and saucer. Ross waited while he poured from a silver gilded pot.

"I knew a bit about the captain from his papers," he said. "His name was Captain George Pitkethly, but I'd only met one of the crew personally. He was a young sailor by the name of Jimmy Morrill." He sipped his coffee and replaced the cup on the table, careful not to spill any on the starched white tablecloth. "It's really getting to me, Maurie. I mean Captain Russell of the *Pleiades* said that the *Peruvian* hadn't broken up on the reef and he thought it looked like at least some of the crew might have survived the collision. Someone had tried to launch the longboat, - and failed, - the wreckage of it was still hanging from the stays, but it looked like they might have constructed a raft because a couple of the masts and quite a few spars were missing."

"Don't you think it's a bit of a long shot to suggest someone had built a raft old man? It was a total wreck, wasn't it?" O'Connell was bemused by Ross's agitation at the fate of *that* particular ship, for ships went missing all the time with whole crews lost at sea. It had been mentioned in the Sydney press that she had gone down in the cyclone that had borne down on the coast as far south as Moreton Bay in the week after her departure.

Ross continued in a hollow tone with his eyes downcast, almost as if he was thinking out loud. "There were no signs of *any* bodies on board and the cabins had been ransacked of clothes and blankets." He looked up and O'Connell saw a gleam of hope in his eyes. "Some of the crew could still be…alive, Maurie," he said hesitantly.

O'Connell held a hand up in protest. "Hold on, Rossie," he said. "That ship left Sydney in late February and went missing a few days later. It was found wrecked in late May – more than 300 miles from the coast on the outer reef. Even if they *were* able to build a raft in the middle of a storm or shortly after it, as you're apparently suggesting, it's unlikely that anyone could have survived the journey they then had to embark on to get to the coast."

"They *could* still have made it with an ounce of luck," Ross persisted. "What about your own grandfather, Maurie? Captain Bligh managed to sail 4000 miles to safety in an open boat after the *Bounty* mutineers set him and his loyalist crew adrift."

O'Connell winced and shook his head, for his maternal grandfather was not someone he liked to be reminded of. It was certainly a great feat of endurance and good fortune to sail through the cannibalistic islands of Fiji and on to Kupang Harbour and Batavia, but O'Connell had always considered that William Bligh had brought most of his troubles on himself with his rigid and uncompromising discipline.

Thankfully O'Connell's mother Mary hadn't inherited her father's obdurate nature. "That's different Clem," he said. "Grandfather Bligh had plenty of provisions and a seaworthy sailing launch that could be steered, and he had favourable winds that drove him directly through a gap in the northern end of the Great Barrier Reef. What's the chance of something like *that* happening to any survivors of the *Peruvian* wreck drifting on a makeshift raft, eh?" He paused and then as an afterthought added, "and even if they did get to shore by some miracle, it's all forest and mangroves with sharks patrolling the sea and alligators guarding the shore."

"We don't get alligators in Australia, Maurie," Ross said absent-mindedly.

"Oh, then why have we got an Alligator River on the map near Port Essington?" O'Connell was slightly miffed by Ross's matter-of-fact attitude.

"…It was named by Phillip Parker King and he'd done some exploration in Central America before he came to Australia. He wouldn't have known the difference between crocodiles and alligators."

O'Connell looked at his friend and grinned, his moment of irritability forgotten in an instance, for he had a genuine fondness for Clem Ross. "You're a strange one Rossie," he said. "The natives are probably cannibals anyway. We might not have alligators in Australia, but we do know for sure we've got cannibals, *don't we*?"

"No, we *don't* know that for sure either, Maurie," Ross said emphatically. "There *are* cannibals in Fiji and New Caledonia, as your grandfather found out, but that's a long way from the east coast of New South Wales. The Aborigines of the north east coastline could be the same as the Dharuk's of Hawksbury or the Eora of Sydney, - and what about the Moreton Bay tribe, - the Badtjala? They looked after that shipwrecked lady, Eliza Fraser didn't they?"

O'Connell laughed scornfully and shook his head. "*She* said they murdered her husband and took her prisoner, Rossie."

Clem Ross wasn't to be put off so easily. "Some of the other people who survived disputed her story. They said her husband died from the injuries he received in the shipwreck and that the Aborigines had looked after her well, just like they'd done on a few occasions before her episode. The chap who brought her back had lived with another tribe in the area for six years."

"That's true, Clem, but he was an escaped convict, called John Graham, - *and* he was half-savage himself. If he'd gone back to the Moreton Bay settlement, which he could have quite easily done, he would have been flogged…"

"…But the point is that he had the *option* of staying with the tribe and he chose that as his best chance of ensuring his own welfare in the long term, Maurie. He only arrived back in Sydney after he was pardoned by the government for organising her so-called *'rescue'*."

O'Connell was becoming a little weary of Ross's persistence. "You're getting yourself a bit worked up over this, Clem," he said. "You need to get it out of your mind."

Ross ignored his comment. "The explorer, Leichardt has just come back from his overland expedition to Port Essington and *he* said the natives on the headwaters of the Burdekin River are friendly."

"I agree that we don't know anything about the Aborigines who live that far up the coast, and of course you're right; Ludwig Leichardt found *some* of them to be approachable and even friendly, but don't forget there were others who murdered the explorer Edmund Kennedy up near the tip of the cape; - and what about William Bryant?"

Ross frowned and shook his head, but said nothing.

"He was the convict who stole the Governor's boat and escaped from Port Jackson with his wife and children and a few others. They got as far as Kupang by hugging the New South Wales coast until they got to the Gulf of Carpentaria, and he wrote in his journal that the further north they went the more hostile the natives became. I think they're probably like Grandfather Bligh found the South Sea Islanders to be - friendly one day, but treacherous the next when they've become weary of the novelty of seeing our white skin."

Ross conceded defeat. "I still can't get it out of my mind though Maurie," he mumbled.

O'Connell stopped the onslaught when he sensed that this meant more to Ross than he'd expected. "You might find out how friendly the Aborigines are soon enough Clem," he said light-heartedly.

"Huh?" Ross was still preoccupied with his thoughts. "What do you mean by that," he said.

O'Connell leaned forward and looked around furtively before answering, although there were few people within earshot who would have shown any interest in their conversation. "You've heard of the North Australia Colony?"

"Of course – everybody in New South Wales has heard of it." Ross was bemused by O'Connell's secretive manner. "It was proclaimed by British Parliament last year and we got to hear about it in February, not long before the *Peruvian* set out on her final voyage.

O'Connell ignored what he thought was his friend's apparently morbid fascination with the demise of *that* ship. "I've got it on good authority that the North Australia project is definitely going ahead. The capital city is going to be at Port Curtis."

Ross shook his head. "Where'd you hear that?" he said. "I thought the explorer, John Oxley, reported that the harbour was too difficult to enter with a decent sized ship and the country was too dry to grow anything? I've heard that Governor Sir Charles FitzRoy isn't in favour of it either."

O'Connell had a smug look on his face. "It *won't* be in New South Wales, - so it doesn't matter what Fitzroy thinks of it. The British Parliament has rushed it through, - mainly because there's an election coming up and *their* opposition is against it too. Nobody in New South Wales thought it would ever happen, but here it is after all and it's not just *sanctioned* by the British Government, but *commanded* by Letters Patent from Queen Victoria to proceed immediately, even though it's been criticised in the Legislative Council. Colonel George Barney is to be the Lieutenant Governor of the *new* colony of North Australia. He's taking a hundred soldiers and a party of convicts to build a settlement there"

Clem Ross brightened up. "I'd like to go on that expedition, Maurie," he said.

Maurice O'Connell studied his old friend closely. "What on earth do you want to do that for?"

Ross avoided his gaze, pretending to examine instead one of the luxurious, leather-covered, reclining sofas across the dining room. "Oh, I think it could turn into a great adventure for me and, as you know, I've been along that coastline before."

"Yes I know, and I know what happened to you on that voyage," O'Connell reminded him. "The merchant ship *Integrity* wasn't it, - wrecked in the Torres Strait in 1841 on a voyage from Sydney to Singapore? You were injured and relegated to a land based occupation, Rossie. You might be killed next time, - and what would your good wife, Daphne and young Eliza Ann do then, eh? They both need you here, old boy. What's young Eliza Ann now, - eight or nine? Don't you think she needs her father more than ever at this time of her life when she's about to grow into a young woman?"

Ross still avoided his gaze, conscious of the fact that his distinguished friend had built his success on his propensity to read between the lines of any discussion that wasn't entirely an honest representation of the speaker's thoughts.

"This is different," he said lamely. "It's country that's been explored already, - and it's not going to be a dangerous operation, - what with a hundred soldiers to protect us..."

"...And a bunch of the worst convicts that we've ever had here in New South Wales, Rossie." O'Connell threw his napkin down beside his coffee cup on the table. "Twenty-five years ago the Sydney settlers wanted to get rid of the wickedest convicts from their upper-class backyards, and even the ex-convicts wanted to get rid of the worst of their own breed. They petitioned Governor Brisbane to fix the problem and he founded the Moreton Bay settlement. Port Curtis is just another penal colony to replace Moreton Bay, now that it's been opened to free settlers, and *they* don't want any more convicts either," he said. "It's caused a huge headache for the British Government and, quite frankly, I don't think it's going to be very successful. Besides all that, do you really think you're up to it physically?"

Ross's humourless look told O'Connell that he thought he was. "Moreton Bay was successful," he scowled. "Some *positive* people in Sydney have been talking about Port Curtis as a new challenge; *the most northerly city in the great south land,* - like it was here sixty years ago when Sydney was founded."

O'Connell nodded, ignoring his friend's inference about his negativity. "Yes, and it's going to be as tough at Port Curtis as it was for the first fleet when they landed at Botany Bay." He was amused by Ross's apparent enthusiasm. He'd only mentioned Port Curtis in passing to take his mind off that infernal ship that he seemed so fretful about. "What about the ports the British Government founded twenty-five years ago on the Tiwi Islands to trade with the Malays? Fort Dundas and Fort Wellington both only lasted a year each and then they were abandoned, and now there's the Victoria settlement at Port Essington. What a great venture that was going to be; brick barracks, a brick Government House, a stone pier into deep water and cottages for the soldiers families. The town of 1,280 acres was divided into half-acre allotments for the settlers who were going to come in their thousands, but it was all fine and dandy on paper, Rossie; - nobody came. The government tried to sell the land in 1841 and then again two years ago, but they've almost given up. The Malays said they'd come to trade, but they didn't come either, and as I'm sure you'd know, Ludwig Leichardt, on his recent return, called it one of the loneliest outposts in the world. Those who are still alive are sick with fever, including the Commandant John McArthur, and now, - it's going to be tried *all over again at Port Curtis*. It's madness, I say."

"I suppose you're right," Ross said, "I just thought being on the North Australia Expedition would have given me a lot of satisfaction."

O'Connell's attitude softened a little again as he studied Ross's crestfallen appearance. "What do you want *me* to do about it, Rossie?" he said. "Colonel George Barney is a hands on sort of leader, so I expect he'll keep a tight control on who he takes with him to the new colony."

"I know." Ross shook his head. "But you're a friend of Governor FitzRoy's."

O'Connell fell silent for a moment, his face pensive, and Ross felt that he was on the verge of saying something, but then he obviously changed his mind, for he shook his head and absent-mindedly folded the white napkin he'd tossed on the table before he replied. "I doubt if even Fitzroy would have any influence on George Barney's selection of sailors. Anyway, I don't think Sir Charles would be concerned with the project since he's been snubbed by the British Government. He's got another problem now too that's going to keep him busy for a while."

Ross frowned. "You mean his wife's carriage accident?" he said.

O'Connell nodded. "Mary's a lovely woman. I hope she gets over it, but it doesn't look good at this stage." He looked at his old friend shrewdly. "It seems to me that you've never really got over that young sailor's disappearance, Rossie? What was his name again, - *Jimmy Murphy*?"

Ross's face reddened in embarrassment. "Jimmy Morrill it is, - or *was*," he said.

"You wouldn't be thinking that you might have a better chance of finding out what happened to him if you're a bit closer to the action, so to speak?"

"Maybe!"

"Let go of it Clem. Let it slip from your conscience, old man," O'Connell said. "It'll wear you down in the end. You couldn't have done anything to stop the lad from going on that voyage." He paused, as if debating in his mind whether he should continue, and then he leant across the table. "I can't do anything for you about getting on the Port Curtis expedition, but I promise you I *will* make sure you're on my staff on my next assignment."

Ross stared at him, surprised. "Your *next* assignment, - you know already where you're going to be posted?"

O'Connell looked around again cautiously. "This really is a secret, Rossie," he said. "I've been causing a lot of concern amongst the settlers at Port Phillip with my stance against the use of the Native Police force to take part in the dispersal of other Aboriginal people in the western districts. Their commander, Henry Dana, has been ordering them to shoot rather than make arrests and I've objected strongly to his methods. The settlers don't want me interfering and Superintendent La Trobe has asked Governor FitzRoy to *remove* me from the district. To his credit, FitzRoy stood by me, but under pressure he's asked me to take on the role of Commissioner of Crown Lands for the Burnett district, - and I've accepted the appointment."

"The *Burnett*?" Ross sighed. It was more than he could have hoped for. The Burnett was centred on a newly thriving settlement on the Wide Bay River, about halfway between Moreton Bay and the proposed Port Curtis, and it had been recently in the news because Governor FitzRoy had renamed the river, the *Mary*, in honour of his ailing wife. A post office, recently opened, had been named Maryborough, but what made it such an attractive proposition to him was that the community had been founded by free settlers for trade with the inland districts, - *not*, as in the case of Moreton Bay and now the proposed colony of Port Curtis, - as penal settlements.

Daphne would like it there, and Eliza Ann would too, he felt sure. These were real pioneering families, the salt of the earth, not the trumped up gentry that he'd been forced to do business with here in his daily office tasks. He loved Sydney, of course, and he felt that he would always consider it home, but for now his promised inclusion in Maurie's new assignment had given him a sense of optimism that he hadn't felt for a long time, - *and hope, - yes,* he'd been forced to admit to Maurie that he still retained *some hope* of solving the mystery of what happened to the crew of the *Peruvian*. What Maurie didn't realise though was that it was somewhat more than mere hope; it was a premonition that continually gnawed at his reasoning and left him with the gut instinct that the story of the *Peruvian tragedy was not over with yet.*

On the 25th day of January 1847, one day short of the fifty-ninth anniversary of the arrival of the first fleet at Port Jackson and the ceremonial raising of the flag of Great Britain, the *Lord Auckland* arrived off the southern entrance to Port Curtis harbour. Unfortunately for Colonel George Barney and the jubilant soldiers and crew, - and the not so enthusiastic convicts aboard, - the entry was not as grand, nor as successful, as that of Governor Phillip into Sydney Harbour. On the contrary, it was quite the opposite, for the *Lord Auckland* ran aground on shoals off the tip of Facing Island. Despite the setback, however, Barney was sworn in as Lieutenant Governor of the new Colony of North Australia on the island at a proclamation ceremony on 30th January.

Seven weeks later the entire complement was rescued and delivered to the site of the intended settlement on the mainland, but barely two months after that, a change in government in Britain ended the North Australia experiment.

25

Bunginna and Obungella were gathering malboon on the lower slopes of Mandilgun. The heavy rain and storms of the monsoon season had provided an abundance of food as expected, and there would be plenty for the visiting tribes to eat after the next round moon. Today, however, injin had appeared from behind his curtain of clouds and his bright face heated the ground below their feet and glistened off the drops of moisture that were shaken from the stems of the waist-high blady grass as they passed.

'You, - one too quiet Bunginna, - what you thinking, sister?' Obungella looked at her friend with a twinkle in her eye, for she'd noticed that Bunginna had tried to conceal a secretive smile on her lips as she worked. *'Wanye and other uninitiated warriors been away for...'* She held up one hand, *'...these many round moons, - soon return to be initiated at the boree, - remember, sister, - they not allowed to see any mujus before boree, - you no go looking for him. If Wanye see you before boree he waste away and not give you nunga.'*

Bunginna looked away, a little embarrassed that Obungella had noticed the change in her behaviour. *'I no want see Wanye before boree,'* she said, *'not thinking about him.'*

Obungella grinned shrewdly. *'You thinking about another warrior, sister, - who is it?'*

'I was thinking about Jemmy Morl.'

'Oh, sister, - you not be thinking about that ghost-warrior,' Obungella said in a shocked voice. *'Jemmy Morl is Karkinjib Wombil Moonie, - come back to avenge his own death, - he kill Wurunga warrior soon and go away again, - fly away back to sky.'*

Bunginna shook her head and laughed. *'Ngaw, Obungella, only you and old Maneba think that anymore.'*

'What ghost-warrior say about it, sister?' Obungella's voice had a touch of sarcasm to it.

Bunginna flinched in surprise, but said nothing and gazed out over the headland and the dull, grey flat sea that was visible beyond it.

Obungella must have realised immediately that her tone had been too harsh and may have hurt the younger woman, for she gestured to her, and when Bunginna came to her she embraced her warmly, hugging her to her breast. *'If not Karkinjib Wombil Moonie, then who, Bunginna?'* she said softly.

'A warrior from far distant tribe,' Bunginna whispered. *'Far away, - maybe more than injin or werboonburra.'*

'If from that far away, - he not come here take Bunginna for mujumuju? Not initiated through the boree, - seen more wet seasons than any other un-initiated warrior.'

Bunginna nodded. *'Jemmy not try come here, - only here because big canoe broken in storm, - Yiay, not been through the boree, - Jemmy tribe not initiate warriors like Bindal. No boree, - a skool they go, - learn weave baskets, - count numbers more than two hands.'*

'Hah!' Obungella snorted. *'What help that to warrior? Count numbers more than two hands? – that one not help spear fish, - feed nungas, - save Bunginna from Warungu when come steal mujus from Bindal.'*

Bunginna sighed. *'Jemmy not take me for own muju, - not yet.'*

'You want him to, yiay?' Obungella persisted. She pushed away slightly and held Bunginna at arm's length so that she could look into her eyes. *'Why you not want Wanye? He be initiated Bindal warrior soon, - take you at initiation maybe, - Wanye, he like you sister.'*

Bunginna dropped her gaze to avoid Obungella's searching eyes. *'Wanye good friend, - but Jemmy...!'*

'That one Jemmy Morl, too much counting fingers to make nunga, maybe,' It was obvious to Bunginna that Obungella was finding it increasingly difficult to conceal her scorn, but she moderated her tone enough to add, *'And he have pain. I see on his face, - plenty pain.'*

Bunginna looked out to sea, and a slight smile played on her lips. *'Jemmy not too much count to make nungas, - Bunginna teach Jemmy Bindal speak, - Jemmy teach Bunginna, - many things,'* she said, her voice almost a whisper.

'Yiay, - Jemmy Morl teach things elders say Bindal must not listen to, - speak ideas maybe not good Bindal to learn, - maybe have him killed for odd things he teach.' She laughed, but it was a hollow sound that contained no humour.

Bunginna suspected it was unlikely Jemmy would be killed on the orders of the elders. He was too valuable to the tribe, but she also knew that if he was found to be consorting with a young muju, another warrior might harm him out of jealousy, or might ask the council to have him killed for disrespecting the law of the tribe. *'Old mujus not want kill Jemmy, - love him too much, - make good nets, - weave good malboon basket,'* she said uncertainly.

Obungella had sensed her lack of self-assurance. *'But maybe not long time elders get their way.'*

'Ideas not all bad for Bindal.' Bunginna said, *'Jemmy come from powerful tribe, - have canoes like Wulgurukaba, - but much bigger to carry many warriors, - great canoe have small canoe inside, - come*

ashore collect fresh water maybe, - let Jemmy know if see, - want speak with them.'

'Jemmy Morl go away in great canoe, maybe, - Bunginna not see him anymore.'

Bunginna shook her head. *'Jemmy say he happy here, - sad for Jordee and Betsee,'* She looked at Obungella defiantly. *'Jemmy make nunga with Bunginna, maybe, - take Bunginna to his far away tribe.'* She brightened at the thought of venturing beyond her tribe's country and even beyond the country of the *Warungu,* the stone warriors who caught that playful warrior Werboonburra each morning when he fell to earth behind the mountains.

Obungella's voice became indulgent and her tone sympathetic, but there was no mistaking the warning that hung in her words. *'You would be sorry, Bunginna, but in the end, - maybe best thing to go if make nunga with Jemmy, - Wanye kill him no matter old mujus wail, if Jemmy Morl not initiated Bindal way, - not can make nunga with Bindal muju.'*

Bunginna fell silent, unwilling to continue what she felt was a conversation that would not end well for her own dreams. She would have added that Jemmy had told her the elders were wrong. He said *Werboonburra* was called *The-moon* in his country and that it wasn't a great warrior playing hiding games, but a *big* rock floating in the sky. How could that be so? Rocks don't float – not even in water – but which one is most believable? The elders could be right, but so too could Jemmy.

He also said that the tribes who live in his country are white only because injin, the great ball of fire that heats the Bindal country, is not so great in their country. He said that sometimes it doesn't appear at all for many of *his* round *The-moons'* and when it does it is nothing more than a small, red ball hidden behind dark clouds, but the clouds are not at all like those that bring our wet season when the storms roll in and the wind howls. No, Jemmy said the clouds in his country are more like the swirling dark smoke from many cooking fires when the wood is damp and their injin peeps from behind them like a dying ember of one of those cooking fires.

He said that if he sat the whole *Wulgurukaba* and the *Bindal* and the *Juru* and even the *Bandjin* tribes side by side and counted all their fingers together it still would not be enough to count the cooking fires in that far off country.

They pay a terrible price too, for having to live in a country with no injin to warm them, he said, for they have to cover their bodies with many Kangaroo skins about their shoulders and legs, just like Betsee and Jordee do, and sometimes even on their heads when it is very cold, and then when Injin is hot they still have to cover themselves to keep Injin from burning their white skin. He said they build very large gunyah's too that they use for many wet seasons and they use them even in the dry seasons as well because it is so cold.

Obungella looked up at injin as he started his descent towards the Warungu country. *'I go back to camp. Warriors be making fire now, - cooking fish, maybe Kangaroo. You coming now sister?'*

Bunginna grinned naughtily at her. *'Not yet must serve a warrior or nunga, old muju, - I come back soon when ready.'* She sat on a rock and looked out over the glistening ocean. *'Stay here and dream awhile, - you go do old muju jobs.'*

Obungella smiled at her friend and acknowledged her remark with a wave of her hand, but her feelings were made perfectly clear to Bunginna before she turned to go back to the Bindal camp. *'Careful what you dream, sister,'* she said. *'Good living here for Bindal on Mandilgun, - plenty food in bellies now, - Jemmy Morl tribe come, - maybe no more country left for Bindal to dream in.'*

26

The great corroboree had certainly provided them with the information they'd hoped for, Morrill thought with satisfaction. They had carefully watched the various dancers tell their stories, and although they didn't understand the full details of each performance, they were convinced that the five warriors from the Darumbal clan were the answer to Geordie's and Betsy's prayers. They had travelled from the furthest south to tell their important news to the tribes, and the news was considered to be so important that the warriors, all fit young men, had travelled for one and a half round moons, about six weeks in all, without mujus or nungas to slow them down, to get to the corroboree. Their dramatic account overshadowed even the Bindal's vivid description of the rescue of their resident ghost-people.

Morrill sought out their company at the feast that followed the dance and Geordie grew excited as he translated what he could of the Darumbal language into English. "Big canoe, with many, many ghost-people. Canoe lie down on rocks, two round moons stay on island. Other canoe come, take ghost-people, - corroboree on sand at water edge, much bang-bang with thunder sticks."

"We were right then. They *have* seen a ship, Jimmy, and then another one come tae the aid o' the first one that must have foundered on rocks." Geordie thought for a moment and then laughed. "A corroboree at the water's edge an' much bang-bang; surely that sounds like a ceremonial raising o' the flag an' a gun salute?"

Morrill agreed, "Maybe Port Curtis *has* been settled after all."

He frowned and the captain studied him anxiously. "Aye, it's a possibility, laddie, isn't it?" he said, "but why are ye' looking so glum?"

"I'm not sure the settlement was a success, Geordie. The Darumbal also said "Ghost-people build gunyah's, - stay two round moons, - all go away in big canoes."

Geordie groaned, his hopes dashed in an instant. "They all *left* again, after two months?" he said. "I thought fer a minute we might have been saved…"

"…maybe they left to find a safer harbour, Geordie," Morrill said, with a hint of hope in his voice. "Their first attempt at landing obviously failed if they ran aground."

Pitkethly's mood swung around again instantly. *"Of course they would*, Jimmy. Aye, I'm sure yer right, - an' that means they could be even a lot further north than Port Curtis now, *an' a lot closer tae us, -* couldn't they?"

Morrill nodded, but the troubled look on his face showed he still had reservations. "They could, Geordie," he said, "but if none of the other closer tribes have come across them since then, it's probable they've gone a bit further south instead."

Pitkethly was unmoved. "Maybe so, but it's a long coastline an' they might have found a harbour further north that the local tribe hasn't realised they're in just yet. It took the Bindal two weeks afore they discovered we were here, didn't it?" He shrugged. "Anyway, north or south, Jimmy; I don't care; the fact is there's a settlement on the coast somewhere north o' Moreton Bay an' we *have* tae find out where that settlement is."

"Maybe we should wait here and let them find us," Morrill said, but he knew even before he voiced his conviction that the captain would never entertain such a proposal."

Pitkethly shook his head. "I cann'ae dae that," he said flatly. "Betsy's come so far down she's at the point that I think she'd die if I told her we're no' going anywhere." He looked at Morrill and his face contorted as he tried to hold his emotions in check. "An' if she were tae die, Jimmy, then I'd no' see civilisation again either; I'd die right here wi' my wife. I'd like ye' tae come wi' us, laddie; we need ye'; Betsy needs ye', an' so does the boy."

A thousand people on the move is a grand sight, Morrill thought as he, James Wilson and the Pitkethly's prepared to steal away from the Bindal camp. They were now quite well known to many of the warriors from the various tribes and readily accepted as travelling companions. The five fit young Darumbal warriors had moved off swiftly on their long trek south, but the Juru from the lower reaches of the Mall-Mall, the Biria from further upstream and the Gia and Yuwibara from beyond Cape Upstart travelled unhurriedly, stopping regularly to hunt and gather roots.

A week later they were camped for the night on the north bank of the Mall-Mall. The Juru were about to turn downstream to their main camp the next morning and the other tribes were going upstream towards the Biria fish-traps on a shallow part of the river where they could cross and continue south to their own countries.

"I think we need tae split up now too," Geordie said. "That way, if any o' us see any sign o' a settlement we can contact them and let them know there's other people waiting tae be rescued."

Morrill looked around the little group. Both Geordie and Betsy had looks of faith and confidence in their eyes, and James Wilson was beaming with optimism. He shrugged. "Yes, that's it settled then," he said. "We'll split up."

He was surprised that Geordie had grown so much in confidence that he felt capable of journeying on without the support he'd requested earlier, but he supposed it was due in part to the change for the better in Betsy's disposition. He was secretly happy with the resolution, however, because the further south they went the more misgivings he had been having about continuing their journey.

He knew they were not going to be able to travel any further south than the Yuwibara country without assistance and it remained to be seen whether any of the tribes between there and the Darumbal were hostile. It also seemed pointless to move any further away from the tribe that he hadn't really wanted to leave anyway on a mission that he felt was destined to fail.

He knew there would be no opposition to the suggestion that he was about to put to the other three as it was clear they were keen to keep travelling south. "I'll go down river to the coast with the Juru if that's all right with all of you?" he said. There were no objections to his proposal.

At dawn the next day they said their goodbyes, promising to keep each other in the forefront of their thoughts, and if or when relief came to any one of them, whether in the form of a great canoe with billowing white sails, or the discovery of a flourishing settlement on the coast, a search party would be despatched immediately to rescue the others.

27

It was not unusual for small estuarine crocodiles to inhabit the brackish, turbid waters where the clear waters of the stream mixed with the incoming tidal flow, chased upstream out of their own territory by bigger reptiles. For one of the estuarine giants to be so far upstream meant that it was either old, or injured and unable to protect its own environment from other reptiles that were its equal in size. Whatever the case may have been, the massive creature suddenly launched its bulk out of the water, clamped down on Maneba's legs and sank backwards. The old muju let out a long shrill scream of terror as it dragged her down the bank, her fingers leaving deep scrabbling marks in the soft earth as she desperately tried to scramble back to safety. It was to no avail, however, for the animal's death roll cut off her final shriek and the other mujus were left awestruck in the ghastly silence that followed, their eyes wide with fright and fixed on the spreading red stain where bubbles of air still rose to the surface amid the widening circles of ripples.

Minutes earlier Maneba had been walking along the bank of the creek, cheerfully boasting to the other mujus of her returned *dhula* Karkinjib's *s*kill at knotting the close-meshed fishing net that she intended to use that afternoon to cast for the baitfish that came in with the tide. Now she was gone and, what's more, there would be no need for a funeral pyre to be raised for her, for the few remains that would float to the surface after five days or so were not worth the risk of retrieving.

Maneba had been a sometimes prickly member of the tribe, who usually got her own way in any argument, Bindjuk thought, but she had been well-liked and her loss was another reminder to the younger mujus that to stand too close to the edge of a billabong that was too deep or murky to see the bottom of was never a good idea.

He had other more serious matters to occupy his mind, however, for the great corroboree had come to an end. The young warriors had returned from the ordeals that had been prescribed to prepare them for manhood, just as he and Karkinjib Wombil Moonie had done five wet seasons past. They'd spent the last five round moons in isolation from their earth-mothers and each other, providing for themselves in the mountains of the Ayianga river inland from Bandjin country. It was a country that few people cared to traverse unless on such a mission as the young warriors had been, for the mountain tops were rarely glimpsed, hiding behind dense, dark clouds even through the dry season when the coastal plains were bathed in injin's warmth.

The constant drizzling rain that washed those vast misty mountains trickled out of every fissure and joined together to form permanent streams that became roaring waterfalls cascading over massive rocks and into deep gorges. Hordes of leeches wriggled over the wet muddy ground and crawled up onto the branches of trees, where they would lay in wait for any living thing that happened to brush against the leaves, and then, bloated with the blood of their victim, they would drop off sated to start the process over again. The stinging trees and biting green ants would have tormented them too as they foraged for whatever food they could find, and it was impossible to make fire so everything they ate would have been raw.

Bindjuk grimaced, for that was not the end, or even the climax of their ordeal. It was when they returned to the Bindal camp that the real agony began. The cane rings were tightened around their arms to stop the blood flow and they were left to endure the torture all night long, crouched on the ground with their heels firmly planted on their hands to stop their fingers from becoming permanently deformed. It was late in the morning of the next day before their misery came to an end when incisions were cut in their swollen arms to relieve pressure and avoid inflammation, and then they were presented to their earth-mothers to comfort them until the time came to choose a muju. The initiation scars would follow when the union was completed.

Three of the young men had not returned. What had happened to them would never be known, - a slow and lonely death after being bitten by a poisonous snake in the rainforest, perhaps, – or another kind of solitary, agonising death from breaking a leg in a fall. Wanye was one of them, - which was where his current troubles had started, for he'd been preparing the young warrior to take his earth-sister Bunginna as his mujumuju at the boree.

To make matters worse, Bunginna seemed inconsolable, but not for Wanye; that was bad enough, but she was grief-stricken over the loss of Jemmy Morl, who had disappeared with the three other ghost-people after the festivities were over.

Bindjuk reproached himself, because he should have known that their sudden departure was imminent. He'd seen Jemmy Morl having animated discussions with the Darumbal warriors, but had paid no heed as he didn't think for a moment that Jemmy would have left. He'd settled in to Bindal life so well. The old mujus were sad, of course, and so was he, for he'd become quite fond of Jemmy and enjoyed his company on fishing excursions, particularly as he was so good at catching fish.

On the other hand, Jordee and his muju had been desperate to return to their own tribe, which was the reason for their relocation to join the Wulgurukaba on the coast, and he'd noticed that the little ghost-woman, Betsee had looked brighter and exuded more energy than he had ever seen her display previously. She'd tolerated the latest round of inspections with composure, as if, he thought in hindsight, she'd recognised that this would be the last time she'd have to endure the humiliation. He couldn't understand *why* she objected to such an innocent examination of her body, but he knew by her reaction on each occasion that the little ghost-woman was deeply embarrassed by it.

Obungella had warned him that Bunginna was spending too much time with Jemmy and that he was filling her head with ideas that were against the teachings of the elders. Perhaps it was as well that he'd left, because now that old Maneba was not around there was nothing to stop the elders from issuing an order that he was to be killed with the others.

The other disturbing news that had come out of the corroboree was that there were many more ghost-people who had arrived without warning in the country of the tribes across the Mall-Mall, - and they were not friendly. Some had already exhibited aggressive tendencies towards warriors who were just going about their own business hunting for food in their own country.

He sighed deeply and closed his eyes as if to shut out the vision of ghost-people paddling across the bay in many, many great canoes, - the bay in which the Wulgurukaba and the Bindal had fished for countless wet seasons, - and spreading out across their traditional country where they had hunted and gathered fruits and seeds since the dreamtime.

Bindjuk *did* find out what had happened to Wanye, and it was neither the bite of a poisonous snake, nor a broken leg that was the cause of his presumed death. Obungella broke the news to him.

Wanye was doomed even before she'd warned Bunginna not to try to see him before the boree, for she was already carrying his nunga by then and was going to be an ami-muju in four round moons. Wanye had simply wasted away alone in the rainforest because of he and Bunginna's rash departure from the Bindal tradition.

28

Two wet seasons had passed since Jimmy Morrill parted with James Wilson and the Pitkethly's. He had been living with the Juru tribe, patiently waiting for news of a ship anchoring in Upstart Bay, or of a party of horsemen arriving from a settlement further down the coast, for he fully expected that, sooner or later, the other survivors would be able to contact white society and send someone to find him.

He was in no hurry to return to that society, however, and would have continued his pleasant existence, fishing, hunting and making nets for as long as it took for so-called civilisation to catch up with him. That all changed when he received the disturbing message. A warrior from the Gia clan had arrived with his muju for a reunion with her earth-mother of the Juru.

'Ghost-man Jems, - he jump up, - fly up to the clouds now, - up in fire, - he fly away in smoke – two round moons.'

Morrill was distressed at this unexpected turn of events. James Wilson had died two months ago and been cremated, as was the custom of that tribe. The news brought an unfamiliar upsurge of melancholy to his mind. The boy had lived through a terrible tragedy, as they all had, but for his young life to end, possibly alone in a gunyah in an otherwise busy camp, and certainly without the comfort of his own family around him, was more than he could bear to think about.

The Juru were sad to see him go, for the whole tribe had accepted him as part of their community, but the elders understood and showed great sympathy when he explained to them that he had to visit Jordee and Betsee and make certain they were well after the news of Jems' passing.

He retraced his steps over the familiar track that followed the northern bank of the Mall-Mall upstream until he reached the ford near the Biria fish-traps. He crossed to the southern bank and struck out across the river's fertile flood plain, eventually climbing the rugged rocky hills that marked the northern boundary of the Gia country. It was another three days before he saw the smoke of the camp fires to the east, and three more to reach the Gia camp.

The camp consisted of a dozen well-constructed gunyahs set in a lush green valley about a mile from the ocean. It was protected on the seaward side by low tree-covered hills, and on its western side the land rose sharply to thickly vegetated mountain peaks.

The camp was almost deserted when Morrill arrived and he went directly to the circle of elders who sat cross-legged around the camp fire. He produced the gifts that he had brought, several woven baskets and some fishing nets, and was formally welcomed. After a brief smoking ceremony he put his question to them and was directed to a small gunyah on the outskirts of the camp.

Morrill approached the gunyah with some apprehension. Two old mujus sat outside the doorway, one on either side, rocking backwards and forwards and wringing their hands while they quietly moaned a chant, but neither looked up as he passed by and entered the gunyah. The atmosphere inside the gunyah was hot and clammy after the recent rains and the air was stale with the smell of mildew. For a moment Morrill was unsure of what lay against the wall, but as his eyes adjusted to the gloom his heart raced. The body of a naked and emaciated old man, a white man, who looked nothing like the robust Captain Pitkethly that he remembered, lay on a bed of straw. The little woman who knelt by his side turned and stared at her unexpected visitor in bewilderment, her eyes bloodshot and her hair matted. She was almost naked herself except for some scant rags that Morrill recognised as the remains of Geordie's trousers, and her bones protruded through the almost translucent skin of her bare shoulders.

"Jimmy?" She struggled to rise and Morrill helped her to her feet. She fell into his arms and he held her close to him as her small, trembling body was racked by uncontrollable sobs of anguish. At some time later, Morrill wasn't sure how long he'd stood there holding her, her tears began to subside. She looked up into his eyes. "My poor Geordie; I cann'ae believe he's *gone*, Jimmy," she moaned, her words coming between long sighs of misery.

"I'm so sorry, Betsy…," he began.

"No Jimmy, ye' shouldn'ae feel sorry fer *me*." she shook her head and tried to put on a brave face, but it quickly crumbled and she dissolved into more tears. "*I'm* the one who needs tae be sorry, - an' I am, - so very sorry."

Her voice faded away and Morrill became alarmed, but she rallied and looked up at him, tears streaming down her face. "I couldn'ae let go o' my self-consciousness, Jimmy. I know now how senseless that was since everyone else around me was naked, but I had tae keep, what I believed was my modesty, intact." She laughed, a hollow dry cackle that rose from her throat. "*Modesty*; can ye' imagine that? These people don't have any idea o' the meaning o' our Britisher modesty. They're free spirits an' they couldn'ae care less about clothes except tae keep themselves warm on a cold night.

Morrill winced, suddenly aware of his own nudity. It was not something he'd thought about for a long time, for it all seemed so natural to him now. He remembered his first meeting with Bunginna and how he'd been charmed by her natural beauty, - her total ignorance of any shyness regarding her own nakedness. "Geordie always respected your right to maintain *that*, Betsy," he said. "He would have moved mountains to get you back to the society that you were comfortable in."

"I know that, Jimmy, but I was too impatient, an' now I've lost him because he worried himself tae death over my state of mind." Betsy sighed deeply. 'He didn'ae want me tae come on the voyage wi' him at all, ye' know. He knew it was going tae be too hard, - me with my fine clothes an' fussy methods o' doing everything, but I was adamant an' wouldn'ae listen. I didn'ae want him tae leave me alone again in Scotland after being without him fer six long years."

'The captain has his wife on board.'

She tried to smile as she recalled the memories, but her lips twisted and quivered uncontrollably. "It was like we were newly married when I saw him again after that first voyage he made tae this God-forsaken place. Now he's gone an' apart from you I'm the only survivor o' the wreck o' the *Peruvian* left alive now, Jimmy. Even young James Wilson is no' alive anymore. Did ye' hear about him?"

Morrill nodded. "That's why I'm here. I got the message that James had died and came to see how you and Geordie were, but I didn't expect to find you like this."

"Geordie admired ye' right tae the end; I think he'd want ye' tae know that, Jimmy, an' I knew he still wanted tae learn from the Aborigines just like you did, but I held him back. The death o' young James was the last straw fer him. When we got the news I think he realised then that we were never going tae get back home again an' he just gave up. Until then he'd carefully kept count o' the days that passed so we could observe the Sabbath, but he stopped counting an' he stopped praying then, Jimmy."

Morrill sighed and the tears flowed freely from his eyes too, for mere words seemed inadequate to describe his feelings for the little widow who appeared intent on bearing the guilt for her husband's death on her stooped shoulders, and was expressing her regrets in such a heartbreaking confession to him.

"He was a great and pious man, Betsy," he said at last. "I wouldn't have kept the faith for as long as Geordie did." He cringed at the superficial words and the thin sound of his own voice, but Betsy seemed not to notice.

"No, an' neither would I, Jimmy," she said. "I know *that* must sound terrible, but I have tae admit that I lost my own faith long ago. Every morning we'd walk up the track that leads between the two wee hills tae a rise above the beach an' we'd sit an' look out tae sea, praying that God would get Jack Millar tae finally arrange fer a ship tae come an' pick us up, but it dawned on me after a short while that it was highly unlikely that *any* God was listening tae either o' us, an' we were wasting our time praying. I should have told Geordie that I didn'ae think Jack Millar had ever made it tae Moreton Bay, Jimmy; we'd always promised we'd never keep any secrets from each other, but I thought it would have been too much fer him tae take so I kept up the pretence."

'Geordie never told her about Millar being found. He thought it would be too much for Betsy to take.'

"I want tae ask one last favour o' ye' Jimmy." Betsy's body still trembled, but her voice had gained a new determination. "I *am* happy that I came on this final journey with my man. I'd rather be here wi' Geordie than have lived the rest o' my life as a widow in Scotland never knowing what had happened tae him. I *am* going tae die very soon, but I don't want either o' us tae be cremated like young James was."

She gazed over at her dead husband, and it occurred to Morrill that it wasn't the body of a naked and emaciated old man, the wasted corpse of a once proud captain, that she saw lying on that bed of straw, for she was still smiling devotedly when she turned back to face him.

"I want Geordie an' I tae be buried side by side, as close as possible tae each other, on the rise above the beach between the two hills. We'll lie there together fer evermore an' look out on the sea that he loved so much, an' we'll dream that our ship is coming tae pick us up an' take us back tae our family."

Her tone became more urgent. "I told Geordie a long time ago that we'd never be apart again, Jimmy. Would ye' see tae it that we're no' separated, even in death?"

Morrill's voice was at breaking point when he assured her that he would see to it that her wish was fulfilled, but then his mind was drawn back to a dream that *he'd* had on a raft as it drifted helplessly on the ocean currents such a long time ago.

"Don't grieve for me, Jimmy Morrill. You're going to be the one who will live to let the world know what happened to the rest of us after the wreck of the Peruvian.

Betsy had put her arms around his shoulders and comforted *him* in his grief when Nora died. *Nora's in God's hands now, Jimmy,* she'd said at the time, but now even she doubted the existence of any God and he wondered, with the same odd sense of detachment that he'd had in the past, whether Geordie had lost his faith too in his final months and was simply going through the motions for Betsy's sake.

'We can become so familiar with someone we love and yet never really know them at all.'

Geordie's body was wrapped in bark and placed with solemn ritual on a bier of green tree fronds, and four of the most powerful warriors took up the brace poles, although the captain's skeletal form could have been carried by any single one of them. They made their way up the winding path to the burial place between the two small hills, their spears left behind, driven into the ground in a circle at the camp as a mark of respect for their ghost man who had returned to his home in the sky. The remaining warriors marched behind the pall bearers and a party of wailing mujus followed them, with Morrill supporting Betsy as she staggered along resolutely at the rear.

Sleep eluded Morrill for many hours that night and for the next three nights after, as he lay on the sandy ground outside the gunyah and listened with an aching heart to the sobs of the grief-stricken woman inside.

Betsy never uttered another word and refused all offers of food and drink from the sad faced mujus who took it in turns to maintain a constant vigil by her side, and it was something akin to a sense of relief that Morrill felt when he awoke on the fourth morning to find that her misery had ended.

Betsy had been laid to rest to spend eternity beside the man that she had been inseparable from in life, and Morrill stood on the rise between the two small hills and gazed out over the white sandy beach and beyond it across the vastness of the calm azure sea. The wailing mujus and the downcast warriors had already gone back down the track to the camp and he alone remained, contemplating what had turned out to be Betsy's final words from several days before.

'Geordie an' I will lie there together fer evermore an' look out on the sea that he loved so much, an' we'll dream that our ship is coming tae pick us up an' take us back tae our family.'

And then he saw it, - a small white speck silhouetted against the horizon. His first thought was, - *you're a little too late,* - but then he realised immediately that it would have been just another disappointment to Geordie and Betsy had they been alive to witness it, for although it was a ship the like of which they had anticipated for so long, it was passing well out to sea, its white sails billowing in a stiff breeze as it headed south.

He ran down to the beach and watched until it had passed from his vision and then he fell on his knees on the soft sand with his head in his hands, suffering again the same crushing sense of loneliness that he had felt when the news of James Wilson's death was brought to him.

'Your life is wi' us, Jimmy, an' wi' the morals an' standards o' our society. It's no' about whether ye' like it or not; it's what ye' were born intae.'

After some minutes, - he'd lost track of time, - he rose to his feet, scanned the empty horizon one last time, and turned his back on the ocean; he *would* survive; he knew he *must*, for the sake of Nora if nothing else. He silently vowed that the prediction that her wraith had made in his dream would eventually come true, but he had to be patient, for Moreton Bay and the society that Geordie and Betsy had yearned for was still too far away and his chances of making it were slim. And then another thought slipped disturbingly into his mind. *'But wasn't it that very same society, the so-called civilisation of the empire, that I was so desperate to get away from?'*

He decided that his only option was to head north, even though he didn't know if he would be welcomed back to his own tribe. *'Yes Betsy, - my tribe, and the way of life that I have chosen to be mine, in the country and with the people that I've learned to love. I will go back to the Bindal and beg them to accept me again.'*

29

The peaceful relationship that the Bindal had enjoyed with their close kin, the Wulgurukaba, had slumped to an unprecedented low. The corroboree that had been arranged to celebrate Morrill's return had quickly deteriorated into a stand-off between the warriors of both tribes when the Wulgurukaba realised that Jordee and Betsee were not on their way home. They blamed Morrill for enticing their ghost-people away and said that he deserved a crack on the head, but the Bindal mujus, many of whom had been born into the Wulgurukaba and married Bindal warriors, claimed that they were wrong and that Jordee, and particularly Betsee, the little ghost-muju, had been responsible for all of them running away. They pointed out that the young ghost-boy, Jems, who was so well-regarded by the younger mujus of the Bindal, hadn't returned either.

Morrill himself had been in a much weakened state when he'd staggered into the Bindal camp on Mount Elliot, delirious and confused. The long journey from the Gia country had taken its toll. His knees and ankle joints were red and swollen from a swamp infection and boils on his legs had festered so that the mujus had to constantly treat them with heated balemo juice poultices wrapped in soft green eucalyptus leaves.

His recovery was slow and it was a full round moon before the fever eventually left him and he was able to rise from his soft grass cot. He'd seen Bindjuk several times when the anxious warrior had come to check on his health and as soon as he was well enough he went directly to Bindjuk's gunyah. *'Bindjuk not here, Obungella?'*

Obungella sat cross-legged at the entrance and she looked up briefly and smiled, squinting into the sun. *'Ngaw, Jemmy Morl. Bindjuk go hunt kangaroo.'* She turned her attention once more to the baby suckling at her breast.

'Obungella, - mularamun belong you and Bindjuk?' Morrill said.

Obungella nodded, but avoided his gaze. *'Yiay, - Jemmy Morl, - that one, - Buramu, - our mularamun.'*

Morrill grinned. *'Buramu, - butterfly, - that one pretty name.'* He pointed at another child, who looked about eighteen months old and who was playing happily on the ground at her feet.

'Mankara here, - you too, nunga?' he said, as he bent and ruffled the little girl's hair.

Obungella shook her head and quickly raised her eyes to meet his as if she was watching for his reaction. *'Ngaw, - that one nunga belong sister Bunginna,'* She paused, studying his face closely before adding, *'Bunginna and Wanye, - they belong nunga.'*

Morrill was stunned. Bunginna had told him about Wanye, who was expected to take her for his *muju* after the corroboree. He in turn had told her about Nora. *'What else could I have expected,'* he thought bleakly?

He managed to smile again. *'Wanye muju Bunginna, - pretty nunga – both happy?'*

He flinched as Obungella frowned and shook her head again. *'Ngaw, Jemmy Morl, - Wanye, - no more he come, - no come down from Ayianga, - maybe jump up white, - gone up to clouds.'*

A feeling of dread overcame Morrill. Wanye hadn't returned from the mountains. *'Wanye gone, - where Bunginna, - out gather malboon?'*

Obungella looked up at the sky and sighed, hugging her baby to her as tears began to run down her face. *'No gather malboon anymore, - Bunginna jump up too, - fly up to clouds now, - up in fire, - she fly away in smoke, - Obungella nunga ami now.*

Morrill was devastated at this latest turn of events. Bunginna had obviously died shortly after giving birth and Obungella was now the *ami* or mother of the little girl. He looked at the happy child again. *'What name give nunga?'*

'Noora' she said miserably.

'Noora? – Obungella call mularamun, Noora?'

'Ngaw, Bunginna call mularamun name quick before she fly away, - Noora she call, - then fly away quick, - after Noora come, - Bunginna say Jemmy Morl come back soon, back to Bindal, - Jemmy Morl, he know why Noora.' She wiped away the tears and looked intently at Morrill as if she expected him to explain what Bunginna had meant, but he was beyond words and simply stared at her deep in thought.

'Jemmy Morl, he know why Noora'

The wet seasons passed with regular monotony and Morrill lost all sense of time as he went about the usual day-to-day occupations of the tribe. He became even more renowned for his basket weaving and net making skills and his food carriers were a great source of bartering with the neighbouring Wulgurukaba and Jura. He and Bindjuk became closer as time went on and were often seen fishing together in the same canoe, and he spent as much of his free time as possible with little Noora who seemed to have developed a special attachment for *Uncle Jemmy.*

On several occasions ships were sighted sailing through the inner channel, but they were invariably too far out to offer any possibility of hailing a communication from the shore, and their passage so swift that putting to sea in a canoe to try to make tangible contact was also out of the question.

Even if a ship had been anchored in the bay, Morrill reasoned, there was the obvious danger that the intent of the occupants of a canoe attempting to come alongside would have been misinterpreted and met with sudden and fatal force before he'd had an opportunity to present the speech that he'd often rehearsed in his mind.

'Ahoy there, what cheer shipmates? I'm a British subject, sirs; a shipwrecked English sailor no less, and I should like to speak to your captain, please if I may?'

He realised that he would have looked nothing like the British subject that he claimed to be in any such encounter, and he suspected that a naked warrior with matted hair and beard trying to recall English words unspoken for so long would probably not be given the opportunity of a hearing with the captain, even if he did manage, by some remarkable good fortune, to put the words together in such a finely cultivated manner.

He knew too that any such attempt would have to have been undertaken with another warrior to help paddle the two man canoe if there was to be any chance of making reasonable headway, and he wasn't prepared to risk the life of the other innocent paddler to the possibility of a hail of bullets from a nervous and trigger-happy ship's lookout.

It was more likely that any contact would be made with an overland exploration party. The Warungu had encountered a group of heavily armed white men many days walk upriver on the Mall-Mall and they'd described the horses they rode and the bedding they'd laid out around a campfire at night. Eventually the party had crossed the Mall-Mall and headed south, but they were well to the west of the Biria country so there was no news of where they had gone after that.

30

Maurice O'Connell's tenure at Wide Bay had been relatively peaceful compared to what he now faced at Port Curtis. He'd been appointed Government Resident two years before and had seen an influx of free settlers as land was opened up for pastoral use, but the opening up of the new leases and the enthusiastic nature of those who ventured further and further afield presented its own problems. His position required that he arrange for the protection of the settlers against the anticipated depredations of the Aboriginal tribes who, it was supposed, would be just as aggrieved by the presence of trespassers on the land they'd roamed over for thousands of years, as the tribes further to the south had been.

O'Connell paced the floor of Clem Ross's office. "It's much worse than Port Phillip, Rossie, - much worse. I was at least partly successful in getting the Native Police disbanded in the Colony of Victoria a couple of years ago, and now it's happening *again* right here in *my* electorate. They've brought in more Native Police from the Murray and Murrumbidgee areas. They call it *'dispersal'* just like they did in Port Phillip, but it amounts to nothing less than bloody *extermination.*" He threw the folded newspaper down on the desk in front of Ross.

Clem Ross looked at the news banner and sat back in his chair without picking it up. "I've read the report about the Hornet Bank Massacre, as they're calling it, in the North Australian," he said. "I've read the Moreton Bay Courier version too. It's the same story, but a different way of looking at what should have been done about it."

O'Connell stopped pacing and sat down in a chair opposite him. "Oh, why do you say that?" he said. He looked relieved and a little hopeful, like a convict who'd received a temporary reprieve at the eleventh hour. "I haven't read the Courier yet. I assumed they'd *both* be blaming my government for letting it happen. The North Australian correspondent wants us to go out there and kill every Aborigine in the district in reprisal."

Ross opened a drawer in the desk. He pulled out a newspaper and adjusted the spectacles on his nose. "The Moreton Bay Courier, November the eleventh 1857," he read out loud. "Massacre by the Blacks." He shoved the paper across the desk towards O'Connell, but he pushed it back.

"I know the story of the massacre well enough, Rossie. Mrs Fraser, seven of her children, a tutor and a farmhand were murdered by members of the Jiman tribe in the upper Dawson River country just west of here. Just read the parts that are different to what's in the North Australian."

Ross grinned "Forgot your spectacles, Maurie?" He picked up the Courier again. "As you said before, the North Australian correspondent wants the whole tribe exterminated, but the Courier's man is a bit more sympathetic; he says, *The settlers condemn the policy of the government for trying to reduce the Native Police Force; they also claim that an efficient Native Police Force would be a protection for both whites and blacks...*"

"...Hah!" O'Connell's fist came down on the desk, startling Ross. "They want to deal with it the same way, Clem; kill all of them and start out with a clean sheet, - is that it?"

"Not quite, Maurie," Ross said. "He goes on to say that, *...retribute justice should fall with discrimination and on the guilty only. We are therefore bound to discover those who are the guilty and failing this we apprehend we are not justified in killing those who are innocent.*"

"Well, at least he, whoever he is, has thought about it a bit and doesn't want the public to go on an indiscriminate killing spree." O'Connell was beginning to calm down.

Ross wasn't finished reading the article. *"Can we wonder that the Aborigine turns on the intruder when pinched by hunger and depraved by the vices which the white man introduces with his power."*

"Can we wonder indeed, Rossie? Of course I feel sorry for the Fraser family, but do they mention anywhere in either newspaper that twelve Jiman tribesmen were massacred a few months before the Hornet Bank affair for spearing some cattle, because the Frasers had fenced off the waterhole on the Dawson and they were starving, - or that half the Jiman women and children died last Christmas when the Frasers gave them Christmas puddings laced with strychnine?"

Ross shook his head. "That correspondent is a brave man, but I suppose he's not stupid. He knows he'll make few friends amongst the ranks of the settlers and their supporters with his frank opinion, and one of his major critics will be Governor Bowen himself."

31

'*George, Augustus, Frederick, Elphinstone, Dalrymple,*' Clem Ross shook his head and grinned to himself. '*You'd think George's father would have run out of names by the time his tenth son was born,*' but despite the pretentiousness of the man's name Clem had to admit that he was actually an easy enough person to get along with, and besides, he was a friend of Sir Maurice, even naming a river that he had discovered somewhere between Rockhampton and the proposed settlement at Port Denison, the O'Connell River.

Dalrymple had certainly had a meteoric rise to prominence, Ross mused. He'd published his *Proposal for the Establishment of a New Pastoral Settlement in North Australia,* in Brisbane in February 1859. He'd secured capital and received the blessing of the New South Wales government, and had led an expedition to investigate the potential of the Burdekin River watershed for settlement. The area had initially been explored and recommended as suitable for grazing by Leichardt on his outward journey to Port Essington fourteen years previously.

Unfortunately for his syndicate of investors, one of the first acts of the newly appointed Queensland government after separation from New South Wales was to countermand the decision to open up the new district for settlement. Dalrymple complained bitterly, and as compensation for his financial distress was given the position of Commissioner of Crown Lands for the Kennedy district. He promptly set out in the schooner Spitfire with Captain Smith and a crew of twelve to investigate the opening of Port Denison as the port of access for the Kennedy district.

The report of that voyage lay on the bench beside Ross where he'd placed it earlier. He looked down at it absent-mindedly. It was entitled;

REPORT
of the
PROCEEDINGS
of the
QUEENSLAND GOVERNMENT SCHOONER
"SPITFIRE'
In search of the mouth of the
RIVER BURDEKIN,
On the north-eastern coast of Australia;
And of the exploration of a portion of that coast
extending from
GLOUCESTER ISLAND TO HALIFAX BAY.

Ross looked out over the Port Curtis bay to Facing Island and sighed in resignation, for at sixty-two years of age he'd realised that, much as he'd dreamt about taking part in another exploratory voyage along the north-eastern coast, it was now well and truly beyond him and the best he could hope for was perhaps an appointment on Maurie's staff when Port Denison was officially launched for settlement.

As the title suggested, the purpose of the expedition had been twofold; apart from surveying the channel at Port Denison, the government had requested that an examination of the coast to the north of the port be made to ascertain the location and suitability for navigation of the mouth of the mighty Burdekin River.

Dalrymple had come within twenty miles of the coast on his previous overland expedition and had predicted then that the river Captain Wickham had discovered and named after himself when he anchored in the lee of Cape Upstart in the Beagle was, in fact, the Burdekin. On that occasion he'd been forced to continue his journey south without tracing the river to its mouth due to lack of provisions.

Ross was pleased that Maurie was away in Brisbane attending to his political duties, for he doubted that his friend would have considered his reflections worthy of merit and would have gently chastised him as he had in the past for what he considered his, - *morbid obsession with the disappearance of the crew of the barque Peruvian, -* and he was right; it *was* indeed an obsession, although hardly a morbid one; he could admit to that now. The possibility that Jimmy Morrill and the other sailors who had abandoned the wreck of the Peruvian on the reef fifteen years ago and somehow made it ashore had never left him. It was always there in his subconscious mind, coming to the fore whenever he spotted anything in a newspaper or, as in this case, a report, that reminded him of it. And in this particular report there were several records that could easily have triggered his current melancholy contemplation of those events of long ago.

He picked up the report again and opened it at the first page he'd marked, where a comment by Captain Smith had caught his eye. The crew had noticed a canoe with two native fishermen in it in a bay of the Whitsunday Islands, and by means of gesticulations had invited the men to come alongside, eventually persuading one of them to come on board the vessel. Ross read the passage again.

'Our interview, though short, was very interesting, and we were inclined to think that in this region the natives are not as hostilely disposed as was rumoured. We bartered for some spears, and spear heads of a harpoon barb form, about six inches in length, and also for some roasted turtle. A breeze springing up, the two Aborigines left us to

cross over to Hook Island, a distance of ten miles with, no doubt, a wonderful tale for their countrymen.'

It was true that elsewhere in the report there were numerous incidents of aggressive responses to the crew's attempts at peaceful contact, but he reasoned that those could be simply the result of poor communication and misunderstandings by both parties. It was obvious nevertheless, that there were at least *some* tribes who might have taken pity on helpless shipwrecked sailors, - and the other thing that he'd noticed, as a former sailor himself, was that the captain referred to the prevailing wind as south-easterlies and the tides constantly running parallel to the coast in the vicinity of Cleveland Bay. It tied in splendidly with the possible drift of a raft he'd projected on the charts that he kept locked in the bottom drawer in his desk.

He knew, of course, that Maurie would have laughed at his irrational reflections, but surely it didn't take too much imagination, considering where the wreck had come to grief on the reef, to visualise a raft drifting with the wind and tide towards that part of the coast?

The Queensland Government, having finally recognised the value of the pastoral lands of the Kennedy district, and anticipating the procurement of a large increase of funds to the financially troubled treasury, had funded the establishment of a new port at the site recommended by Captain Smith of the *Spitfire* expedition.

The Commissioner of Crown Lands, George Elphinstone Dalrymple, left Port Curtis to the cheers of a large crowd of well-wishers with an overland party fitted out with horse and bullock teams, pulling wagons heavily laden with the necessities that were required to establish a permanent settlement at Port Denison.

Captain Henry Sinclair, in the meantime, had travelled by boat to the new port that he himself had discovered and named less than two years before at the request of the New South Wales Government, but unfortunately for him at that time, when he'd returned to Sydney to claim the reward that had been offered for his success, the separation of the colonies had taken place and the new Queensland Government refused to honour it; he was however appointed harbourmaster of the new port that was named Bowen in honour of the Queensland Governor.

Dalrymple himself had been appointed Police Magistrate and Commander-in-Chief of the contingent of Native Police that had accompanied him on the journey and his repeated requests for an increase in troops for the protection of the new town caused much irritation in the capital. Finally, frustrated at his lack of success, he wrote that, '*...reports of murders and depredations committed by the* *blacks are so frequent and the panic in the district is so great...'* In response the government established a permanent barracks at Port Denison in 1862.

32

The funeral pyre had died down to a pile of smoking cinders and the wailing of the mujus had quietened to a low moan.

Morrill sat with Bindjuk at the edge of the clearing and the newly elected elder looked at him with tears in his eyes. *'Why, Jemmy, - why they kill Gudhala?'* he said. *'Gudhala good warrior, - not bad man.'*

Morrill's shoulders sagged and he shook his head sadly, for he considered himself at least partly responsible for Gudhala's death.

During the previous dry season a vessel had landed on the coast at Cape Cleveland and the sailors had given the fishermen some speckled shirts in exchange for dugong meat. He'd asked them to try to let any other white men who landed on the coast know that there was one of their kind living with the tribe, but unfortunately when it did happen he'd been up on the slopes of Mount Elliot looking for honey and breadfruit. The warriors' eagerness in their efforts to communicate the news of his presence had obviously alarmed the ship's crew and a few shots had been fired, presumably to disperse the tribe. Whether by accident or malicious intent, one warrior had been wounded and Gudhala had been killed. *'Good man that one, - Gudhala,'* he said. *'Jemmy, – Gudhala, brothers.'*

Bindjuk managed a weak smile. *'Yiay, - Jemmy Morl, - you our brother, - ghost-warrior. Why they kill Gudhala?'*

Morrill stood up suddenly and picked up a spear that had been lying against the log. He thrust the spearhead into the earth at his feet with such force that it left the shaft quivering. *'Jemmy Morl, - ghost-warrior,'* he said in a voice that was full of emotion. *'Jemmy avenge Gudhala.'*

Bindjuk looked up at him in surprise. *'Ngaw Jemmy, - too many white men, - too many firesticks. Jemmy get killed too. Not Bindal lose another brother.'*

Morrill placed a hand on his friend's shoulder. *'Jemmy not fight with spear, Bindjuk. Jemmy go into battle for Bindal in lawful way, by way of white man's council of elders, but first Jemmy must make contact with white men, - no more Bindal try make contact, - only Jemmy Morl. Bindjuk tell all Bindal, - tell all Wulgurukaba, Jemmy Morl must know of white men, but ngaw contact in any way, - wait for next time.'*

Morrill looked over at the mujus sitting in a circle around the campfire, not laughing and chattering as they usually did, but subdued, whispering amongst themselves, with the nungas playing unconcerned at their feet. He knew that Gudhala's death had shocked the whole tribe. There was no war to be fought; the Bindal had stolen no mujus from the white tribe and they'd not invaded the white tribal lands. Gudhala had only been trying to tell them that one of their kind was living amongst the tribe as *he* had asked them to. He looked beyond the mujus to where the high ridge of Mandilgun reared above the green canopy of trees. A flock of white cockatoos screeched as they swooped from one to another, the only raucous sound in the quiet tranquillity of the Bindal camp, and Morrill looked at Bindjuk and knew what he was thinking, for he saw a tear roll down his brother's face and his eyes glaze over as he stared trance-like into the distance.

Bindjuk placed his hand over Morrill's that still rested on his shoulder. *'Bindjuk know Jemmy Morl try hard, but afraid for Bindal way of life, - Bindal come to an end very soon.'*

Morrill could feel the grief that hung palpably in the air and he knew it wasn't just the pain of losing Gudhala that was the cause of Bindjuk's sorrow. Bindjuk was an elder now and the future of the tribe was partly his responsibility, and Morrill understood how heavily the insecurity of that future weighed on his mind.

Bindjuk shook his head as if to clear his mind of whatever vision he'd conjured up in his reverie. *'Bindal get message to Wulgurukaba and Juru and Gia, - tell Bindjuk quickly when white men come to country.'*

It was well into the next wet season when news of another shooting was brought to Morrill from the Gia tribe. A white man had been seen on the south bank of the Mall-Mall riding on the back of a large kangaroo with another following behind, both of them bigger than the biggest kangaroo ever seen in the Gia country before. He'd come upon some of the Gia who had been howling a mourning chant over the death of an old man. Morrill listened with mounting anger as the messenger explained how the white man had pointed his firestick and killed the son of the old man who had been lying on top of his father's body as part of the funeral ceremony. The rest of the mourners ran away and hid behind trees, and later, some of the brave warriors returned and made gestures of friendship, but as soon as the white man let down his guard, they dragged him to the ground and killed him. The two giant kangaroos had run away.

Was he a lone wanderer travelling with a pack horse in tow, or had he been separated from a larger group? Morrill thought. *'We'll probably never know, and it would not be a good time to try to find out. If he was part of a bigger exploration party, which is more likely the case, there's no doubt the others will shoot any Aborigine on sight. The tribe doesn't understand the way the white man thinks. Do I even understand how the white man thinks anymore?'*

He dimly recollected a conversation he'd had with a man in Sydney. It was many wet seasons ago; too many to count, and it was just before he'd set out on the voyage that had brought him here.

'After the tribes realised that the weird looking white people, with their strange animals and equipment, were here to stay and had every intention of settling on the land they had occupied for countless generations, some of them turned to violence to let their feelings be known. It was the beginning of the end for them as a nation.'

Was it happening again, Morrill thought grimly, or had it never stopped? Had the killing and depredations been going on throughout all the years he'd been away from so-called *civilisation*?

'It's only settled down here because we've destroyed the local Aboriginal culture in our efforts to civilise them and make Christians of them, Jimmy. Civilise them, indeed? If you were Aboriginal do you really think you would regard us Europeans as civilised?'

He sent the messenger back with a warning to the Gia that there will most likely be other white men seeking revenge and they must move their camp as far up the Mall-Mall as possible.

Not long after that incident four stray beasts were seen on one of the creeks at the southern end of Mount Elliot, - *on the border of Bindal country*. Morrill was on the coast with Bindjuk at the time, but on their return he was shown the tracks and recognised them as the cloven hooves of cattle.

'What these big kangaroos, Jemmy? - Gia say many, many big kangaroos like this.' Bindjuk put his hands up to his forehead with his fingers outstretched mimicking the horns of a cow.

'Big kangaroos called cattle, - white men eat, - same one Bindal eat kangaroo, - Bindjuk tell Bindal ngaw eat cattle, - white men kill Bindal with firesticks.' Morrill said.

Bindjuk frowned. *'Plenty kangaroo-cattle, Jemmy, - why Bindal not eat? – plenty cattle for all, - Gia and Juru no more fish, - waterholes dry up, - kangaroo-cattle drink all water, - no more grass, - kangaroo-cattle trample all down, - no more boan roots.'*

Morrill shook his head in frustration. How could he explain that the white men considered the herds of cattle their own and not for the Bindal to share, and they would defend that ownership with guns if necessary? It was a concept that was totally foreign to any of the tribes and not easily explained. He didn't even try. *'Ngaw eat cattle, - white men kill.'* he said.

Bindjuk frowned again. *'And other big one kangaroo-cattle, - white men jump up, - sit up on top, - the kangaroo-cattle run, - many white men sit on top, - drink all water, - fish die.'*

'Ngaw cattle that one, - white man sit up, - that one horse.'

Morrill lay awake that night, a myriad of thoughts tumbling over in his mind. White civilisation was closing in on the Bindal and their whole way of life was about to change. He was certain Bindjuk knew that and he suspected many of the other warriors did too, and like them there was absolutely nothing he believed he could do about it.

Geordie had expressed it in a nutshell. *'Ye've as much hope o' stopping the march o' progress that'll turn these people's lives upside down as ye' have o' turning back the tide, an' that progress is eventually going tae reach this far.'*

'The march of progress,' Geordie had called it, and why wouldn't he? Geordie was a good man, but like many other good men he'd perceived his own stamp of culture as being appropriate to all nations and had neglected to look at it from the perspective of the victims of the so-called progress. *'Well then, if it is inevitable as Geordie said, we'll just have to make the best of it.'*

Morrill sat on a log facing the circle of elders. He'd made a decision. He was going to meet the problem head on. *'Jemmy Morl go now, - go to Gia camp, - go to white man's camp, - talk to council of elders, - come back to Bindal,'* he said.

Several elders shook their heads in dismay. One had tears running down his lined face. *'Jemmy Morl go away, - Jemmy not return to Bindal camp, - not come back, - white men kill Jemmy,'* he moaned.

Morrill was almost moved to tears himself. Here was the proof that he'd been accepted absolutely by the tribe. Even the elders didn't want him to go and were afraid the white men would kill him. *'Jemmy need see white men, - talk to white men, - Jemmy come back, - bring axes, - fetch glass to make fire, - carry Injin down to the water.'*

'Jemmy come back Mandilgun one half-round moon?' one of the old men said hopefully.

Morrill shook his head and held up four fingers. *'Ngaw, four round moons,'* he said solemnly.

The other elders looked disappointed, but Bindjuk nodded and grinned. *'Yiay, Jemmy, - ghost-warrior, - talk to white men, - Jemmy come back to Bindal brothers four round moons. Bindjuk come to Juru country with Jemmy.'*

Morrill and Bindjuk left the Bindal camp on Mount Elliot the next morning at dawn.

33

Noora laid down her pounding stone and held both hands out in front of her face. She spread the fingers of one hand wide, mentally counting the number of games *Werboonburra* had played since the start of the current dry season. Was it three fingers or four? She tried to concentrate, but it was too dificult for she had so many other things on her mind. She looked across at her younger sister, who was sitting opposite her, cross-legged, on a Wallaby-skin mat. Buramu was engrossed in pounding the boaan roots that had been laid out in the heat of the day to dry, as she herself was. The flour would be moistened and rolled into cakes and then baked in time for the warriors returning from their fishing and hunting forays. It was one of the daily routines she enjoyed, because it gave her a sense of belonging, of fitting in with the other young mujus and being a part of their social group, even though none of the other mujus had ever commented hurtfully on her differences.

She'd always been slightly lighter in colour than her sisters, and they'd said to her many times that she should be happy. *'You look like ghost-muju, Noora, - Look like Uncle Jemmy, - You his favourite.'* But a long time ago, Noora had seen her reflection in the still waters of a billabong and after seeing it she'd cried out in anguish and slapped at the water to make it disappear in the ripples. Her nose was too long. It was certainly not flat and beautiful like Buramu's and most of the other young mujus. Her hair was straight and hung limply to her shoulders, not curly like theirs, and her eyes were too big and round, but perhaps that was from the shock of seeing her reflection.

It was entirely possible that none of the initiated warriors would *ever* pick her for a companion at any time in the future and she would become one of the old women who shambled about the camp muttering to themselves. She shuddered at the thought of that happening to her, but perhaps her hair *would* become curly in time if she continued to secretly twirl it round her fingers at night and her nose would become flatter if she made sure she lay with her face down on her mat. It was an uncomfortable position, though, and she felt a little embarrassed at the thought of how the strange noises her nose made when she tried to breathe in that position must affect the other mujus and nungas sleeping in the gunyah. She consoled herself with the thought that she'd seen some of these once-pretty, curly-haired women with a new-born mularamun on one breast and a nunga more than two wet season's old, hanging from her hip and suckling from the other as she went about gathering roots and berries.

And what of her name, - *Noora*? It was a strange name to give a mularamun. She knew she would never know what it meant. Her ami Obungella had told her that her earth-mother Bunginna had chosen it just before she flew up to the sky in smoke and her earth-father had never come back from the mountains of the Ayianga River inland from Bandjin country.

She'd been looked after very well by her father, Bindjuk and her mother Obungella, but it was not the same as having her earth-father and earth-mother to comfort her. Nothing could ever be the same as that. Obungella had told her that, because she'd had no mularamun of her own at the time she had no milk to offer and Noora had been given to another muju who had a plentiful supply. It was Obungella's opinion that it was the quality of the milk she'd received that was most likely the reason her hair was straight and her nose long. She sighed aloud and realised with a start that Buramu had stopped pounding the boaan roots and was looking at her curiously.

'You dreaming again, sister? Always dreaming, - better start pounding, - warriors be back soon looking for cakes.'

Noora gathered another handful of roots and picked up the pounding stone. She began pounding again, but she slyly looked at Buramu and when she had confirmed that her sister wasn't watching she looked again at her fingers. The old warrior, Jemmy Morl had taught her how to count to more than the fingers on both hands. It was easy, he said, and so it was. She concentrated. Ten and one; ten and two; ten and three. Ah she thought, that's it; ten and three wet seasons since her earth-mother, Bunginna had gone up to the clouds. She was grateful to old Jemmy. He seemed to be interested in teaching her. She giggled to herself; perhaps it was because he too had a long nose like hers and felt sorry for her, but it didn't matter, - lame and sick as he was, she craved the fatherly attention that he provided. He was almost as old as her father Bindjuk, who was his great friend, but Bindjuk was now an elder and as such was often called to the council. Jemmy Morl made a great substitute father when he was here, but both he and Bindjuk had gone away to the Juru. She wasn't sure what it was all about, - something to do with the murder of some Juru warriors by a faraway tribe.

Buramu had stopped pounding the boaan roots and was looking at her again. *'We never get these finished, sister,'* she said with a hint of frustration in her voice. Noora gathered up another handful of roots and picked up the pounding stone.

34

Clem Ross knew that Sir Maurice O'Connell had suspicions about his motive in asking to be appointed to a posting at the new settlement of Bowen at Port Denison. Maurie seemed to have accepted it as one of Clem's little idiosyncrasies that his old friend was obsessed with the fate of the lost passengers and crew of the barque *Peruvian*. They had discussed it a number of times in the past over a coffee and no matter how often Maurie had scorned him and made light of it, Ross was sure he had provoked at least a trifling desire in the mind of the newly elected President of the Queensland Legislative Council to solve the mystery. In any case Maurie hadn't argued against the idea and had expedited the transfer without his customary grumbling protest that Clem's requests caused too much disruption to his staffing constraints.

Bowen had been in existence for a year when Ross arrived to take up his posting and he found that the tiny settlement was a bustling community of more than a hundred permanent citizens. Many more were arriving weekly on the steamers *Ariel* or *Bredalbane* to apply for land licences and organise expeditions to the interior to find runs suitable for cattle and sheep grazing. The town was well serviced with a hotel, half-a-dozen shops and secure government offices, one of which had been set aside for his use.

"It looks like you and Daphne have settled in quite well now Rossie?" It was Sir Maurice's first visit to the settlement and after the official business that had brought him to the port was finalised he had retired to the government built house occupied by Clem and his wife. He and Ross sat at a small wooden table on the front veranda overlooking the port.

"It *is* a nice little town, Maurie," Ross said. "It's fairly quiet, actually, - except for the port, of course; it's always busy down there."

O'Connell looked up from the wicker chair as Clem's daughter came through from the kitchen bearing a tray with a steaming pot of tea, a pair of porcelain cups and a platter of cakes and biscuits.

"Ah, Eliza," he said. "It's good to see you again, young lady."

Eliza smiled. "It's always nice to see you too, Sir Maurice. I hope my father is not boring you again with reminiscences of his past life as a master mariner."

O'Connell laughed. "No, I've managed to avoid the subject so far, dear Eliza, but I must say your father never ceases to amaze me with his vivid recollections. I wish my own memory was as good."

Clem Ross took the compliment silently, but a small turn up of the corners of his mouth betrayed his contentment, and after he'd watched Eliza place the tray on the table and retire once more to the kitchen he looked at O'Connell with pride etched in his lined face. "I couldn't have wished for a finer daughter, Maurie," he said. "Daphne's not been well, as you know, and Eliza looks after both of us so well."

O'Connell nodded. "She hasn't found a young man equal to her father yet, I take it. How old is she Clem?"

"Twenty-four, Maurie."

"Plenty of time then. I wish I was half the age I am now."

Ross laughed. "I don't think she would fit in too well with all the ladies at Government House in Brisbane. She prefers the simple, peaceful life here in Bowen to the rush of the city."

"What about the threat of violence from hostile Aborigines that Dalrymple was so vocal about? He said that we could expect them to attack in great numbers if he didn't get the Native Police he needed to protect the town."

Ross shrugged. "Dalrymple resigned last year, as you're aware I'm sure, and he did succeed in getting an expanded force based here, but the truth of the matter is that there hasn't been any murders or depredations at all in the town's first year of existence, - apart from, perhaps, the disappearance without trace of a New Zealander named Humphries."

"Oh, and has that *definitely* been assigned to Aborigines?" O'Connell raised an eyebrow. "Maybe he just fell off his horse or something."

"That's what I thought, but the more vocal settlers are insisting that he met with foul play, - *while going about his lawful business, -* they say. It boosts their arguments for retaining the Native Police to *disperse* any Aborigines found guilty of such atrocities.

O'Connell snorted, but it was with disdain. "And there's nobody who can argue on the side of the Aborigines that the atrocities usually start with the Native Police, right?"

Ross nodded. "Apparently this Humphries was out with a party looking for a good run for his sheep and the others were too slow for his liking. He went out on his own and never made it back to their base camp. He was supposed to be an experienced bushman and his friends argued that, because of his bush skills he was presumed to have been ambushed and murdered rather than having met with an accident. The Native Police trackers couldn't locate any remains, although his horses were found wandering close by where he'd been last seen near the mouth of the Burdekin."

35

Morrill and Bindjuk travelled to the Biria fish traps on the Mall-Mall and then down river to the Juru country where they were welcomed as brothers at the main camp and treated well, and in the following two months Morrill received almost daily reports of white men's activities south of the river.

Bindjuk travelled back to the Bindal camp on a weekly basis and always seemed happy to see that Morrill was still at the Juru camp when he returned. Morrill bided his time, fishing and hunting with the Juru, but eventually he learned that there were two white men and a black man who had been seen regularly about a two day march from the Juru main camp.

The Juru were as reserved about his chances of success as the Bindal had been when he told them of his intention to try to make contact with the white men, and they tried to persuade him to stay, refusing to show him where the white men's camp was.

'Plenty black men on horse-kangaroos, - have firesticks like white men, - shoot Juru warriors down dead, - no understand why. Where their country? Juru not know. Kill Jemmy when see him. Black-white men on horse-kangaroo shoot Jemmy down dead.'

Everything changed when a fishing party of the Juru was murdered. Fifteen men, strong able-bodied fellows, were on the Mall-Mall and a party of black horsemen had come suddenly out of the scrub on the south bank and confronted them. The fishermen hailed them with signs of peace, but it was to no avail. The horsemen opened fire.

A meeting of the elders was held and Morrill put his case. *'Juru be all dead if not show Jemmy white men camp, - Jemmy try talk, - Jemmy try save Juru.'*

The hut was on the north bank of the Mall-Mall, which was running in flood, and Morrill approached it cautiously. It was just before dusk, but the sky was overcast after recent storms and the flickering light from a tallow lamp that had already been lit in preparation for the coming night threw moving shadows between the cracks in the wooden window shutters.

He'd washed his body thoroughly in a creek to make himself look as white as possible, but he was still not confident that his appearance would prevent anyone who was startled from shooting him on sight. He slipped by the empty sheep pens and climbed onto the top rail so that the dogs that he'd heard growling nearby couldn't get to him, and from that precarious position he peered apprehensively at the hut that held his first link with the civilisation that he'd left so many years before.

Grey smoke drifted from the stone chimney and the aroma of roasting meat filled his nostrils. It could have been any cottage in the damp English countryside around Maldon, except for the narrow slits in the walls that were just wide enough to poke a rifle barrel through.

Voices came from within, floating on the slight breeze, laughter, Britisher voices, merry and cheerful. A wave of nostalgia threatened to consume him as the memories of his childhood came flooding back, memories that he'd been compelled by circumstances to push to the back of his mind in order to fully embrace his new life with the Bindal. And was it so wicked of him that he'd been able to make that transition and effectively erase all thoughts of his former family from his mind when he'd supposed he would never see them again? Betsy had certainly thought so.

Ye' need tae consider that ye've got yer real family back home who are suffering because they think yer dead an' buried at sea.

But Betsy had died longing for the day *she* would be reunited with her family, and those whom she'd yearned for had no doubt given her up for dead and had ceased to suffer long ago. His family would be the same; their sorrow over and done with and he, nothing more than a memory to them now. Was it any less wicked to reappear in their midst and then repeat and heighten their grief by telling them he had no intention of coming back to live in Maldon, but preferred to spend the rest of his life amongst his new family?

What to do now? His courage almost deserted him and he would have jumped off the fence and gone back to the tribe, but he thought of Bindjuk who had shown so much faith in him; Bindjuk who had shown him and the other survivors so much kindness when they had landed on his shore many, many wet seasons ago. They had become closer as the years passed; like brothers.

It had to be done. He could not go back to the tribe without having at least tried to mediate on their behalf. He steeled himself for his rehearsed speech

'Ahoy there, what cheer shipmates? I'm a British subject, sirs; a shipwrecked English sailor, no less, and I should like to speak to your leader, please if I may?'

"Ahoy there, what cheer shipmates?" His voice rang out in the stillness of the late afternoon and seemed to echo from the damp trees along the riverbank. Dogs began to bark and the laughter stopped suddenly inside the hut. After a few moments of silence the door was half-opened and a man peered cautiously from behind it, his burly figure silhouetted in the light thrown by a lamp on the table behind him.

Morrill heard him gasp and then he turned and spoke in an urgent voice to someone inside. "Come out here Bill; It's not Jock Creek with the sheep; there's somebody up on the rail."

"What?" the voice inside the hut was slurred. "Not the Scot? Somebody *up on the fence*?"

"A naked red man or yellow man maybe, - I don't know. Bring the gun."

Morrill was petrified with fear and held his hands high in the air. "Don't shoot me; I'm a British *object*," he called out hoarsely. "I'm a shipwrecked sailor."

The man edged out from the doorway a little further. He called out to the other man inside. "It's okay Hatch; he's not armed, - says he's a shipwrecked sailor, - a British *object* no less. I think he means he's a British subject." He came further out and the other man followed him on unsteady legs.

"What's this Wilson? Are ye' sure it's not a black fella' sizing us up fer an attack? They can be tricky ye' know; his dusky chums might be biding their time among the trees waiting fer his signal before they rush us. It's happened before." He brandished the gun towards Morrill. "Where's Jock Creek anyway? The shepherd should've been back by now; murdering thieves might have got him already."

Wilson scanned the darkening scrub beyond the figure perched on the rail. His voice was gruff with anxiety. "Come on down from the rail, feller an' come around the stock yard. The dogs are tied up, but Hatch's got his gun on ye', so don't make him use it."

Morrill jumped down from his perch and paced around the fence as he'd been instructed, all the while aware that the man called Hatch had a rifle pointed at him. It was little comfort to him either, that the way Hatch was wobbling and holding on to a rail for support, that any bullet he fired, deliberately or accidentally, could have gone anywhere. The pair came around and met him halfway and they stopped half a dozen paces apart.

"A shipwrecked sailor, ye' say, eh?" Wilson looked Morrill up and down. "Must've been quite a while by the look o' ye', an' ye've forgotten some o' yer English words too. Can ye' tell us yer name an' how long ago ye' were wrecked then?"

Morrill shrugged. "Jemmy Morl, - ah, - Morrill," he said, stammering over the words. "Don't know how long, - long time, - many wet seasons."

Hatch cackled. "Many *wet seasons*? Ye' sure yer not a black fella' that's picked up a bit o' English from somewhere? Tom here wants to know how many weeks, months or years ye've been lost."

"I lost count, - many years, - too many to count," Morrill said, glancing uneasily at the rifle barrel that continued to swing around in little arcs as Hatch spoke.

Wilson must have noticed where Morrill's frightened gaze was directed for he motioned to Hatch to lower the rifle barrel without looking at him. "I'm Tommy Wilson, Jemmy," he said mildly. "I was a sailor too a few years ago. Can ye' remember the name o' yer ship?"

Morrill looked blankly at him for a moment as he fought to remember the details of the voyage and the subsequent wreck of the…

'A lot of sailors won't sail on Fridays. They reckon it brings bad luck to the ship and all who sail in her. To be perfectly honest, that's why it was so easy for me to get you a berth on the Peruvian…'

"The *Peruvian*, - that's it," he looked at Wilson nervously, wringing his hands together. "I almost forgot the ship's name; it's been long time, that one, - 1846, I think. Yes, it was; I remember now, - there was a big storm. The *Peruvian* was wrecked; we built a raft, abandoned ship."

Wilson's eyes widened. "1846? Are ye' sure about that? Do ye' have any idea what year it is now, Jemmy?"

Morrill shook his head and looked at his fingers. "Ten years maybe, - or two more, maybe three?"

"It's January 1863 now. If what yer telling me is right, then ye've been wandering about here fer *seventeen years*." Wilson said.

Hatch was sceptical. "I think yer either mistaken, Jemmy boy, - or maybe yer lying to us, eh?" He raised the rifle again and pointed it in Morrill's general direction. "Nobody could've survived out here that long without starving to death, or more likely, being made into a tasty stew by the blacks."

Morrill was scared. Hatch looked trigger-happy, but it gave him a little relief to see that Tom Wilson seemed to be in control. "They're not cannibals," he said, addressing Wilson.

"Ye' must think ye' know them *very* well then?" Hatch still had the rifle pointed at him.

"The Bindal saved us when the *Peruvian* was wrecked and the raft landed on their shores. We lived with them."

"*We*, Jemmy?" Wilson said. "Are there more shipwrecked sailors out there?"

"Not now," Morrill said. "Not for many wet seas…, - I mean not for many years past."

"Put that rifle down, Bill," Wilson said to Hatch. "Yer making *me* nervous too."

Hatch pointed the barrel of the rifle towards the floor, but his eyes still shifted uneasily at the slightest sound from the surrounding scrub.

"I think I *have* heard o' the *Peruvian*," Wilson said to Hatch. "It was wrecked on the reef with *no* survivors ever found." He looked at Morrill again. "Until now that is. Better come inside, lad; it sounds like ye've got quite a story to tell."

The three men entered the hut, Hatch taking up the rear. He paused and trained the rifle on the lengthening shadows, scrutinising each thicket and tree until he was satisfied that nothing moved, before he closed and latched the sturdy wooden door.

Morrill looked around the sparse furnishings in the hut. It had been built from split logs and was divided into four rooms, the front two serving as a kitchen with a rough table and three chairs in one, and a wood fired stove and storage area in the other. The back two rooms were fitted with two low beds in each and he chuckled as he felt the comfortable wool filled mattresses that the men slept on.

"Haven't slept in a bed fer a while, eh?" Hatch said, amused at Morrill's simple delight.

Morrill shook his head. "Long time." He pointed to the swollen joints of his knees and ankles. "Too many nights sleep on wet ground."

Wilson shook his head. "But the natives build shelters don't they? The southern ones do anyway."

"Build gunyahs with broad leaf palm. I tried build good bark hut first wet season, - warriors take it over; not like this *big one* house."

"This isn't a big house, Jemmy; only a small hut Mr Antill's had built for us on his Jarvisfield station," Wilson said. "We're just some o' his shepherds. Mr Antill's going to build a real *big* house very soon fer himself. He's got five hundred head o' sheep an' a hundred head o' cattle here right now, an' there's another fifteen hundred coming in the next month or so. When he's done he'll have a hundred an' fifty square miles o' good grazing land to his name on the northern side of the Burdekin."

Morrill stared at him in confusion. "*The Burdekin?*"

Wilson grinned. "That's the river out the back o' the hut here. Haven't ye' ever heard it called *that* before, or had ye' just forgotten?"

Morrill shook his head. "It's known as *Mall-Mall* by my tribe," he said.

Hatch laughed, a hollow sound. "*Your* tribe, Jemmy?"

Morrill looked at him unashamedly, but thought it better to remain silent, for Hatch seemed resentful about his affection for the tribes. He remembered Betsy's similar reaction to that very same expression.

'Yes Betsy, - our tribe.'

"It's called the Burdekin River now," Wilson assured him. "It doesn't matter anymore what *your* tribe called it."

"No," Hatch agreed. "Doesn't matter much now, does it? They'll have to get used to the names we've given to every hill and every stream in Kennedy district."

Wilson could see that Morrill was still confused. "You've got a lot o' catching up to do, Jemmy," he said, not unkindly. "I know a hundred an' fifty square miles sounds like a lot o' land for one person to lay claim to, but it's needed fer the stock Mr Antill's expecting to move on to it, an' Jarvisfield's not the biggest run either. John MacDonald owns a hundred an' forty square miles on the southern side o' the river, but there are much bigger properties pegged all the way on both sides o' the Burdekin fer a good hundred miles or more upstream o' here."

Morrill's mouth fell open and his eyes widened in disbelief. "A hundred miles upstream? That's past Biria, - into Warungu country. Not heard about this from Warungu, - Gia and Juru not heard of this happen either," he said. "News usually travels fast between our tribes."

"No, I suppose most o' yer tribes haven't heard o' it yet..." Wilson said.

Hatch laughed. "...or if they have they might not be in any condition to tell anyone else."

Wilson gave him a sour look. "Ye' see, it's mostly on paper at this stage, Jemmy," he said. "Sure, some o' the settlers have organised expeditions to survey the land they've been licenced to occupy an' a few individuals have already taken up their blocks, like Mr Antill has, but that's all going to change soon. In the next few months we'll see a huge transformation in the country around here. I've heard that Mr Antill's neighbour, John Black, is taking upwards o' five hundred head to stock his run at Cleveland Bay next month an'...."

The rest of Wilson's conversation was lost on Morrill. *His run at Cleveland Bay?* His heart sank, for he realised there was no hope for the Bindal now, - or for any of the other tribes north of the Mall-Mall for that matter.

Jock Creek, the Scotsman who was the third of Antill's shepherds stationed at the hut, arrived.

"You're late, Jock," Hatch grumbled. "We were worried the Blacks might have got ye' and ye'd disappeared like Antill's partner, Salisbury Humphries."

Creek laughed. "Yer always thinking the wurst, wee Bill," he said. "Ye' don't even know fer sure it was the Aborigines that did Humphries in, dae ye' now? He could've just fell off his horse, couldn't he?"

"No!" Hatch was adamant. "That Kiwi was much too good a horseman to fall off, Jock, - an' they found his mount an' packhorse wandering along the riverbank, so *somebody's* got at him fer sure." He glanced in Morrill's direction meaningfully. "Anyway, if he'd fallen off his horse they would've found his body, wouldn't they? *No* Jock, I'm sure the blacks have made a stew o' him."

Morrill knew Hatch's remarks were said for *his* benefit, for he was certain the other men would have known all the particulars of the man's disappearance.

'So that was it then,' he thought; *'the reason for Hatch's apparent agitation; the man was scared, and if he was as trigger-happy as Humphries had been, - for he was sure now that Humphries was the lone rider who had murdered the Juru warrior, - then he had every reason to be scared. No warrior of any tribe would fight the white men for the country they occupied, - they would be willing to share it and the abundance of food that it provided, but if a warrior was killed then the murderer would have to atone with his own life, that's the way it was, - the way it had always been.'*

Creek laughed again. "Any good horseman can get careless too, Hatch." He shrugged. "Maybe he stopped by the Burdekin tae fill his waterbag or have a drink an' a croc' took him. I've been out there by meself fer a couple o' days an' the natives didn'ae even show their hides, although I *could* feel they were watching me." He sneered at Hatch. "I *was* careful, but I didn'ae go shooting madly intae the bushes like a loony as I've known some o' yer own kind tae resort tae."

Hatch shrugged and looked away.

'Perhaps he's embarrassed because he's been guilty of just such a foolish act himself,' Morrill thought.

"You can't be too careful, Jock," Hatch said. "Not when yer dealing with the blacks; they're treacherous as ye' know very well. Dalrymple found that out when he went up the Burdekin on his first expedition, - treacherous, he said, - ye' can give them presents an' next minute they're trying to steal yer stores from under yer very nose."

'You don't understand; that's because it's their way of life. Nothing belongs to an individual; they share everything.'

"Aye, but it could've been a lot wurse than pilfering a few stores," Creek said. "They probably could've killed Dalrymple if they'd wanted tae, but they didn'ae, an' I'll bet they'll soon wish they'd done it when they had the chance." He turned away from Hatch in disgust and walked into the back room where he threw down his swag, but not before he had a parting shot. "You an' Dalrymple are like a pair o' startled lambs. Both o' ye' are always jumping at shadows. Ye' need tae keep yer finger *off* the trigger, Hatch, an' think before ye' cause any unnecessary harm tae our black neighbours. If ye' treat them wi' a bit o' respect ye' might be able tae get along wi' them just fine, but if ye' don't then ye' might very well end up the way ye' think Humphries did."

Wilson went into one of the rooms and returned with some clothes which he threw over the back of a chair. "Get these on Jemmy," he said. "We can't have ye' walking around naked as the day ye' were born like one o' them savages."

Morrill's eyes strayed again to the now sulking Hatch. *Savages?* He hesitated, his mind in a blur. It was all so sudden; so final. Here he was at the brink of a return to the society that he'd lived in as a child and learned to despise all those years ago as a young sailor; the civilisation of the Empire that Geordie and Betsy had yearned to re-join and died without ever attaining.

'... it's no' your way of life, Jimmy. Your life is wi' us, an' wi' the morals an' standards o' our society. It's no' about whether ye' like it or not; it's what ye' were born intae, - ye' can't just throw away all the things ye've learned an' throw away yer clothes as well tae go frolicking around naked wi' these people...'

But even Betsy had understood in the end. She'd realised that the culture of her forefathers was not necessarily the only one that could bring happiness and contentment and that those whom she'd been thrust into the midst of were not savages at all, but merely people leading an equally fulfilling life under much different circumstances. "I must go back to the Juru, tonight," he said. "They will be waiting for me to return to them. They say I must tell them what they have to do to keep the peace with you."

Hatch gave him a suspicious look that told Morrill he still had grave doubts about his sincerity, and even the down-to-earth Wilson was silent as he weighed up the circumstances. "Well then, that sounds very obliging o' them," he said at last. "Ye' can tell them that if they don't interfere with us, or our sheep an' cattle, we won't interfere with them, Jemmy. We're not like some o' the other hard-headed settlers from down Bowen way, who'll shoot any native on sight..."

"…but we will if we have to," Bill Hatch added.

Morrill was curious. "Bowen way?" he said. "Is that what Port Curtis is called now?"

Wilson frowned and shook his head. "Port Curtis is a long way south o' Bowen," he said. "I'm surprised ye've even heard o' it since ye' hadn't heard o' the Burdekin River. The town at Port Curtis is called Gladstone now."

"Our captain told us about Port Curtis on the *Peruvian*," Morrill said. "After we were wrecked it was his goal to try to reach it, but it was too far away."

Wilson was amused. "There are several settlements north o' Port Curtis now. Bowen's the nearest one, - about two days ride to the south o' here. We'll get ye' there as soon as we can when ye' return from the tribe…"

"…*if* ye' return," Hatch muttered in a low, scornful tone.

Wilson ignored him. "The Land Commissioner's Orderly will be coming through from the Fanning River in a couple o' weeks so ye'll have to stick around here until then."

Morrill nodded. "I'll tell Juru they must go away to the coast, - to swamp lands, - not kill your cattle or sheep, - I'll come back here soon, maybe tomorrow or the next day, - wait for Orderly to take me to, - Bowen."

Hatch had unlatched and opened the door. He still had the rifle in the crook of his arm as he held it open, but when Morrill made to go out into the night, he stopped him. "Three days ye've got then, Jemmy," he said. His voice was calm, but there was no doubting the threat that lay behind his mild-sounding words. "If yer not back by then we'll have to assume ye've been lying to us an' ye've come here to spy on our layout." He grinned. "We're allowed under the law to disperse any troublesome natives fer our own safety, ye' know." He winked at Wilson, and then he added, almost as an afterthought. "An' if we need them, the Native Police can be here by the end o' the week."

'There are black men on the kangaroo-horses too and they have the firesticks that the white men have. They shoot our people down dead.'

"The Native Police?" Morrill said. "Which tribe are they from?"

Hatch's grin broadened. "They're not from any o' *your* tribes, Jemmy. They've been recruited from away down south an' they don't mind *dispersing* their northern cousins when they're called upon, - an' another thing yer tribal friends should know is that they don't care much about taking prisoners. Your tribe an' all the others around here will get to know them soon enough though, if they persevere in spearing our animals, I can assure ye' of that, lad."

Wilson intervened. "Don't worry, Jemmy. Just do what ye' have to an' then come back here after ye've sorted it out with yer friends. As I said before, we won't harm them if they leave us alone to get on with our business."

Morrill closed the door behind him and he felt a cold shiver run down his spine, but it wasn't the decisive rasping of timber on iron as the latch was pulled across, barring him from any further communication with the white men in the hut that made his whole body shudder. It was the outburst of harsh laughter from Hatch that he could clearly hear as he set out across the damp grass.

36

'What you see, Jemmy Morl, - plenty white men?' The tribe was jubilant on Morrill's return and gathered round him. *'You see plenty white men? You see plenty kangaroo-cattle? Black-white men on kangaroo-horse?'*

Morrill nodded *'Yiay, plenty white men, - plenty firesticks, - Juru ngaw go near white men or black-white men either, - Juru get killed all together one time.'*

Bindjuk had returned from the Bindal camp while Morrill was away and they sat together on a log at the edge of the camp after the Juru had drifted off to their gunyahs. *'Jemmy not happy with white men council?'* he said quietly.

Morrill's elbows were on his knees and he hung his head wearily. It had been a taxing couple of days. He looked up at his friend and shook his head slowly. *'Ngaw, Bindjuk. White men take your country, - too many white men, - black men too from tribe far away who will kill you and all Juru and Bindal warriors.'*

Bindjuk nodded gravely. *'Yiay, Jemmy, - Bindal ngaw war with white men, - we live together in peace, - white men take all country near Mall-Mall, - good for kangaroo-cattle. Bindal live swamp land and high up Mandilgun, - no good kangaroo-cattle. White men let Bindal fish in rivers, dig for roots in swamp near coast. No kill white men kangaroo-cattle.'*

Morrill's heart was breaking. What could he say? The leader of the tribe that he'd come to love was simply pleading for his people to be able to live on land that was useless to the white men, but Morrill knew that such a plan would never be agreed to by the land hungry settlers. It was written on pieces of paper now that they owned the land the Bindal and the Juru lived on and the tribes were about to be suffocated out of existence by a growing swarm of zealous land seekers. They would take up every piece of bare earth, every inch of swampland, no matter that not a patch of useful fodder for their cattle would grow there, in some vain hope that one day it might be to their advantage, and there was nothing, *absolutely nothing,* he could do about it.

'Juru must go further away from white men camp now,' he said. *'Full day walk, - all Juru, - burn gunyahs, - all nungas, all mujus go. Bindjuk must return to Mandilgun, - prepare to move camp.'*

'You come too, Jemmy?'

'Ngaw,' Morrill said. *'Jemmy must go back to white man camp, - white men say they will track Juru and shoot all tribe if Jemmy not*

come back, - say Jemmy must be too much look out for tribe, - spy on white men camp.'

Morrill watched despondent the next morning as the Juru made preparations to leave their main camp. It was a sad farewell and the nungas gathered round him, even the youngest seeming to know that they were unlikely to see Uncle Jemmy ever again. When it was time to go each of the muju's shyly embraced him, and then led their children away, their eyes downcast and tears streaming down their faces. The elders were next and each of them, for the most part, wizened old men with straggling white hair and beards, came to him one by one, looked dejectedly into his eyes, hugged him and then turned away without speaking a word.

Morrill brushed away the blinding tears with the back of his hand. There was only one person left to say goodbye to now, and he was the one that he dreaded leaving the most, for although he was a great warrior and a friend, above all he was a brother. Across the clearing, amid the clamour of the shouts of the warriors, the squeals of the mujus and nungas breaking camp and the hissing and crackling of burning wood he heard a voice.

'Jemmy Morl.'

He peered through the swirling smoke; a tall muscular warrior glided between two burning gunyahs like an apparition and placed his spears and his shield carefully on the ground beside him. He slowly raised his arms and shuffled unhurriedly across the open space between them, holding his hands out in front of him, palms upward. Morrill stared at him for a moment and then with a gruff cry of greeting he too shuffled forward, his own arms raised in the same way. When they were about ten paces apart both stopped and regarded each other in silence and then Morrill grinned, dropped his hands to his sides, and stepped forward, letting the fond memory of his first meeting with Bindjuk on the beach that day so long ago sweep over him. Bindjuk stepped forward at the same time and when he was within arm's length he reached out and touched Morrill's forehead. A grin then spread across his face too and the two warriors clasped each other's shoulders.

Binjuk's grin clouded over. *'Bindjuk go back to Bindal now, - back to Mandilgun, Jemmy Morl.'*

Morrill nodded and looked at him in silence for a moment and then he frowned. *'Bindal maybe go one time another camp, brother? How Jemmy Morl find Bindal camp, - when back to Mandilgun in two round moons?'* he said.

Bindjuk smiled half-heartedly, but Morrill could see the sadness behind his brave facade reflected in his dark, moist eyes.

'Bindjuk maybe no more see Jemmy Morl, - Jemmy Morl go white men camp, - live white men ways, - not Bindal ways anymore, - country now belong white men, - Bindjuk no live same one white men.'

Morrill shook his head vigorously. *'Ngaw, Jemmy belong Bindal, - ghost warrior come back Mandilgun two round moons, - live Bindal way with Bindjuk, Obungella, - Jemmy more teach Noora.'*

Bindjuk looked away towards the faint blue line of the distant mountains and heaved a sigh. *'Bindjuk maybe take Obungella, Noora, Buramu, - young warriors, Gimiru and Dabu, maybe old men, new country, - maybe safe country where Injin fall from sky, - no good for Jemmy.'*

Morrill knew Bindjuk was right. He was a proud Bindal warrior, proud of his people, proud of his heritage, and as an elder it was his duty to pass on that heritage to the younger warriors and the nungas as they grew into manhood in a country that they belonged to and without any meddling in the customs that they'd adhered to for countless wet seasons.

'Maybe safe country where Injin fall from sky.'

He realised that Bindjuk had probably voiced a desperate plan that he'd formed in his mind, to take his family and anyone else who would follow him and head west across the mountains into the setting sun, but he knew, and he suspected his brother did too, that it was an impossible dream. They both understood that the new masters of the land would spread beyond the mountains too and eventually there would be nowhere they could go and live in the peace that he craved for his tribe. The white men had little respect for the land that they occupied, and even less for the traditions of the people who had been dispossessed of it, and much as he loved Bindjuk as a brother and he knew that Bindjuk felt the same way about him, he, Jemmy Morl, was a white man and would inevitably bring the white man's ways with him no matter where the tribe went.

Bindjuk's voice was breaking, but he was adamant. *'Long way to safe country, - no good Jemmy come, - white men kill Jemmy Morl, Ghost Warrior, – kill all Bindal too.'*

Morrill sank onto one of his swollen knees and covered his eyes with his hands. He grunted at the sudden discomfort it brought, but the pain in his legs was nothing compared to the ache he felt in his heart as the tears rolled down his cheeks and dropped unimpeded into the dust.

It was the end of his time with the Bindal; the end of a great chapter in his life with the people that he'd grown to love, but if Bindjuk was prepared to sacrifice their bond of brotherhood to strengthen the prospect that the Bindal way of life continued for at least *his* lifetime, then so must he. Perhaps his plan to move his tribe to a new and faraway country *would* be just enough to ensure the survival of the Bindal.

'*Goodbye my brother,*' he said. '*Go to safe country for Bindal, - my body goes back to white men, but my heart goes with you, - tell our story in the corroboree, - tell the warriors that not all white men bad, - Jemmy Morl try to live in peace, - other white men too, but too many not.*'

Bindjuk placed a hand on Morrill's bowed head and then on his own chest. '*Yiay, Jemmy Morl, - Bindjuk remember always, - wadda mooli, - goodbye Ghost Warrior,*' he said softly. He turned, picked up his spears and shield, and strode quickly away into the scrub.

37

The whole population of Bowen was abuzz with the news that had filtered in from Antill's run at Jarvisfield that a shipwrecked sailor had been rescued from the clutches of the wild blacks and would, as soon as he'd recovered enough of his former strength, be brought into town. Many were sceptical though, of the rumour that the poor man had been held captive for seventeen years and cited the case of the now mostly discredited details of the liberation of the infamous Eliza Fraser as an example of how gullible people could be. Mrs Fraser had been feted in high society and had made a small fortune from recounting the harrowing details of her husband's murder, her capture and debasement by a brutal Aboriginal chief, and her ultimate rescue, - until it was discovered that she had made most of it up.

It was generally agreed though that if it *was* true then this was just as important an event as that of Mrs Fraser, which had made national and worldwide headlines twenty-six years ago and had helped to highlight to the world the perils of life amongst the savages of the Australian colonies. Some of the settlers too were particularly interested in verifying the privations that the sailor was reported to have suffered at the hands of those who stood in the way of their empire-building, as just another proof that the methods undertaken for their dispersal were completely justified.

Clement Ross was excited. It had been seventeen years since the wreck of the *Peruvian* had entered his life to haunt him; seventeen years since the first seed of speculation about the fate of those aboard her had insinuated itself into his mind and remained embedded there. Now it seemed that he was on the verge of learning the truth about what happened to Jimmy Morrill and the other crew and passengers of the ill-fated barque, for he was sure that this shipwrecked sailor could have come from no other ship.

Seventeen years was the key. Sure, there *were* plenty of other ships that had been wrecked along this coastline, but he'd known about all of them through his position in Sydney and the fate of their sailors had been mostly verified. It was too much of a coincidence, and wasn't this the very location he'd reasoned that a raft launched from the wreck of the *Peruvian* on the southern extremity of the Great Barrior Reef would have drifted ashore?

He knew it was premature to speculate on which one of the *Peruvian's* complement of sailors had been the lucky survivor, or how rational the man's memory might be after the great length of time he'd spent in captivity, if indeed that was the case. Perhaps he wasn't the only survivor and there were more to be discovered yet, but he allowed himself the indulgence of feeling a little self-satisfied when he considered what he would say to Maurie when next he visited Bowen.

'Oh, ye of little faith, Sir Maurice O'Connell; I was right all the time.'

The residents of Bowen had already been informed that the dray carrying the Land Commissioner's Orderly back from an official visit to George Dalrymple's Fanning River station was due in that afternoon and that the shipwrecked sailor would be travelling with him. A crowd of curious onlookers had already gathered to witness what many considered to be a significant event for the town and a cheer went up as a young horseman, barely into his teens, galloped down the dusty main street of Bowen on his piebald pony. "He's coming," he yelled at the top of his voice. "The sailor's on his way."

The dray came into view at the end of the street and the tired horse pair plodded along, suddenly pricking their ears at the sight of so many people forming an intimidating gauntlet that they had to pass between.

"Stand back, come on stand back." The police sergeant and his constable had met the dray on the outskirts of town and they escorted it through the milling crowd, clearing a gap that quickly closed after the dray had passed.

Clem Ross craned his neck to catch a glimpse of the miracle survivor, and as the dray passed him he saw the Orderly wave cheerily to the bystanders as if he'd assumed that the fanfare was about him and not his passenger. A sallow-skinned gaunt figure crouched beside him, slumped in the seat, peering out from beneath a broad-brimmed hat that looked like it was a size too big for him. His eyes, sunken in his cheeks, darted from side to side, much, to Ross's mind, like those of a cornered animal wildly seeking a means of escape. He heaved a sigh and sat down heavily on the wooden bench that was the only furniture on the veranda, and a feeling of guilt dulled his initial excitement, for he was forced to admit to himself that he'd dearly wished that the survivor might have been the young Jimmy Morrill. It filled him with remorse to realise that he felt disappointed that it was some other poor sailor who had finally been saved.

The dray stopped outside the Magistrate's Court building and a brawny saddler with a leather apron wrapped around his waist took the reins from the Orderly and secured them to the horse rail. The tired animals immediately dropped their heads in the trough and began to suck in the cool water. The Orderly stepped down and walked around to the other side of the dray. He motioned to the crouched figure, who hadn't made any effort to move from his position, and the man slowly edged towards him.

"Come on Jemmy," he said. "It's time to meet the Magistrate and tell your story to the world."

The crowd had gathered round the dray again and Ross's view of the proceedings was obscured, but he heard the clapping and cheers and then a chant went up. "Come on Jemmy. Come on Jemmy."

A voice called from inside the building behind him. "What's going on there, Clem? I can hear cheering."

"It's all right Daph," he called back. "It's the shipwrecked sailor. They've brought him to the Magistrate's office."

38

Jimmy Morrill leant with his arms folded on the portside deck rail of the Customs cutter, *Ariel* and looked out over the four miles of blue water that separated his ship from the long, curved spit of sand that formed the southern extremity of Bowling Green Bay. Beyond that low, sparsely wooded coastline, he knew, lay twenty miles of wetlands criss-crossed by mangrove fringed saltwater inlets until the swamp gave way to gradually rising grasslands that rose to the great ramparts of the back mountainous country.

To the north the headland of Cape Cleveland projected out into the bay, rising abruptly from the low land that separated it from the remarkable natural prominence that Cook had named the Mount Elliot Range, and that his tribe knew as Mandilgun. Its lower slopes rose up in the long easy incline that he remembered so well, climbing gradually from the low coastal land to level out in a series of high ridges that terminated in the summit of the main peak at its northern extremity.

He studied the lower slopes intently, looking for the telling sign of a column of smoke that would indicate the location of the Bindal camp. It had been more than two years since he'd last set foot on the mountain and nineteen years almost to the day since he'd last seen it from this position when the raft had drifted helplessly towards Cape Cleveland.

Now, as the *Ariel* ploughed through the calm seas, he could clearly make out the narrow stretch of sand they'd called The Landing and he remembered how they'd gazed longingly at it. He remembered too the sense of elation that he and Captain Pitkethly had felt when they scrambled ashore on that day after more than forty days at sea.

'We might be saved after all, Jimmy.'

Poor Geordie; the captain had had so much faith that he and Betsy would find the strength to sustain them through their ordeal, but it was not to be, for he was long gone now with Betsy and the other survivors who'd endured those weeks of misery on the raft after the *Peruvian* was wrecked.

Morrill scanned the lower ridges of Mandilgun once more. There should have been the smoke of at least one campfire somewhere on the mountain and he was both puzzled and then alarmed that there was no sign of the usual thin wisp curling lazily towards the sky. He was about to turn away in frustration when he saw it, barely distinguishable in the heat haze of the day, but it wasn't on the slopes of Mandilgun where he'd expected it to be. It was down in the lowlands behind Cape Bowling Green, in the swamp country. His heart sank; was this the Bindal's fate now? Had Bindjuk come to an agreement with the station owners?

'*Bindal live swamp land and high up Mandilgun, - no good kangaroo-cattle. White men let Bindal fish in rivers, dig for roots in swamp near coast. No kill white men kangaroo-cattle.*'

Bindjuk had been desperate to retain the culture of the Bindal that had been adhered to for thousands of years for the generations that he hoped would come after him. It was his duty as an elder, and Morrill remembered that his brother had even voiced a desperate plan to take his family and anyone else who would follow him and head west across the mountains into the setting sun, but it had seemed like an impossible dream at the time. Had Bindjuk achieved his dream? He realised he couldn't rest until he'd found out the truth.

The Ariel rounded the headland and glided into the smooth waters of the channel between the lofty mountains of Magnetical Isle and the familiar imposing red granite bluff that the white men were calling Castle Hill.

This was Wulgurukaba country, the home of the canoe people who fished these waters and traded with the Bindal. His nets and lines had proved to be popular with them in the past, but where there should have been a dozen, there was no sign of *any* canoes in the channel on this day.

The crew took the *Ariel* through a narrow gap in the mangroves which was the estuary of the Ross River, not named after his friend Clem, but another Ross who was in the party that *discovered* it. He grimaced when he thought of the word, *discovered*. He could have told them it was here.

The mangroves had been cleared for a mile along the northern side of the river and a sturdy looking jetty constructed, and a number of buildings were in various stages of erection along the street and up on the ridge of a rocky projection that overlooked the river.

The crew was greeted with great fanfare, and a toast to the first delivery of goods from Bowen was offered by a Mr John Melton Black who seemed to be a man of great standing in the port. And then, with the festivities over, Morrill began to supervise the unloading of the Ariel.

At high tide next morning, the cutter continued on its way to pick up a load of cedar from Port Hinchinbrook further north. Jimmy Morrill wasn't on it. He'd obtained leave of absence for that part of the voyage, intending to reboard the ship on its return the following week.

The place they'd called The Landing looked just as it had nineteen years ago, when the raft carrying its seven exhausted survivors grounded itself on the sandy beach, and Morrill closed his eyes and revelled in the feeling of the cool white sand under his feet, as he had back then. He listened to the soft regular sighing of the tiny rollers breaking mildly on the rock strewn sandy shore, punctuated by the sporadic cry of a seabird gliding overhead on the light breeze that fanned his face. Nothing about this magnificently wild stretch of coastline had changed in many thousands of years, and it would probably remain untouched for many more while the country around it was transformed into cattle pasture. Could the Bindal exist in this secluded part of their country, a spear throw from the settlements that had been established to service the Empire's needs? It seemed that they were going to try.

He opened his eyes and immediately returned to reality, for a ship had appeared around the headland. It was passing well out to sea, its white sails billowing in a stiff breeze as it headed south, and he remembered the disappointment that he'd felt the last time he'd seen such a sight, for although it was a ship the like of which Geordie and Betsy had craved for so long as they kept watch on a beach further south, they'd not been alive to witness it. He recalled too the crushing sense of loneliness that he had felt *then* as he watched it pass from his vision, and he wondered absent-mindedly whether their ghosts still watched the passing ships from their lonely graves between the two small hills, yearning in vain for one that would take them home.

He walked slowly along the beach to the cave that had been their temporary refuge and the wretchedness returned in force as he thought of Bindjuk and his two attendants shuffling, with outstretched arms, along this same stretch of sand towards the ghost-people who'd arrived unannounced in their country. They'd been almost child-like in their innocence and curiosity and when he'd shown Bindjuk the locket that had belonged to Nora it was obvious from the way he'd gazed at it that he didn't understand, but readily accepted that Nora and her Da' were alive and living blissfully in their home in the little golden Injin.

He remembered he'd tried to imagine it in the way that Bindjuk had, and what he'd seen in his mind's eye was an uncomplicated world within the little sun where everyone was happy and contented, where all people, no matter what faith they were born into or what colour they were, lived side by side in harmony. He'd buried the little sun reverently, knowing that he didn't need to carry it around with him to absorb its wisdom, but the time had come now for him to look into it again, because he may never pass this way again and he knew he needed to see Nora's happy smile once more.

The little sun nestled in his shaking hands when he took it from its resting place in the cave and he carefully brushed the sand from it, his fingers fumbling at the clasp. When he'd finally succeeded in prising it open he studied its contents with some concern, for the difficulty in opening it had led him to consider that it may not have been completely sealed. His fears seemed to be unfounded, however, and it was with a sense of relief that he gazed into that happy little world from where Nora and her Da' smiled back at him, the place that would remain in his dreams until his earthly life was over and he could join them, along with Bindjuk and the Maori, and all the other outcasts of the Empire.

It was then that he detected something that had escaped his notice previously, or perhaps he'd just forgotten it was there. It was a dark shadow in the background behind Nora's Da', as if someone had come up behind him and was standing near his shoulder. He studied it closely, glancing at it from one angle and then another just as Bindjuk had done all those years ago. He ran his finger over it, but the shadow seemed to be ingrained into the image and he shrugged off the odd premonition that gripped him and made him shudder involuntarily as he closed the locket.

The Bindal camp was strangely silent. No nungas played games or ran to meet him as he called out from the edge of the swamp. He'd removed his clothes and laid them in a neat pile on a log a mile down the track from where the wisp of smoke had told him the exact location of the camp, although he could have found it without even that assistance. He looked around apprehensively; perhaps the warriors were out hunting, but he'd noticed that the commonly plentiful rock wallabies that climbed about the low ridge of Cape Cleveland were nowhere to be seen as he'd travelled over it to get to the swampland behind Bowling Green Bay.

There were plenty of signs of cattle though, for the grass was low and trodden and the muddied freshwater lagoons he'd passed were ringed with deep, cloven hoofmarks and soiled ground. It was a typically warm day, but a few old men were huddled around the small campfire silently contemplating the ashes. None of them looked up as he approached.

An old muju sat on the ground outside a rough gunyah, feebly pounding some boaan roots that had been laid out to dry in the sun. She was thin and emaciated, her bony shoulders stooped over pendulous breasts that hung like empty leather gourds over her abdomen. She stopped and laid down her pounding stone when Morrill spoke to her, but her eyes were still fixed on the ground in front of her.

'*Where nungas and other mujus?*' he said quietly, not wishing to disturb the tranquillity of the trancelike state of the elders nearby.

'*All gone, Jemmy Morl,*' she said, waving a skinny arm in an arc above her head. She looked up at him and there were tears welling up in her sunken eyes. '*All gone, Jemmy.*'

Morrill was stunned that the old muju had recognised him, and he searched her lined face. There was something familiar about her. She raised her eyes to meet his and all of a sudden it sank in. '*Obungella?*' he said. His voice was still hushed, but it was not out of respect for the elders now. '*Obungella, - my sister?*'

She nodded. '*Obungella.*' Her brow furrowed as she studied his face. '*Jemmy Morl come back to stay Bindal camp? - too late, Jemmy, - Bindal way all gone.*' Tears had formed quickly in her eyes and began to trickle down her wizened face. '*Gimaru and Dabu work on station, - big station, - plenty work, - ride horse, - plenty food. Buramu cook and clean, - take on white man's ways, - no more Bindal ways.*'

Morrill's voice was rising. '*Where Noora, Obungella?*' He crouched on the ground in front of her. '*Where Noora?*'

Obungella raised her arm again and pointed back along the track in the direction that Morrill had come from. '*Noora gone, - white man come, - say Noora not Bindal, - must be nunga white man settler, - take Noora, - Noora cry and run, - take her anyway, - don't know where.*'

Morrill's eyes were wild with shock and despair. '*What about Bindjuk? He work on station too?*' he pleaded, hoping against hope that the answer would be yes, but Obungella shook her head.

'*White men say Bindjuk too old, - maybe too much wild Bindal warrior, - cause trouble - no work on station.*' She pointed to the circle of old men. '*White men say all elders too old, - give elders plenty rum, - say it make elders more wise, - Obungella no like, - maybe white men want elders gone away.*' She nodded gravely as if she'd thought about it very carefully and often. '*Yiay, white men want elders gone away, - need Bindal country for cattle, - give plenty rum.*'

Morrill's eyes darted to where the old men still huddled around the fire and then he noticed something that he'd missed before. Beyond them was a midden, a heap of discarded shells and bones, and strewn around it lay empty bottles, - many bottles. He realised then that the old men weren't in a spiritual trance as he'd assumed.

'*Where Bindjuk?*' he said. His voice was hoarse and his fingers tightened about the locket that hung around his neck.

'*The shadow in the little injin!*'

Obungella looked at him desolately. '*Bindjuk, - he fly away, - he jump up, - fly up to the clouds now, two round moons.*' She wiped away the tears and tried to smile, but the effort was too much and she only succeeded in sighing deeply. *'Bindjuk happy now, - not long Obungella join Bindjuk, - soon join Bindjuk little injin.'*

Morrill's mind was reeling. *'Obungella join Bindjuk in little injin? How Obungella know about little injin?'*

'Bindjuk say Jemmy Morl come back one day, - Jemmy promise, - Obungella, Bindjuk say go wait for Jemmy little injin, - plenty kangaroo-cattle there, - plenty cattle for Bindal, - Gia and Juru too - plenty fish for Wulgurukaba, - all live together in peace.'

Conclusion

In compiling my father's notes for posterity I have not only complied with his last wishes, but in doing so I have also learned some fragments of the Jimmy Morrill story that I may have been better off *not* knowing. It is done now, however, and it leaves me nothing else to do other than review the final chapter of Jimmy's life.

Jimmy had become quite an unwilling celebrity after his sudden arrival in Bowen from the shepherd's hut on Jarvisfield Station and with subscriptions raised by the fascinated community he became a freehold land owner at Bowen. He never wanted or sought out any measure of attention from the beginning and would have been content to slip back into the realm of comfortable obscurity had it not been for the persistent notion that he, and he alone, was the only one who could do something positive to lessen the indignities suffered by his dispossessed people. He was tireless in his pursuit of justice for the Aborigines of the northern coast of Queensland and became a thorn in the sides of many politicians with his relentless submissions on their behalf.

Jimmy's growing prominence in the community was raised to even greater heights when my father introduced him to Sir Maurice O'Connell, and with the help of Clem and through Sir Maurice, his plea to the Queensland Government to legislate to improve the welfare of the tribes was finally heard. He succeeded in presenting a petition, signed by the majority of the fair-minded residents of Bowen to the Governor who had given his name to the town, Sir George Bowen. Bowen himself had displayed little interest in changing, what to him, was a system that was providing a reliable and profitable income for the government from the Kennedy district, but at least the struggle for peaceful conciliation and disbandment of the Native Police gained some momentum amongst the more humanitarian members of the Legislative Council.

Jimmy was appointed Bonded Warehouse Keeper in Bowen, a position which he always alleged was part of Governor Bowen's plan to get him out of the metropolis of Brisbane and give him something to occupy his interests outside of the relentless pursuit of justice for the tribes. He accepted the appointment, however, believing that it would give him a better opportunity to keep a close eye on events in the district that might affect his brothers. It did, for it was in that capacity that he delivered the first shipment of bonded goods to the new settlement at Cleveland Bay and visited his tribe for the last time.

His death in October 1865 at the age of 41 shocked Bowen's population. The Port Denison Times recorded it in the following terms;

'It is our mournful duty to record the death of the pioneer white man in the north, - James Morrill, - which took place on Monday, 30th October. For some time he had been suffering from the effects of a wound received in the knee during his sojourn among the Aborigines, which had been attacked with rheumatism, and ultimately brought on inflammation and fever, which resulted in his death...'.

The article, which was quite extensive for a small newspaper, went on to say that;

'...He was a general favourite throughout the district and when his death became known on Monday, the whole of the flags of the ships in the harbour, and at the various stores throughout the town were lowered to half-mast. The funeral took place yesterday and was attended by a large number of mourners, including many of our influential citizens The men belonging to the pilot station had asked for, and obtained permission to act as bearers to their old comrade's remains; the police also attended and moved in the procession next to the hearse; then came the Mayor and the Police Magistrate, followed by a long string of vehicles, horses and pedestrians...'.

I was present at the service of course, and it was quite solemn and beautiful to see the number of Bowen citizens who were reduced to tears by its end, but perhaps the most tears were shed in the weeks and months after that by those who would have learned of Jimmy's death through the corroborees of the tribes who clung to their way of life in the swamps and on the higher slopes of Mount Elliott.

The correspondent for the Port Denison Times had the last word on the matter;

'...Could the Mount Elliott blacks learn that their pale-faced brother was dead what howling and woe there would be...'.

The doctor who attended him in his final days and hours stated on the death certificate his opinion that Jimmy's premature death was due to a combination of the rigours placed on his body from the years of exposure he'd endured. Perhaps he was right, but as far as I am concerned Jimmy died of a broken heart, and I was in a position to know.

Jimmy had searched for Noora over the length and breadth of the Kennedy district and beyond, but he was destined never to see her again in the limited time he had left in this world, and his grief at her abduction was only equalled by his grief at the demise of his tribe, and especially the death of his brother Bindjuk.

As I said at the beginning of this narrative, my father, Clement Ross sailed back to Gladstone on the *Ariel* after the double heartbreak of Jimmy Morrill's death and that of his much loved wife, my mother, Daphne, which transpired within months of Jimmy's. In time, and with the benefit of our mutual support, we both recovered somewhat from the sorrow that only time can heal,

The decision to leave Bowen was a poignant one for us and had nothing to do with the amenity of the town, for Captain Sinclair had chosen the location well and it remains a lovely little village with a deep, enclosed natural harbour and spectacular views, both on its landward and seaward aspects, but it held too many sad memories for both of us, - and I had another reason too.

There were a few people, - only a handful, - in the town and in the surrounding stations who believed that my father had been too outspoken in his advocacy for the protection of the Aborigines, and that Jimmy was nothing more than an emissary for the tribes. These few deluded, but vociferous people maintained the conviction that *his* tribe had sent him back to Bowen to create conflict and cause disruption to the *honest* settlers who were merely trying to establish and work the cattle runs that they'd hewn out of the unforgiving scrub. With Jimmy's death their opinions became more openly aggressive against anyone suspected of harbouring an intention to carry on the struggle, and my father, nearing seventy years of age by then, had been covertly threatened on more than one occasion. It was primarily for that reason that I knew I had to take action to ensure the welfare of both my ageing father and my new-born son. He remained in Gladstone with me and his grandson in our cottage overlooking the bay and beyond to Facing Island in relative ease and relaxation for the remainder of his life.

Indeed, the struggle for the abolition of the Native Mounted Police and the associated butchery they were responsible for in the name of dispersal of a perceived horde of savages *did* continue without us and I am both elated and dejected at the outcome. I am elated that certain other right-minded people, like the Clapham Saints, for example, experienced a reasonable measure of success in promoting a better covenant for the poor, displaced original inhabitants of this beautiful country, but at the same time I am dejected that the wanton destruction of their way of life, so unsophisticated, but so pure in its simplicity, has resulted in an enormous decline in their numbers.

One other important fact that I have so far declined to mention, - *deliberately*, - is that Jimmy Morrill entered the matrimonial state, late in his life as it turned out. The reason that I have concealed this until now is that I did not want you, the reader, to form the impression that I have embellished his exploits to further my own financial gain.

You see, as a government employee, Jimmy's widow was eligible to receive an annuity from the government to the amount of fifty pounds, - and I was that widow. Our son, who was born after Jimmy's untimely death, was also entitled to fifteen pounds each year for his welfare and education, but if I *have* cast any doubt in your mind as to the legitimacy of our relationship, it may restore your trust in my integrity to know that I never asked for, nor was offered, any support from the government fund.

I believed from the moment I met Jimmy as an adult in my father's house in Bowen that I had fallen in love with him. (I had met him as a child in Sydney, you may remember.) Perhaps, in hindsight, it wasn't love, for it was a very long time ago and my opinion of the complexities of one's love for another has changed over the years. It may, in fact, have been simply *compassion*, for even though he appeared to my twenty-five year old eyes to be like a captured wild creature with fear and confusion emanating from sunken, haunting eyes that stared out from a face darkened by the sun and pock-marked with the ravages of scurvy, there was something about him that evoked a tenderness in me. As I got to know him better, in a very short time, I came to realise that there was so much more to the man than just a simple shipwrecked sailor who'd spent seventeen years of his life in privation with a primitive tribe.

Oh yes, I knew before we became intimately involved that he'd had loves in his life before me, for he would sometimes call out their names in his delirium when he was ill, but I fancied that they were hallucinations in his mind from long ago and were due to circumstances he'd found himself in at the time. I had, of course, wondered about his relationship with the young Aboriginal woman, Bunginna and I am no wiser now than I was before I transcribed my father's notes. What became of her daughter Noora? Was she removed from her ostensibly less than wholesome surroundings by some well-meaning campaigner to a safe place where she was educated and nurtured? There were certainly plenty of these champions around in later years to force our brand of doctrine on the survivors of our misguided self-indulgence. Is she still alive and well somewhere? I sincerely hope she is. She would be over thirty years old now, but my fear is that we've done nothing in the meantime to prolong the lives of the Aborigines who've been struck down by the diseases we've introduced to them over the last century.

What if she *was* Jimmy's daughter, though? And don't tell me *that* possibility hasn't crossed your mind too, as it has mine on many occasions when I've seen an unusually light skinned Aboriginal lady approaching me. If she was, then she may have inherited the immunity from diseases that the European body has developed over time and that have had such a severe effect on those who have not been exposed to them previously. It's absorbing now to think I may have a step-daughter somewhere near who is not many years younger than I am.

Some of Jimmy's little habits used to leave me curious as to their meanings; for example, no matter how sick or feeble he felt, when the bells of our little church in Bowen rang the angelus at noon on Sundays he unfailingly struggled out of bed and wound the clock, and then he would take hold of the tiny gold locket that he always wore around his neck and kiss it as tenderly as he ever kissed me. I was naturally a little upset at what I supposed in my girlish youth to be an affront to his young wife's feelings, but I'd been told that Aboriginal people have an aversion to looking at images of those who are deceased. I grasped at *that* vindication of his apparent disrespect without the slightest hesitation, choosing to accept that it was one more of the Aborigines customs that he'd taken on. I know differently now, of course, but the real explanation is no less a hint of his true character.

It wasn't until I transcribed my father's notes that I understood fully the significance of those little gestures, and I knew then that the locket was not simply a tender memento to evoke memories of Nora by, but a window into that unsophisticated and happy place where Nora and her Da' resided, and Jimmy's mother too, along with Bindjuk and the Maori, and all the other outcasts of the Empire.

I was given the locket by the funeral director after Jimmy was buried, due to a misunderstanding of my request that it remain with him. I refused to open it even then, not because I held any bitterness that he'd never shown me what it contained, or allowed me to be part of the private world of his past. It was simply because in Jimmy's mind the little sun was a place of peace and tranquillity, an uncomplicated world where everyone was happy and contented and all oppressed people, no matter what faith they were born into or what colour they were, lived side by side in harmony, - and I wasn't quite ready to accept that such a wonderful place could possibly exist. Jimmy's hopes for a better future for all God's creatures lay within that tiny world, and isn't that what we all dream of for ourselves in the end, no matter whether we call it Heaven, Nirvana, The Promised Land, or the Little Sun?

'He fly away, - he jump up, - fly up to the clouds now, - all live together in peace.'

Eliza Ann Morrill.

Gladstone, Colony of Queensland, July 1880

Addendum

The bulk of this manuscript was completed in July 1880. That was, as I said at the time, not long after the death of my father, Clement Ross, but then, perhaps predictably, for I was so much my father's daughter, I put it away in a drawer to gather dust for the next forty years. You see, I was doubtful that I could face the scrutiny and possible litigation that I suspected the narrative might provoke amongst those who undoubtedly would have felt bitterness regarding its content.

Now, as I am well past my eightieth year and the infirmities that seem to afflict my aching body more often than not these days alludes to a limited duration for me on this earth, I feel that the time is long overdue for me to dispense with my fears of any such scrutiny or legality affecting my future life.

Most of the challengers to the account's credibility, and those who may have felt vexed at its publication are already in their graves by now in any case, and I have long ago become immune to the whining of politicians who perceive their own insignificant agendas as being of the utmost importance in a world that has just emerged from a war; one that is already being called *The Great War*. Many of us who have been fortunate to have escaped relatively unscathed from its devastating effects anticipate, - or pray, if we are of that ilk, - that nothing like it will ever happen again in the future.

I am content that I have at last accomplished the promise I made to my father over forty years ago and which has weighed heavily on my mind ever since. I now beg of you, dear reader, to leave me in peace to contemplate the providence that brought together my late father, Clement Ross and my late husband, Jimmy Morrill, and to enjoy my own life's memories in the few years that I may have left to indulge in them.

Eliza Ann Morrill.
Of Charters Towers in the State of Queensland,
July, 1919

Editorial Comment.

Eliza Ann Morrill re-married many years after the death of her first husband, Jimmy Morrill, but it was her desire that her former matrimonial name be retained for this publication. This was done, I suspect, not only to preserve the acknowledgment in the reader's mind of her relationship with Jimmy Morrill, but also a clever ploy to protect her anonymity and privacy in the final years of her life.

Eliza wore the tiny golden locket she insisted in calling *'Jimmy's little sun'* around her neck until the day she died in Charters Towers in 1923 aged 85 years. The nurse who attended her in her final hours filed her report and in part it read;

'…She clasped that little locket in both hands, closed her eyes and sighed deeply. I knew she was close and I thought that was the actual moment of her passing, so I raised myself from my chair and lifted the sheet to cover her face. I saw her eyelids flutter and then open wide, but she didn't look at me. She smiled serenely and seemed to gaze beyond me, possibly further than any living thing in this world. I heard her whisper a few words, but her voice was so soft that I couldn't quite make out all of her words. It sounded something like, 'We…all together in peace and harmony.'

'It was then I noticed that the locket had dropped from her grasp and was lying on the sheet, ever so slightly open. I closed it and placed it back in her hands, but by then she had passed away very peacefully.'

In accordance with Eliza Ann Morrill's previously expressed wish, 'Jimmy's little sun' was buried with her.

Laurence Joseph Murphy (Author)

The Sound of Liberty

ISBN 978-0-9923046-5-2

The Sound of Liberty
is also available as an Ebook.

Felix Reitano arrived in Sydney, Australia from Naples, Italy in 1896 as a young teenager. He quickly learned to speak English after a chance meeting with an equally young aristocrat from England. Felix travelled to Queensland, first to the sugar cane town of Mossman and then to Halifax, a small cane farming settlement about 100km north of Townsville. In Halifax he met and fell in love with a Scottish lass, Sarah Livingstone.

Sarah's journey to Australia at the age of nineteen, having grown up in a small poverty-stricken village in Scotland with limited knowledge to prepare her for what lay ahead, was also truly remarkable and was only matched in true pioneering spirit by the man she married.

Felix and Sarah's story would have been similar to that of many pioneering families and therefore tremendously admirable, but not independently productive in the retelling. What set them apart, however, was their unusual (at that time) inter-racial marriage and the unique complications they were confronted with due to the rise of Mussolini's Fascism and the effects of Italy's entry into the Second World War on the side of the Axis powers.

www.ingramcontent.com/pod-product-compliance
Lightning Source LLC
Chambersburg PA
CBHW061034120726
47910CB00006B/2241